FOUR THOUS

Also by M.J. Trow

A Geoffrey Chaucer mystery

THE KNIGHT'S TALE *

The Kit Marlowe series

DARK ENTRY *
SILENT COURT *
WITCH HAMMER *
SCORPIONS' NEST *
CRIMSON ROSE *
TRAITOR'S STORM *
SECRET WORLD *
ELEVENTH HOUR *
QUEEN'S PROGRESS *
BLACK DEATH *
THE RECKONING *

The Grand & Batchelor series

THE BLUE AND THE GREY *
THE CIRCLE *
THE ANGEL *
THE ISLAND *
THE RING *
THE BLACK HILLS *
LAST NOCTURNE *

The Peter Maxwell series

MAXWELL'S CROSSING
MAXWELL'S RETURN
MAXWELL'S ACADEMY
MAXWELL'S SUMMER

* *available from Severn House*

FOUR THOUSAND DAYS

M.J. Trow

SEVERN
HOUSE

First world edition published in Great Britain in 2021 and the USA in 2022
by Severn House, an imprint of Canongate Books Ltd,
14 High Street, Edinburgh EH1 1TE.

Trade paperback edition first published in Great Britain and the USA in 2023
by Severn House, an imprint of Canongate Books Ltd.

severnhouse.com

British Library Cataloguing-in-Publication Data
A CIP catalogue record for this title is available from the British Library.

ISBN-13: 978-1-78029-134-5 (cased)
ISBN-13: 978-1-4483-0741-8 (trade paper)
ISBN-13: 978-1-4483-0740-1 (e-book)

Typeset by Palimpsest Book Production Ltd.,
Falkirk, Stirlingshire, Scotland.

ONE

'This is absolutely disgusting!'

'I hoped you might like it.'

'I don't. And no, Veronica, it's not going to "grow on me", as you young people say. If I live to be a hundred, I'll never get used to this. What on earth is it?'

'It's called Syrup of Coca-Cola, Dr Murray and it's all the rage in America.'

'So is lynching, but I'd hate that to become a British custom. All in all, it's rather worse than that ghastly Sarsaparilla concoction Signor Luigi keeps trying to press upon me in Market Street. Thomas!'

Margaret Murray was not much taller than the ailing queen, but in the hallowed halls of University College and the cafes and bookshops of Gower Street, her word was law and her voice, never raised above what was acceptable, brought minions rushing from all directions. Such a one was Thomas, the proprietor of the Jeremy Bentham coffee house and he stood at the lady's elbow now, hair carefully macassared, apron just so.

'Is there a problem, Prof?'

'This.' She held up the bottle. 'Quite an attractive shape, in an early Hittite sort of way, but its contents . . .' She looked at it again, as if to make sure it was real, and smacked her lips to rid them of the lingering taste. 'What's it made from?'

Thomas had come up the hard way, from a barrow boy in Smithfield, where the blood ran in the gutters, working his way upwards and westwards to the exalted heights of the Jeremy Bentham in darkest Bloomsbury. To certain clients, it was the Tea Rooms; to others, it was the Coffee House. What it was not, at least in Margaret Murray's eyes, was an emporium of the undrinkable. What the Jeremy Bentham had in common with the Monster Hotels of the West End was opulence. Everywhere gleamed in brass and cut glass. Chandeliers sparkled from the ceilings and the chairs were padded with velvet of the deepest crimson. For all that, Thomas knew his clientele; most of them were students and he kept his prices low.

'It says "Coca-Cola",' Thomas said solemnly, reading the bottle's label.

She smiled. 'I see all those years at the Board School were not wasted. I hoped you could go further.'

Clearly, Thomas couldn't and Veronica helped him out. She was a beautiful girl, her copper-coloured hair swept up in the new Gibson style and this was her first term at university. She felt sorry for the man and leapt to his rescue. 'I believe it contains the essence of the coca plant,' she said.

'As in cocaine?' Margaret quizzed her. Margaret Murray had never visited an opium den in her life and now was probably not the best time to start. Her dirty secret, however, was an addiction to the yellow press and she knew of such places – and practices – from the murky pages of the *Illustrated Police News*.

'As in cocaine.'

'Well, take it away, Thomas and bring us something more acceptable; a pot of Tetley tea perhaps, which contains tannin and hot water. Oh, and two of those delicious little butterfly cakes . . . or are you watching your figure, Veronica?'

The girl laughed. If she wasn't, most of the men in the room were, even those sitting with other women. Not for her the nainsook camisoles and trimmed torchon lace of the Army & Navy Stores. With Veronica, all this beauty was of God.

Thomas sighed. He had a soft spot for the Prof, as he called her, although she was not yet of that status. Margaret Murray was a kindly soul and it was impossible to guess her age. What with Thomas's new-found gentility, he knew that gentlemen never posed such questions. All he knew was that the Prof had a mind like a razor and it was her own. She was a woman in a man's world; but then, weren't they all? She didn't suffer fools gladly, if at all. And, rather like the pope, she knew what she liked.

'Tea it is, Prof. And don't worry, miss, my butterfly cakes are as light as . . . well . . . butterflies.' Phrasemaker, that was Tom.

When he had gone, Margaret leaned towards the girl. 'Salt of the earth, that man,' she said. 'You can rely on him. Now, the drawings.'

Veronica had been putting off this evil hour for as long as she could. Resting against the table leg under the lawn cloth and doilies was a large, flat case. She lifted it up while Margaret moved the sugar bowl and the little pot of flowers and she edged out a sheaf of papers. They were her first attempts at archaeological drawings, an arcane skill which very few had ever mastered. One by one, they passed under the practised eye of Margaret Murray, junior lecturer at University College, London. Veronica's heart was pounding under her corset. She barely knew that she was gnawing her lower lip as though her life depended on it. Two or three minutes passed – or was it years? She didn't hear the noise around her, the mindless gossip of students and booksellers and the collected academe of this particular part of London; bohemian Bloomsbury at its best. She didn't see Thomas hovering in the background with his butterfly cakes until the table should become available again. All she could see was Margaret Murray's face, inscrutable under the thatch of mousey hair, her grey eyes twinkling in the morning sun. Outside in the street, cab horses snorted and jinked their way through the crowds, the bustle and hum punctuated by the odd klaxon screech of a De Dion proclaiming its modernity. It was Thursday and there was a pause between the lectures in the Godless Institution that was University College. In the wider world still, the Boers were still being beastly to Lord Roberts and his staff, nearly six thousand miles away. There were rumours that the war was nearly over, that 'Bobs' was about to hand over his command to that objectionable boundah, Kitchener. And nobody had much confidence in him. The century was coming to an end, or it had come to an end, depending on how you measured it. The mathematics professors at University College and beyond argued long into the night as to quite what year would herald the twentieth century, but that was mathematicians for you. But none of this mattered in the Jeremy Bentham that Thursday. All that mattered was Margaret Murray and the judgement of Solomon.

She leaned back in her chair. Her eyes flicked upwards and

she smiled at the girl. 'Not bad,' she said. 'For a first effort, not bad. The cross-hatching needs a heavier shade, to convey depth and . . . what's this?' She pointed to a series of black lines.

Veronica tilted her head to see it properly. 'My assumption of what the rest of the beaker would look like.'

Margaret smiled. 'Never assume, dear girl; it makes an ass out of you and me.'

'Don't you think, Dr Murray,' Veronica ventured, her mentor's kind words having boosted her confidence, 'the "beaker folk" is rather a silly name for the people who made these pots?'

'I do, as it happens – although "the pot people" is equally silly. Never lose sight of the fact that the artefacts themselves are by the way. The testimony of the spade only tells us so much about the people who made them, were buried in them, or with them, depending on the artefact itself. They had dreams, these people, hopes, loves and hates. Most of their children died before they could walk. A man was old at thirty. But at least they had one advantage over us.'

'Really? What was that?' Veronica never missed an opportunity to gather pearls of wisdom from her mentor.

Margaret Murray looked under her eyebrows at the girl. 'They didn't have to drink Coca-Cola.'

Veronica laughed as she gathered her drawings together and slipped them back into their folder. 'Seriously, though,' she said, 'do you think Professor Petrie will like them?'

'Flinders?' Margaret smiled as Thomas finally could put his cakes down on the table. 'Good Lord, no; he'll hate them.'

'I'm sorry, Miss Halifax; I hate them.'

Veronica's mouth gaped. For all Margaret Murray had warned her, the blow, when it fell, was heavy. The only sound in the great man's study was the ticking of the grandmother in the corner. William Flinders Petrie was a legend in his own lifetime, a man who looked to Veronica as old as Methuselah with a nearly white beard, a waxed moustache and a shock of greying hair. He wore a silk bow tie which was beginning to show signs of having been tied once too often and the shoulder of his gown had slipped to one side, making it easier for him to reach his pipe. The elegant churchwarden lay on its cradle among the debris on his desk, scrolls of hieroglyphs, potsherds, the odd bone and a curling sandwich.

'What did Dr Murray think?' He fixed his ferocious stare on to the girl.

'I believe she rather liked them,' Veronica said.

'Hmm.' Flinders Petrie was rarely that non-committal. 'You see, this cross-hatching' – he pointed to the offending article – 'far too heavy-handed. In archaeology, Mr Gibbs, what do we need?'

Piers Gibbs was as new to all this as Veronica Halifax. Product of Harrow he may have been, but men like Flinders Petrie had always put the fear of God into him. 'Umm . . .'

The grandmother's voice held centre stage again.

'Thank you, Mr Gibbs,' Petrie said, when it was clear that nothing more would be forthcoming. 'Tell him, Mr Rose.'

Andrew Rose was not a product of Harrow. He had come to University College from Manchester Grammar School in the grim industrial North and had the flat Northern vowels to prove it. He also had a bachelor's degree in archaeology, which gave him a definite edge over newcomers like Gibbs.

'The light touch, sir,' Rose beamed with the smugness of the class swot. 'The finesse of the feather.'

'Yes, all right,' Petrie scowled. 'Don't overdo it. The Beaker Folk, Mr Crouch? Any thoughts?'

Ben Crouch rarely had any thoughts that didn't centre on food. All right, Mr and Mrs Crouch had not realized when they christened him that an earlier Ben Crouch had been the leader of a gang of body-snatchers right here in London in the not-that-distant past and the little baby who grew up to be an annoying slob could hardly be blamed for that. He could be blamed for almost everything else, however.

'Er . . . an enigma, Professor.'

'Hmm,' Petrie murmured. 'I seem to remember that was your response to earlier questions of mine relating to the Minoans, the Illyrians and the Second Punic War. Help him out, Miss Crossley.'

Anthea Crossley was everything that Ben Crouch was not.

She was tall, elegant, vivacious and attractive. Above all, she was a woman and therefore altogether preferable, in Petrie's eyes, to the hapless Crouch. 'I found Professor Flaxman's arguments on them particularly compelling, Professor,' she said, secretly longing for a cigarette to which she had recently become addicted.

'Did you?' Petrie raised an eyebrow. He might have to revise his views of Anthea Crossley.

'Miss Friend?' The great man swivelled in his chair to face the girl. She too was a graduate, articulate and intelligent, but with an air of calm and common sense that made her stand out from the others. The undergraduates in the room were mere children, after all; the graduates no better than they should be; but Angela Friend was rather different . . .

'Puerile,' she said, 'the work of the Beaker Folk. In comparison, that is, with the treasures of the opisthodomos of the Parthenon.'

'Quite.' Petrie glowed with archaeological pride. 'Quite. Now, who haven't I asked?'

All eyes swivelled to little Janet Bairnsfather, a girl of the Presbyterian persuasion from Abergeldy. No one quite knew what Janet was doing here, at London's oldest college, so far from home, intending to matriculate one day in a subject that was *so* dominated by men.

'Miss Featherbum,' Petrie clasped his hands across his waistcoat. 'You've not been with us long. Has Dr Murray introduced you to the delights of ancient Britain? I should have thought bogs and cairns and so on would appeal, in a Pictish sort of way.'

'Well, I—' but the Scots girl got no further because William Flinders Petrie was, after all, a middle-aged man in a hurry. He had a rendezvous to keep in Egypt and the sooner he could rid himself of these ghastly Thursday tutorials, the better.

'Absolutely,' the professor said. 'Well,' he sighed and hauled the half-hunter from his waistcoat pocket. 'Dr Minton will be anxious to pass on his words of wisdom on the villas of the later empire and their place in the Aristotelian dialectic, so I won't keep you.'

They shambled to their feet, mumbling their goodbyes and he slipped his hip flask from his desk drawer. This bunch of no-hopers were Margaret Murray's 'gang', as she called them, a motley crew if ever Petrie had seen one. Still, he valued Margaret's judgement, in this as in all things. For instance, she thought that he was a genius; the woman was never wrong.

The next day and a perfect Friday afternoon was nearly over as far as Angela Friend was concerned. Professor Flinders Petrie was in full flow at the bottom of the raked seats in the auditorium, holding up an amphora as if it were the only one in the world, tracing its whorls and loops with his experienced fingers.

Angela had sat in this theatre and walked the corridors outside it for four years now. It was, after the real one in Berkshire, her second home. She loved the smell of the Godless Institution, the echo of its halls, the silent marble busts of its founders looking down at her. As an archaeologist, she even loved the living statue of Jeremy Bentham in his glass case. His thigh bones jutted through the canvas of his breeches and his carpals glowed ivory through his worn gloves. His head was a wax copy, the horsehair wig that was once his own hanging lankly down from the broad wideawake hat. Angela knew that the greatest of the college's founders could see nothing through his glass eyes. But she also knew that he watched her nonetheless, because his actual head was in the hat box between his feet. And this was the point of it, after all; in his will, Bentham had expressed a wish to look out over his students – and somebody had taken him literally.

'And the next time,' Petrie said in his stentorian voice, 'we'll examine the ships that carried these beauties. In the meantime, all of you, have a look at my paper on Graeco-Roman commerce and its place in linguistic cosmography. Trust me, it knocks the stockings off anything written by Heinrich Schliemann.'

There was raucous applause as there was at the end of all Flinders Petrie's lectures, but Angela was yawning as she closed her writing pad and she wiped her nib. It was no disrespect to Petrie, but someone had noticed.

'Long day, Miss Friend?'

She turned to the young man across the aisle. She'd seen him here before, always on Fridays, always in the lectures open to the public. He was good-looking in a plebeian sort of way and had shoulders like a dray horse. 'How do you know my name?' she had to ask.

'Sorry,' he said, genuinely apologetic. 'It goes with the territory, I'm afraid. I'm a policeman.'

She glanced down at his feet. Yes, that was entirely possible.

'Constable Adam Crawford, A Division.'

'Scotland Yard?' she queried.

''Fraid so,' he said. 'That goes with the territory too.'

'I've seen you here before.' She stuffed her notebook into her satchel.

'Every Friday,' he said. 'The public lectures. Archaeology's a bit of a hobby of mine.'

'Good for you.' She stood up and he stood up with her, towering over her even without the helmet.

'Look . . . er . . . I know this is a bit forward,' he said, 'but, well, it's teatime. Could I buy you a cuppa at the Jeremy Bentham?'

She looked into his eyes. They were hazel and watchful and kind. 'No, thank you,' she said, and swept past him. At the top of the stairs, as the other students made their way out of the auditorium, she half turned. 'Let me buy you one.'

Constable Adam Crawford was a man of two worlds. By day, whenever he could get away from the endless shifts, he roamed the bookshops around University College, soaking up the culture of the ancients and chatting to the students, most of whom were only a year or two younger than he was. By night, however . . .

He walked his beat along Tothill Street, listening to his hobnailed boots clattering at the regulation two and a half miles an hour. He knew every inch of this street and the others around it. It was a warm night, for all it was already October and high clouds scudded under the moon, vanishing in turn above the silhouettes of the rooftops. From somewhere, a dog barked. He checked the time by the Abbey clock; half past two.

He became aware of it, faster than most people, because that was what they trained and paid him for. Raised voices around the corner, and shouting. By the time the glass shattered, he was at a full run, his truncheon in his hand, his heart pounding. Under an awning across Storey's Yard, he could make out an altercation between a man on the pavement, swaying and shouting obscenities up at another man, sticking his head out of an upstairs window.

'It's got bloody nothing to do with me,' the upstairs man was insisting. Then he caught sight of Crawford. 'Oh, about time,' he said. 'I've been shouting for help for bloody hours.'

'Bollocks!' retorted the man on the pavement. 'Get down and let me in, you shit, or I'll have the law on you – this one, in fact.'

Adam Crawford hated to be the man on the spot, a wind-up tin toy that the public could operate at will. Yet, so often, he was exactly that. He had to play Solomon in the most complex of situations and he usually had a split second in which to do it. At moments like these, even the most academically minded copper resorted to the well-worn truisms of the station-house. 'Now then,' he said to the pavement man, 'now then, what's all this?'

The man squared up to him. 'All this,' he said, 'is that I've got a bloody job to do. And that arsehole up there is preventing me doing it.'

Crawford looked up to the arsehole in question. The man was in his nightshirt and cap, not unreasonably at that hour of the morning. He dropped his gaze back to the man on the pavement. 'And what is your job, exactly?' he asked.

The man drew himself up to his full height, frowning at the constable's collar badges. 'I'm a rent collector. And her inside owes me five weeks' back rent.'

'Nothing to do with me!' the man in the window thought it best to remind everybody.

'Have you been drinking, sir?' Crawford asked the man on the pavement. He kept his truncheon handy, just in case.

'I may have been,' the rent collector said, 'at some time in the past.'

Judging by his breath, some time in the present would be more accurate. 'Only, the only reason I ask,' Crawford said patiently, 'is that it is half past two in the morning and that, you'll agree, is not a usual time to collect rent.'

'It may not be usual to you, mate,' the man said, 'but, trust me, it's the only time you're likely to find some of those bastards home. Catch 'em when they're half asleep, not ready for any malarkey or smart answers, and you *may*, just *may*, get a bob or two out of 'em.' He threw his head back. 'That's if helpful arseholes don't mind opening the front door, of course.'

'Bollocks!' the man above grunted.

'You don't have a key?' Crawford asked the rent collector.

'Not to this door, no. I have to her room, of course, in fact all of 'em on the ground floor. It's a bitch, ain't it? Welcome to London!'

'Would you mind unlocking the door, sir?' Crawford called to the man above. 'The sooner I let this man in, the sooner I can arrest him for disturbing the peace.' He felt glass under his feet. 'And breaking windows.'

'Arrest him?' both men said simultaneously.

'That's marvellous,' said the upstairs man. 'I'll be down.'

''Ere' – the rent collector swayed – 'you can't arrest me for doing my job.'

'There's a long list of jobs I can arrest you for doing,' Crawford told him, 'from breaking and entering to interfering with sheep. Now, stand still and don't be a nuisance.'

The bolts slid and rattled and the upstairs man had become the downstairs man. 'You stay with him,' he snapped at Crawford. 'He don't have access to anything not on this floor. And, yes, I'd be happy to press charges.'

Crawford followed the rent collector through the gloom of the passageway. As it got darker around the corner, the constable lit his bulls-eye and it flashed its beams over the walls and flooring, once expensively papered and lino-leumed, now a little shabby. 'Elegant,' he muttered, as the light fell on an obscene message scrawled at eye level. The rent collector ignored him. He had been called worse a dozen times on any given day.

'Here we are.' He knocked on a black-painted door, pressing his ear to the woodwork. 'There you go,' he mumbled. 'Nothing.'

He pulled a bunch of keys from his pocket, and fumbled

with two or three before he found the right one. 'I'm glad you're here, in a way,' he said. 'You can arrest the bitch for non-payment of rent.' He kicked the door open and waited until Crawford's lantern beams lit the place. There were two rooms leading off a tiny inner hallway, with cheap painted furniture and heavy fringes. They were both visible from the door. The constable couldn't help noticing that above the bed was a framed picture telling the world that God is Love. On a whim, he turned it round and on the back, in gilt lettering, were the words 'Love Conquers All'. But it was what was on the bed that held both men's attention. A young girl lay sprawled on the covers, her eyes wide open and dull, her mouth slightly gaping. Her arms and legs were thrown wide like the da Vinci drawing of Vitruvian Man that Crawford knew well. He carefully lifted her head on to the mattress and, pointlessly, felt for a pulse. There was a glass phial on the bedside table, beside the red-fringed oil lamp. The dead woman's clothes were hanging in a deal wardrobe. The smell in the room and the cold of the limp corpse told Crawford that she had been dead for about a day, perhaps two.

The shock of the sight seemed to have sobered Downstairs Man up. 'My God,' he whispered, and then, 'Poor little Alice.'

'Alice?' Crawford repeated, frowning at him.

'Yes. Alice Groves,' the rent collector said.

'That's right,' Upstairs Man nodded. 'Alice Groves.'

'Well, that's odd, gentlemen,' Crawford said, 'because I happen to know this woman.' He played his bulls-eye's beam on to the dead face, just to make doubly certain. 'And her name was Helen Richardson.'

TWO

The night had brought the damp cold of impending winter, creeping north-west from the sullen river, dark and brooding in front of the wharves and quays to the East. Joseph Bazalgette's ornate dolphin standards stood sentinel along this stretch of the Thames and it was already dawn before the vergers of the Abbey came to light the tapers and the gas.

Constable Adam Crawford had done what he could in the dead woman's room, then he had secured the premises, as his superiors had it, and stood at the door until one particular superior turned up.

Inspector Athelgar Blunt of A Division was not known for his concern for his underlings. Seen one man in uniform, seen them all, in his book. He was a dapper little man, only just tall enough for the Metropolitan Police, and he had the baggy eyes and drooping jowls of an out-of-sorts bulldog; at this time on a cold morning, a bulldog chewing a wasp. The tenacity that went with the breed was wholly missing in Athelgar Blunt, however, and he intended to make short work of this.

'You first finder?' he grunted at Crawford as he alighted from the hansom.

'Yes, sir. Constable Crawford, A-four-three-one.' The man saluted.

Blunt looked up at the building, one of several identical ones that ran the whole of the east side of Storey's Yard. 'Well, come on, man,' the inspector snapped. 'What have we got? I don't have all day.'

Crawford led the detective along the murky passageway and into the dead woman's rooms. The inspector took off his bowler and sniffed. 'Knocking shop,' he said. 'Smells like a tart's boudoir.' Only then did he see the body. He walked around the bed, passing his hat to Crawford to hold. Then he paused. 'Have you touched anything?' he asked.

'I felt for a pulse,' the constable told him, 'and moved her more on to the bed.'

'How much more?'

'A few inches. Her head was dangling over the edge.'

'What difference would that have made?' Blunt asked. 'She *was* dead, I take it.'

'Yes, sir. As a dodo.'

'What time was this?'

'Shortly after half past two this morning by the Abbey clock.'

Blunt thrust out a hand and felt the cold, clammy flesh of the woman's neck. 'When will you uniform people ever learn?' he muttered. 'You don't touch a body at a crime scene, ever.'

'Sorry, sir. I was very careful otherwise. The glass phial on the bedside table. I used my cuff on that.'

'What for?' Blunt picked up the item in question – and not with his cuffs.

'Er . . . I was thinking fingerprints, sir.'

Blunt exploded with laughter, a less-than-respectful sound perhaps in that dead room. 'Don't be ridiculous, Constable. Oh, I know the Assistant Commissioner believes in all that mumbo-jumbo, but those of us at the sharp end know better, don't we?' The inspector was peering hard into the constable's face. 'Now, then. For the benefit of your own promotional prospects, should you have any.' He dipped his nose towards the phial's open top. 'What do you smell?'

'Er . . . almonds, sir,' Crawford told him.

'No, Constable, you smell cyanide. Do we have a name for this?' He was looking at the corpse.

'Her rent collector believes it was Alice Groves.'

'You've met him?'

'Yes, sir, he was here as I arrived on my beat, trying to collect the rent.'

'At half past two in the morning?' Blunt was incredulous.

'He implied that rent collecting has no timetable, sir.'

'Did you detain him?'

'No, sir. I have his particulars.'

Blunt shook his head in despair. 'Well, I just hope they pass muster, Constable. Not that this is a case for us.'

'It isn't?'

'God, no. It's suicide. Look at this hell-hole, rough even by Storey's Yard standards. She's on the game, your Alice Groves; gets by giving blokes one on this very bed. What is she? Twenty-three? Twenty-four? Maybe she was a good girl once – most of 'em were. They aren't born with their legs open, metaphorically speaking. She's not happy with her life. She gets an attack of the consciences. See that picture?' He pointed to the wall. 'God is Love. She's a convent girl or somesuch. It all comes flooding back, the bell, book and candle bit. And then she takes her own life, while the balance of her mind is disturbed. That'll be the coroner's verdict, you mark my words. I don't know what those blokes get paid for; we do all their work for them. Right. No need to waste any more time. Send for a Maria; we'll get her to the mortuary – St Vincent's is the nearest. You look a little put out, Constable. Is this your first dead body?'

'No, sir,' Crawford said. 'It's just . . .'

'Yes, I know.' Blunt retrieved his hat. 'Life's flotsam and jetsam, chaff blown on the wind. It comes to us all in the end.' Blunt paused, checking whether he had any other clichés in his armoury, but there was nothing. 'Now, get that Maria and we can say goodbye to your Alice Groves.'

'But she wasn't my Alice Groves, sir,' Crawford said. 'She was my Helen Richardson.'

Blunt frowned and the bulldog looked ready to snap. 'What are you talking about?' he asked.

'I attend archaeology classes, sir,' Crawford admitted, a little shame-faced, 'at University College. Every Friday before my night shift. So does . . . did . . . this woman. I spoke to her quite often. Only she wasn't there yesterday . . .'

'No,' said Blunt, eyeing the constable with suspicion. 'That's because she was bollock naked and twice as dead.' He closed to Crawford. 'I don't know what game you think you're playing, lad,' he said, 'but as a rule I would say it's better not to know suicide victims, especially when they're unfortunates, ladies of the night.' He turned to go, then spun back with a wry smile on his face. 'Archaeology, my arse! Get the Maria and close this place up and we'll say no more about it. You're lucky I'm in such a genial mood this morning.'

It was nearly midday before the Maria turned up and two burly coppers carried what was left of Alice Groves out of her last known abode and into the black wagon. The horses snorted and shifted as they felt the extra weight. Crawford had padlocked Alice's rooms in the absence of the keyholder and was about to get himself home after a long night when a face he knew came bobbing along the road.

'Constable Crawford.' The man raised his hat.

'What are you doing here, Fenton?'

'My job, Constable. You?'

Crawford looked down at the ferret of a man in his loud chequered suit. 'Trying not to step in the horse-shit.'

Fenton ignored him. 'What have we here?' He tried to peer into the glazed, barred windows of the Maria.

'That is a horse-drawn police vehicle,' the constable told him, 'affectionately known as a Black Maria, named after—'

'Come off it, Adam!' Fenton laughed. 'This is me, Freddie. We go way back, you and me.'

'That was before you started working for the gutter press,' Crawford told him. 'Get lost.'

'Gutter press?' Fenton repeated, with all the outrage of Fleet Street behind him. 'I resent that!'

'Shame,' Crawford shrugged.

'Look, the *Illustrated Police News* may be a shade on the yellow side . . .'

'A shade?' Crawford's eyes widened. 'It's yellower than a bunch of bananas.'

'Come on, Adam,' Fenton wheedled. 'For old time's sake. What have we got? Murder? Rape? Anything unmentionable?'

'What's unmentionable,' Crawford scowled, 'is people like you. Why don't you lurk around a graveyard somewhere, like the ghoul you are?' And he walked away.

'Well,' Fenton said to the air beyond Crawford's shoulder, '*he* wasn't very friendly, was he?' And he looked up to an overhead window, where a face peered out. 'Good morning,' he called cheerily, with a triumphant look at the disappearing Crawford. 'Freddie Fenton, *Illustrated Police News*. Can I have a word?'

'But this is . . . awful.'

It was the best that Angela Friend could do. Her Monday morning had begun well. Together with Anthea Crossley and Janet Bairnsfather they were met at the doors of University College by Constable Crawford. He was not in uniform, but neither was this the day of the public lectures. She had been on her way to the library when she saw him and there was something about the expression on his face that alarmed her.

The charming and slightly diffident man she had taken five o'clock tea with only last Friday was stiff, awkward, at a loss to know how to begin. And, yet, he had to; that was why he was here.

All thoughts of the library forgotten, she had gone with him to the Jeremy Bentham and they found a quiet corner.

'Did you know her well?' he asked her. 'Helen, I mean.'

'Probably no better than you.' Angela paused and looked at him, looking for the tell-tale flicker of a man not sharing everything, but there was nothing and her heart skipped a beat. In the middle of bad news, she felt unaccountably happy. 'She was very keen on Roman stuff, I do remember that, particularly the first century. My speciality is Corinthian Greece, as you know, so I really wasn't much help.' She looked at him again. 'I just can't believe this. Murdered, you say?'

Crawford held up his hands. 'The CID are calling it suicide,' he said, 'but, although I didn't know her well, in the chats I've had with Helen there was never any indication of that.'

'Telephonist, wasn't she? With the Central Exchange?'

'Er . . . perhaps,' he flustered.

'Adam,' she raised an eyebrow. 'What is it you're not telling me?'

He took a breath, looked around him and launched into it. 'I believe that she was an unfortunate,' he said.

Angela's eyes widened. 'A prostitute?' The word was delivered a little too loudly for anyone's liking. Arguably the only person in the building except Crawford familiar with the word was Tom and he used a whole thesaurus of alternatives.

'I could be wrong,' Crawford whispered, anxious to keep the conversation between just him and Angela, 'but her rooms bore all the hallmarks.'

Angela didn't have a clue what they might be and she suddenly felt just a little afraid to be dragged into a world in which she had no place – Crawford's world; his day job. 'I don't understand, Adam,' she said, her tea neglected, her choux pastry untouched. 'Why are you telling me this?'

'Because something's not right,' he told her. 'Because in the police we're told that if you want to know how and why a person died, you need to understand how they lived. At the moment, you and I are the only two who knew Helen, however slightly. I need some answers.'

Angela took a deep breath. She reached for her cup, took a swig and stood up. 'Well, then,' she said, straightening her hat, 'the cleverest person I know, who has provided more answers to more questions than you and I have had hot dinners, is sitting just around the corner from here.' She held up her hand. 'Come on,' she said. 'We'll talk to Em-em.'

'Who?'

'Dr Murray. She's the only woman I know who can tell a substantivized verb from a semantic object.'

Margaret Murray sat with a chisel in one hand and a piece of teak in the other. She looked up from her cluttered desk in the bowels of University College and fixed Mrs Plinlimmon with her fiercest stare.

'Well,' she said softly to the stuffed owl high on the shelf, 'what's it to be? Amenhotep or Ozymandias?'

The owl, as always, was stuck for an answer, but Margaret Murray, as the college's only junior lecturer in archaeology, was short of colleagues whose opinions she could seek, so Mrs Plinlimmon it was.

'You're right, of course,' she said. 'Amenhotep it is,' and she began to chip away at the wood with an expert hand.

The tap on the door stopped all that.

'Dr Murray, I'm so sorry to bother you.'

'Angela.' The lecturer put the chisel down. 'And . . .?'

'Adam Crawford, Dr Murray. I attend your Friday lectures for the public.'

'Delighted, Mr Crawford,' she smiled. Then she looked at Angela. 'Is the library closed for refurbishment, my dear?'

Angela laughed, despite the shock she had had some moments ago. 'We have a problem, Dr Murray,' she said. 'Adam and I.'

'Oh dear.' Whatever else Margaret Murray was, she was not a lonely hearts counsellor and knew at once that she was seriously out of her depth.

'Did you ever come across Helen Richardson at the Friday lectures?'

'Helen . . .?' Margaret frowned. 'Tall girl – well, you all are to me – blonde. Not unattractive. Interested in . . .' – she paused and tapped her chin, remembering – 'Roman archaeology, I believe.' She looked up and Angela nodded. 'What's the problem?'

'She's dead,' Crawford said, flatly.

'Oh dear.' Margaret put down her piece of wood and ushered her visitors to chairs.

'I found her,' Crawford told her.

'You did?'

'I should explain, Dr Murray,' he said, 'that I am a constable of the Metropolitan Police. A Division. In that capacity, I came across her body last Friday night . . . well, Saturday morning, speaking accurately, I suppose . . .'

'One must always be accurate,' Margaret reminded the room.

'Um . . . yes. I was called to an altercation and when investigating that, I discovered her body in her rooms in Storey's Yard.'

'Adam thinks she was murdered, Dr Murray,' Angela said, 'but the detectives believe it was suicide.'

'How distressing,' Margaret said. 'But I don't see—'

'Dr Murray,' Adam cut in, 'Neither of us knew Helen very well, but as a fellow amateur archaeologist I feel a sense of . . . I don't know. I need to do right by her.'

'And you are the most capable person I know,' Angela threw in, 'used, if it doesn't sound too ghoulish, to dead bodies.'

'*Long* dead,' Margaret reminded her. She looked at Crawford, then at Angela. Then she whipped a notepad and pencil from under a pile of parchment and passed them to the constable. 'Draw the position of the body,' she said.

'What?' Crawford's mouth hung open. Such a command from a hard-bitten copper or a bewhiskered police surgeon was one thing; but from a woman who barely, when standing, reached his collar badges, was altogether something else.

'Mr Crawford' – Margaret leaned towards him – 'I have studied the corpses of Celtic warriors, Egyptian pharaohs and Finno-Ugric concubines. Without wishing to belittle human-kind or question the sanctity of life, we are all the same length lying down.'

Anatomically, that wasn't true, but Crawford knew what she meant and started sketching. When he'd finished, he passed the pad back to her.

'Arms like so?' Margaret checked. 'Outspread?'

'Yes.'

'And the legs?'

'Likewise.' Crawford found himself blushing.

'Wounds of any kind?' the archaeologist went on. 'Cuts, abrasions, bruising?'

'None that I could see.'

'Very well.' Margaret leaned back, still looking at the sketch. Flinders Petrie would have hated it. 'This is a bed, is it? On which the poor girl was lying?'

'That's right.'

'Now,' she said, 'concentrate. Was there a table, beside the bed, perhaps?'

'There was.'

'Anything on it?'

'A lamp. And a bottle. Well, a phial, really.'

'Size? Shape? Come along, Mr Crawford. An archaeologist is nothing if he can't observe.'

'Er . . . it was about four inches high.' He subconsciously mimed it with his fingers. 'Square sided.' His face was screwed up with the effort of remembering. 'It was empty.'

'Did you sniff it?'

'As a matter of fact, I did.'

'What did it smell of?'

'Almonds,' Crawford told her.

'Cyanide,' Margaret nodded. 'Tell me, Mr Crawford, did you see anyone at those premises in . . . sorry, where?'

'Storey's Yard, Westminster. Yes, a neighbour and a rent collector. It was their altercation which drew my attention.'

'And did you learn anything from them?'

'I learned that they both knew her as Alice Groves.'

'Interesting,' the archaeologist muttered. 'Do you have an explanation for that – the two names of the deceased?'

Crawford shifted uncomfortably. 'I believe that the woman known as Alice Groves was . . . an unfortunate, a scarlet sister, a woman of the night.'

'Hmm,' Margaret nodded. 'A policeman and a prostitute. I had no idea the public lectures on a Friday drew such a colourful audience.' She smiled at Angela. 'Makes the rest of the week appear quite dull, doesn't it, my dear?'

'Dr Murray.' Crawford was still uneasy. 'I shouldn't have brought this problem to you. I—'

But the woman held up her hand. 'Mr Crawford,' she said. 'Have you ever been to Ephesus in Turkey?'

The constable hadn't. The furthest east he had been was Margate, though he lived in hope.

'It's a marvellous place, for an historian or an archaeologist. Or for anyone to commune with the past. It has the most wonderful library, once famous throughout the world. And as you look at its stupendous Greek façade, you will see a small door to the left. That was the entrance to the brothel that operated just behind it. When St Paul was writing to the Ephesians, up to a third of them weren't listening because they were enjoying themselves in what I believe the hoi polloi of today would call a knocking shop. Academe and the bohemian world have always gone hand in hand. The late Miss Richardson's profession doesn't actually surprise me at all.'

'I thought she was a telephonist,' Angela remarked and the archaeologist and the policeman both looked at her. 'Well, I did,' she said, huffily. 'She didn't look like . . . well, she looked just like a telephonist . . .' She gave up and folded her arms.

'I met someone else at Helen's place,' Crawford said. 'Freddie Fenton, a journalist, for want of a better word, with the *Illustrated Police News*. Freddie looks like and behaves like a ferret – he has his teeth into it now and won't let go until he has sucked every ounce of blood from it.'

Margaret Murray looked at the constable with admiration. 'I think you have missed your calling, Constable Crawford,' she told him.

'As an archaeologist?' he asked, brightening.

'No. As a dime novel writer. No, no' – she saw his crest fall – 'that is far from an insult. It is a skill not shared by many.'

'Dr Murray.' Angela was keen to get the conversation back

on track. 'I can't forget that I talked to Helen nearly every week. She was funny and fascinated by archaeology. Can we do anything? To catch her killer, I mean.'

Margaret chuckled to herself. 'All kinds of people come to "learn archaeology" as they put it – the pyramid theorists; the ladies who come to be taught, not to learn; the Bible cranks; the believers in curses and spells. But . . . a lady of the night.' She smiled at Crawford. 'I believe that's a first, Constable.'

'As far as we know.' Crawford knew that not everyone was quite what they seemed.

She leaned back and looked at them both. 'You know the most rewarding thing about being an archaeologist?' she asked. They shook their heads. 'It's about filling a gap – oh, it might not be large and it might not be very important, but it is a gap, nonetheless. And, little by little, we archaeologists fill it. It's one of the purest joys in life. So, let's fill in a gap for Helen Richardson, shall we?'

Margaret Murray was not the only woman in the Boys' Institute at St Vincent's the next morning, but she was the only one taking notes. Inquests drew the flotsam and jetsam of London, not merely the coroner and his flunkies but the litany of ghouls who crowded on pavements after road accidents and who watched bodies being fished out of the Thames.

She carefully noted the names of the witnesses – Jacob Lawrenson, who lived in the rooms above and acted as general caretaker for the house in Storey's Yard; Abel Turner, who collected – or tried to collect – the dead woman's rent; Dr Richard Lambert, the Police Surgeon of A Division, who spoke in disinterested terms of cyanide poisoning and its effects on the human body. There were any number of men in that crowded hall who may have known Helen Richardson in another context, but, almost by definition, they were not coming forward with any information at all. Margaret was singularly unimpressed by the dismissive tones of Detective Inspector Athelgar Blunt of A Division, whose cursory account of the finding of the body, which in reality ought to have been Constable Crawford's job, appeared to elicit from the coroner far more gravitas than it actually deserved.

As the proceedings drew to a close and the coroner thanked the jury, twelve men and stupid, for their time, the inevitable verdict was solemnly announced. 'Suicide, while the balance of the mind was disturbed.'

It was the balance of the murderer's mind that bothered Margaret Murray rather more; and to that end, she tapped one of the journalists leaving St Vincent's on the shoulder, looking carefully at his Press badge. '*Illustrated Police News?*' she said cheerfully.

He tipped his hat. 'Freddie Fenton, madam,' he said. 'At your service.'

Margaret stifled a smile. Adam Crawford was quite right; the man was almost exactly like a ferret. She held up the previous week's edition. 'This.' She tapped the lurid drawing of a woman drowning in Regent's Canal. 'Is it your work?'

'The article, madam,' he gushed, 'not the illustration. Although I can vouch for the fact that our artist spent many a gruelling hour on the towpath of said canal accurately sketching the scene.'

'How accurate will it be for Helen Richardson?'

'Eh?'

'Has your artist already trampled over the pavement in Storey's Yard, quite possibly contaminating a crime scene?'

'A crime . . .? Oh, come now, madam, did you not hear the coroner? A case of suicide.'

'If it were a case of suicide, Mr Fenton, you wouldn't be here. Neither would your nasty, spurious little magazine. Tell me, what do you know about Helen Richardson that I don't?'

Fenton eased himself out into St Vincent's vestibule, secretly longing for light and freedom. 'Who *are* you?' he felt bound to ask.

'A seeker of the truth,' she said. 'Unlike the columnists of the *Illustrated Police News*. Do I assume you have no information on the late Miss Richardson?'

Fenton grinned and tapped the side of his nose. 'You'll have to buy next week's edition to find out,' he said.

'I shall look forward to it,' she told him. 'There will no doubt be a ghoulish wraith standing in Storey's Yard with a bloody knife dripping from his clawed hand.'

'What?' Fenton clutched her arm. 'You mean, she was stabbed? I couldn't get in to see the body . . . I . . . No,' he laughed. 'You're having me on!'

'Am I, Mr Fenton? You'll have to read the letters page of next week's *Telegraph* to find out. And, by the way' – she tapped the front page of the rag again – 'this advertisement "To Married Ladies – Try the French Remedy – not a dangerous drug but a wonderful secret invention." I hardly know where to begin to point out the impropriety of all that. But I think I'll start with the Press Agency. Good morning.'

Margaret Murray could have quietly kicked herself. The inquest had told her precisely nothing and in latching on to the equally useless Freddie Fenton, she had missed her chance to collar Detective Inspector Athelgar Blunt. There was nothing for it; the mountain would have to go to Mohammed and she took a hansom to Scotland Yard.

This was the second – or was it the third? – building to go by that name. And it had once been intended to be an opera house. Appropriate, though, that during its building a headless body had been found in its foundations; after that, what else could the building be used for *but* the headquarters of the Metropolitan Police? For most of the afternoon, Margaret Murray sat in the outer vestibule, the shortest person in the whole building by a country mile. A kindly desk sergeant had brought her a cup of tea and the afternoon shift provided ginger biscuits. No, she had not contributed to the Police Benevolent Fund nor to the Seaside Home in Hove for Distressed Constables; neither did she wish to do so. She merely wished to talk to Detective Inspector Blunt and so, after only three hours, there he was.

People often said that senior detectives looked like bank managers; Athelgar Blunt looked just like a policeman, from his outsized brogues, via the obsolete Dundrearies that framed his face, to the severest of Teutonic haircuts. Margaret knew she could never entrust her savings to a man like that.

'Madam.' He nodded. The man and his entire office smelled of pipe smoke and the pale sun of Westminster barely penetrated the room.

'Doctor,' she corrected him.

'I didn't know there were any,' Blunt said, clearly an oaf to his fingertips.

'Of medicine, I believe there are four. But I am a doctor of archaeology. Helen Richardson was one of my students.'

'Who?'

'The dead woman in Storey's Yard. You attended her inquest this morning.'

Blunt narrowed his eyes at her. He prided himself that he was an observer par excellence, but he had no recollection of this diminutive woman at all.

'I'll come to the point, Inspector,' Margaret said. 'Aware of how busy you must be. On what grounds do you believe that Helen took her own life?'

Blunt blinked, reaching into his pocket for his pipe. 'I am not at liberty to divulge,' he said.

Margaret waited until the match had been struck and the flame hovered near the bowl. 'Must you?' she asked, clutching her breast as though the oxygen in the room had disappeared.

'Oh . . . er . . .' and Blunt blew the match out.

'Perhaps I should explain,' she said. 'Helen was only a part-time student of mine. She was nevertheless, in a strange way, my responsibility.'

'Ah.' Blunt came as close to a smile as he ever did, though it was hard to tell. 'Am I my sister's keeper?' There was no change of expression on his listener's face. 'To paraphrase the Good Book.'

'Yes, I understand the allusion, Inspector,' Margaret said. 'And, in this instance, yes, I am.'

'I'm very sorry,' the inspector said, laying the derelict pipe down on his desk. 'I suppose you wouldn't know a great deal about her, though. Being just part time and all? Do you know of any family, for example? We've been unable to trace anybody so far.'

'That isn't the kind of conversation my students tend to have with each other, Inspector, unless they become especially good friends, or perhaps share a house, as many of them do. I understand she was particularly interested in the early Roman period in Britain, if that's any help to you.'

Blunt raised an eyebrow.

'No, I thought possibly not. One of my students thought that perhaps Helen Richardson was a telephonist. Another, though . . .' She gave a cough. Although she had no problem using the word prostitute or any alternative to it, she had a sneaky feeling that perhaps Athelgar Blunt had other expectations of ladylike behaviour.

Blunt did indeed lower his eyes slightly before embarking on his next piece of information. 'This didn't really come up at the inquest,' he said, 'but . . . and I appreciate that this is rather indelicate. The late Miss Richardson made her living on immoral earnings.'

'She was a prostitute, yes.' Margaret thought the word had to be used or they would be dancing around each other until midnight struck.

It took Blunt a split second to come back from that. 'Well, there you are; another motive for self-slaughter. Guilt. Shame. Believe me, I've seen it all.'

'I'm sure you have,' Margaret said, suddenly seeing Athelgar Blunt as the brick wall he was. She stood up. Blunt did not. 'So, you can't help me further?' she asked, just to be sure.

He shrugged and pulled a pile of paper towards him, already on the next task. 'No. But if you'll take my advice, madam, I'd stay well out of this. Leave it to us; it's what we're paid for.'

'I see.' She smiled. 'Well, don't get up. I'll see myself out.'

'Just appalling about Helen,' Anthea Crossley said. 'I can't quite believe it.'

'Did you know her well?' Veronica Halifax was sipping her cocoa in the homely lounge of Angela's house in Bloomsbury. Veronica had begun the term lodging with some family in cramped rooms somewhere at the end of the Northern Line, but from the first day she had hit it off with Angela, who had invited her to move in. She had told her landlady that a family crisis had made it essential she went home forthwith and had made a happy nest with Angela. Anthea Crossley and Janet Bairnsfather were both something she could put up with; moving again because they weren't particularly congenial would have been like throwing the baby out with the bathwater. And as it happened, that was another thing she liked at Angela's – plenty of hot water on tap!

'Not well, exactly.' Anthea was blowing smoke rings to the ceiling. 'The public lecture people aren't quite "one of us", are they?'

Veronica nodded. If truth were to be told, she was a little in awe of Anthea Crossley. The woman was older than her, with a degree in archaeology now that the University allowed such a thing *and* she smoked cigarettes. Not only was this woman trying to get others of her kidney the vote, she would probably be blowing smoke circles up to the ceiling of Number Ten, Downing Street one day. And, of course, Anthea was right; Helen was not really one of them.

'Angela,' Anthea called. 'Stop fiddling about in the kitchen and tell us all that the gorgeous Constable Crawford has confided.' She gave a rather louche smile that Veronica promised herself she would practise in the mirror later. 'Not everything, of course. Just what pertains to Helen or whatever her name was.'

Angela Friend had not knowingly blushed in ten years and she wasn't going to start now. She came into the sitting room, her cocoa mug in her hand, her hair still wet from the bath. 'That, darling Anthea,' she said, 'is absolutely no business of yours.'

'Oh, come on,' Anthea urged as the girl sat down. 'You don't keep a policeman and bark yourself – or am I mixing my metaphors there?'

A shrill screech from across the room indicated that Janet Bairnsfather had just got the joke. No one paid any attention.

'All I can say,' Angela said, 'is that Dr Murray is on the case.'

'Em-em?' Anthea sat up a little. 'Why?'

'Well, if you must know, I went to see her – *with* Constable Crawford, before you ask. Apparently, the official line is that it was suicide. I don't believe it.'

The others looked at her.

'Neither does Adam . . . er . . . Constable Crawford.'

They continued to look at her.

'And neither does Em-em.'

'What's she going to do?' Veronica asked.

'I haven't the faintest idea,' Angela said, 'but if Margaret Murray is involved, you can bet we're going to get results.'

'Norman was truly awful today.' Andrew Rose reached for his cigarettes. 'Never known him worse.' Students all clapped for Flinders Petrie; no one did for Norman Minton.

'Well, you would do the Roman stuff.' Ben Crouch wagged a finger at him, one of those not wrapped around a sandwich.

'What *is* that?' Piers Gibbs had to ask. He had been looking at it for some minutes.

'Supper,' Crouch told him through the wedge of bread.

'Yes, but *specifically*.' Gibbs wouldn't let it go. To any details forthcoming, he could add that it was the thing dripping grease on to his mother's second-best sofa, but it seemed churlish and also redundant, since Crouch sat in a slick of goo wherever he went.

'Bacon,' Crouch said, 'mainly. Egg. A bit of black pudding I found at the back of the meat safe.' He checked again, lifting a corner of the rather soggy bread. 'I think that's a mushroom . . . yes, a mushroom. All held together by a generous dollop of HP sauce.' He held it out. 'Want a bite?'

'I'd rather cut my own throat.' Gibbs turned away, a fastidious handkerchief to his nose. Then, curiosity kicked in. 'Did you fry all that?'

'Of course.' Crouch hitched some of his bulk on to his high horse. 'I'm not an animal.' He took another bite. 'What about this Helen Richardson business, eh? Rum do.'

Gibbs guessed the general gist of the question. Living with Crouch meant learning another language – Mouthful of Bread. 'Did you know her?' The college had been buzzing with the name all day.

'Sort of,' Crouch said. 'She was one of the public of course, what you public schoolboys call the hoi polloi, I believe. She was keen on Roman finds, though. Didn't she bend your ear, Andy?'

Rose was lighting up his Pall Mall cigarette – to be more exact, one of Piers Gibbs's Pall Mall cigarettes, but who was counting? 'Don't remember,' he shrugged.

'Yes, you do.' Crouch took another bite. 'I saw you only last week in the Fox and Grapes. Head to head, you were.'

Realization dawned. 'Oh, that was Helen Richardson, was it?' he said. 'I didn't catch the name.'

'Did you catch her calling, though? If you did, that probably wasn't all you'd catch.'

'What?' Gibbs had lost track of this conversation.

Crouch sighed. 'I don't suppose you got out much at Harrow,' he said. 'No chance to enjoy the fleshpots of Uxbridge. Rumour has it that our part-time, public lectures archaeologist was a whore.'

'No!' Gibbs was appalled, but in a good way.

'So.' Crouch threw in the last remnants of his sandwich and wiped his mouth with his sleeve. 'How far did you get, Rosey, my boy?'

Andrew Rose laughed at his fellow students with cold contempt. 'Not far beyond the reign of Marcus Aurelius,' he said.

Disappointment was writ large on Ben Crouch's face. Rose got up and made for the door. 'Anthea Crossley, now,' he said, his hand on the handle, 'was an altogether different proposition.'

'You've done it with Anthea?' Crouch was open-mouthed, not an attractive sight.

Rose smiled at Gibbs, who nodded. 'Hasn't everybody?'

THREE

For Margaret Murray, it was an intellectual puzzle. At least, that was how it all started out. But it was one thing to enquire into the life of Nefertiti or Ptolemy the Piper; to uncover a more recent past was altogether more disturbing. But what dismayed Margaret – and what drove her on – was the fact that Helen Richardson had been, however incidentally, one of hers. And the fact that nobody, beyond a tiny coterie of students, seemed to give a damn, as our American cousins were all too fond of saying.

So Margaret approached the problem, at least at first, from an academic point of view. She would go to the foremost authority on the subject and that meant taking the South Eastern line to Camberwell, where the Salvation Army Citadel loomed over the station like the Tower of Babel. There was a lingering fog over London that morning. It had wreathed Bloomsbury like a ghost, hovering in the squares and alleyways, floating with Margaret Murray's train to the south. The lighters honked and bellowed on the river, but the city carried on regardless, as it did no matter what the weather; as it had for centuries.

The Citadel's roof was lost in the mist, but at ground level, all was bustle and laughter, as it always was when the General was in town. The Egyptologist was shown into an ante-room, the walls of which were hung with wise saws from the Bible, the one book that gave this place its purpose. Cheerful men in braided jackets with cherry-coloured collars and cuffs came and went, each of them smiling at Margaret Murray and wishing her a good morning.

'The General will see you now,' one of them said, and led her down a long corridor to a large, airy room at the far end. The object of her visit got up from a fireside chair at her arrival. William Booth looked like an engraving from the Old Testament, his long hair and chest-length beard snowy white, his eyes bright and kindly. He wore a cavalry officer's frock coat, braided in black, and he stooped a little now that the years had finally caught up with him.

'General Booth.' Margaret whipped off her glove and shook the man's hand. 'It's good of you to see me.'

'The pleasure is mine, madam,' he said. 'Please,' and he ushered her to a chair. 'What can I do for you?'

She sat down and got, as she always did, to the point. 'Prostitution,' she said.

Very little over the years had ever fazed William Booth; not the poverty of the Mile End Waste; not the licentious drunkenness of the East End; not even the gangs of the Nichol. He

had taken it all on his patriarchal chin and had sent his Sally
Army angels out from their Alley with a tambourine, a bowl
of soup and, most importantly of all, hope. So his response
to this rather bizarre opening was the result of all this. He
simply said, 'Ah.'

Margaret ferreted in her handbag. 'You are the foremost
authority on the subject in Britain today,' she said, and
produced a well-thumbed book. 'In here' – she tapped the
cover – 'if memory serves on page seventy-nine, you make
the point that prostitution is the only profession in the world
where the young make the most money.'

'I'm flattered that you've read *Darkest England*,' the General
said, 'but I'm not sure I can really offer anyone a way out yet.'

Margaret smiled. 'If you can't, General,' she said, 'I don't
know who can. Let me explain. One of my students at
University College was found dead in her lodgings recently.
The higher echelons of the police believe it was suicide. I
believe it was murder.'

'Sad,' Booth said, 'but I don't see how . . .'

'She was an archaeologist by day, General,' Margaret told
him, 'but a whore by night. It was in that guise that she was
found. I could bore the pants off you with the burial customs
of the Fourth Dynasty of the Old Kingdom, but I'm afraid
that I am woefully ignorant of today's ways of the flesh, for
money at least.'

Booth smiled. 'Will you take tea, Dr Murray?' he asked.

'Thank you,' she said. 'That would be delightful.'

He rang a little silver bell and waited while Margaret gave
him as many details as she could. Within minutes, an army
girl came in, carrying a tray with two china cups and a large
brown teapot. The sugar bowl and the milk jug didn't match
each other or anything else on the tray. Somehow, in this
setting, anything else would have looked wrong.

'Gertie,' Booth said, 'get yourself a cup and join us. Dr
Murray here needs some information. About your erstwhile
employment.'

The girl raised an eyebrow and left, only to return moments
later with another cup. In the meantime, Booth had become
mother and poured for them all, with practised dexterity.

'Tell Dr Murray how you started out,' Booth said.

Gertie raised startled eyes to his. 'Everything?' she asked, dubiously.

'Everything,' he told her. 'If Dr Murray finds it all too much, I am sure she'll tell you.' He smiled across at the archaeologist; ten minutes and he already seemed to know her inside out.

'Well,' Gertie began, 'I was one of eight children. I never knew who my dad was and I doubt my mother did either. He was supposed to be a duke or something. She put me on the game when I was nine. This was in Spitalfields. Then I was stolen by the gypsies.'

'Gertie,' Booth growled and the girl stiffened like a rabbit in thrall to a stoat. 'What was that little chat we had the other day about a little thing called the truth?'

Gertie scowled. In an instant, the little girl lost from the East End with the blue blood and the Romany ways became her usual self. 'I went on the game because I wanted to, mum,' she said. 'Most of us girls do. Well, whatever they tell you, it's better than gutting fish in Billingsgate or getting phossy jaw at Bryant & May's.'

'Did you . . . work alone?' Margaret didn't really know how to put it.

'For a bit, yes,' Gertie said, 'but that's a mug's game. There are lunatics out there, mum, and they get madder still when there's a bit of red on offer.'

'Sexual favours,' the General translated for Dr Murray's benefit.

'That's when I realized I needed some protection. I got into Mrs Prothero's in Turks Row.'

'Middle class brothel,' Booth chimed in. 'Well known to C Division of the Metropolitan Police.'

'Yeah, we had lots of them as regulars,' Gertie chimed in.

'That is in fact true,' General Booth told Dr Murray, 'though that may shock you.'

Margaret shook her head. 'Not in the least,' she smiled. 'Tell me, Gertie, did you have your own regulars? Apart from C Division, I mean.'

'Yes, we all did. Mrs Prothero insisted we were all clean

and nicely turned out for them. She was always very fair, was
Mrs Prothero. We could keep presents; even though not
everyone was as understanding. But she knew that if we were
happy, we'd work harder.' Gertie smiled. 'Because it *is* work,
just like any other job. Even if some of the men are . . . well,
we don't get the handsome ones, not as a rule. Although there
was one . . .' Her smile became distant, remembering old
times.

'Thank you, Gertie,' the General said, tapping her knee.
'Just stick to the facts, please.'

The girl shook herself and came back to earth. 'Sorry,' she
murmured.

'I suppose some girls worked on their own, though,'
Margaret persisted. 'Not everyone would be chosen to work
in a . . . in a . . .' She wasn't sure whether the word 'brothel'
was polite.

'Going freelance?' Gertie pulled a doubtful face. 'Lots of
girls did that, but they weren't in our league at all. They were
mostly skirts up over your head, be quick about it and get the
price of a bed for the night in a doss and a bloater to toast if
you're lucky. Some of them have other jobs, just going out of
a night if they need some extra.'

'Does that sound like your friend?' the General asked.

'In a way, in that she certainly had another life. But I don't
believe she went out on the streets as such. It must be a
dangerous life, Gertie, surely, however you follow it.'

'Except for coal-mining, the fisheries and the army from
time to time, yes, I suppose it is,' Gertie acknowledged. 'Why
do you want to know about all this?'

Margaret looked at the girl. She wasn't pretty in the conven-
tional sense, but it was probably any port in a storm as far as
her gentlemen friends were concerned. 'A girl I know,' she
said, 'was murdered in her rooms.'

'By a client?' Gertie's eyes were wide.

'That's what I'm trying to find out,' Margaret said.

'Some of 'em are weird,' Gertie said, sipping her tea. 'Want
you to do funny things.'

'Really?' Margaret said. 'Such as?'

Gertie looked at her, then at Booth, who nodded. She leaned

across and whispered in the archaeologist's ear. Margaret's eyes widened till they would go no wider, then she said, 'Good Lord!' The only other example of that she had come across had been in an Assyrian bas-relief and that had been fragmented by water erosion so the details were unclear.

Gertie moved back, nodding. 'And that was without the hose-pipe,' she said. There was a silence.

'Look, mum,' Gertie downed her cup. 'It ain't my place to say. The General here, he found me, made me see the error of my ways. Oh, I still get the odd stirrings sometimes – any red-blooded girl will – but now, well, I've got Jesus. And He's all I want – apart from Sergeant Major Poultney, a' course. What you're doing – asking questions about this dead girl – believe me, it's not healthy. In fact, I'd go further – it's downright dangerous.'

Margaret Murray smiled. 'Asking questions about dead people is what I do, Gertie,' she said. 'It's all I've ever done.'

'Dr Murray is an archaeologist, Gertie,' Booth explained.

'Yes, but your dead people have been dead for long enough for them to not have a pimp come knocking on your door, haven't they, though?' Gertie said. She appealed to the General. 'That's right, ain't it?'

Booth sat upright. He had by and large left the conversation to Gertie. 'She is right,' he said quietly. 'Dabbling in this world could get you hurt, Dr Murray. Do you, for instance, have the young lady's client list, assuming, as I think we should, that she didn't go out on the streets?'

'Client list? No.'

Gertie chuckled and dipped her head at the General. He always knew what was what, the General did. 'She'll have a list somewhere. Names. Addresses, sometimes, if the gent was not too discreet.'

'What would it look like?'

Gertie shrugged. 'I never had one. Mrs Prothero did all that kind of thing for us and I trusted her. Some of the other girls kept them, though. They could be a little book, or just a piece of paper. One girl showed me what she did and it was clever, I give you that, though she ended up married to a pork butcher from Mile End, so her ideas of catching one of the bigwigs

didn't come to anything. Where was I? Yes, she put her list
in an envelope and scrumpled it up and smoothed it out and
whatnot and then hid it in a pile of other letters, tied in ribbon.
That was very clever, don't you think?'

Margaret smiled. 'Yes, it certainly was,' she said. 'Very
clever. But if I understand you, *if* my friend kept a list, and
it's only an if, I might never find it.'

Gertie gathered the tea things together and stood up. 'I think
that's about the size of it, mum. Sorry I couldn't be more
help.'

She opened the door with practised ease and left the Salvationist
and the archaeologist alone on either side of the fire. The General
threw on another log and they sat companionably, looking into
the flames.

'Thank you, General,' Margaret said, stirring herself. There
was something about the old man's company that was very
comforting, like having a warm bath while drinking laced
cocoa. 'That was very . . . enlightening.'

Booth chuckled. 'Gertie can be a little blunt, but I assumed
that you wanted a warts and all story, not sanitized.'

'Indeed,' she said, feeling for her handbag down the side
of her chair. 'I must admit I had hoped for more specific
information, such as that a list of clients was always made in
a bright red book the size of a table with "List Of Clients"
written on it, but that was always a faintish hope, I concede.
Hopefully, I will find it.'

'These girls can be very cunning, I'm afraid.' The General
levered himself out of his chair and went to the door. Before
he opened it, he turned and spoke, low and quickly. 'I wish
you all the best, Dr Murray, in finding your friend's killer. I
only hope that what you find will not tarnish her memory.'
He looked at her solemnly. 'Many of the women we save have
a low opinion of themselves and sometimes for good reason.
I see the best in everyone, but that best is not always what we
would wish it to be. Do you understand me?'

Margaret nodded. 'I do,' she said. 'Human beings are not
always very good examples of the Lord's work, I agree. But
I try not to think ill of the dead. I know so very many of them,
you see.'

The General looked at her from under his beetling brows and smiled. He took her hand and squeezed it gently. 'God go with you, my dear,' he said. 'And do come back and see us sometime. I know Gertie would like to see you again.'

'Perhaps I could meet her Sergeant Major Poultney,' Margaret said.

'Hmm, yes. Probably not.'

'Oh?'

'I think perhaps Sergeant Major Poultney will have been transferred by then. He and Mrs Poultney and all the little Poultneys. Sometimes, Dr Murray, old habits die a little bit too hard. Goodbye.' And he gently closed the door behind her.

Damn! Margaret Murray could have quietly kicked herself. She had meant to ask the General for his autograph in her copy of his book.

'What are we looking for again?'

'A client list, Mr Crawford. Something that your superiors should have been looking for all along.'

Night had fallen over the grey splendour of the Abbey and the mist wreathed the Thames beyond. October was dying and the deep twilight reflected it. Constable Crawford's hobnails were the only ones clattering on the cobbles at this hour and Margaret Murray made no sound at all. They turned left into Storey's Yard.

The last time Crawford had been there, it hadn't been hard to spot the house in question; it had been the centre of somewhat of a fracas. This time, he let his feet take him to what looked like the same door and pounded the doorknocker and waited. It seemed an eternity but eventually the sash window above grated open and the same raddled head of Upstairs Man poked out, minus the nightcap.

'Not today, thank you,' he called down.

'In your own time,' Crawford said and listened to the mumbled expletives as the window closed again. The front door opened eventually with much rattling of bolts.

'I've had these fitted,' the man said, 'after all what's happened. They haven't let the room yet. I thought there'd be a queue round the block – you know what people are like;

"Line up here to see where it happened" sort of thing. Ghouls, they are.' He looked at Crawford and repeated the word with relish. 'Ghouls. Who's this?'

He was looking sternly at the little woman at Crawford's elbow. She was too young to be his mother and there weren't any of the female persuasion in the police, despite the odd protest.

'This lady,' said Crawford, 'is helping me with my enquiries.'

Upstairs Man glanced down. He couldn't see any bracelets on the woman's wrists, so he assumed he was not at risk; you heard such stories.

'Good evening, Mr Lawrenson,' Margaret said. She had a thing for faces and Upstairs Man had stood near her, giving his evidence, such as it was, at Helen Richardson's inquest.

'How do you know me?' the unneighbourly neighbour wanted to know.

'As Constable Crawford says,' Margaret smiled, 'I am helping him with his enquiries. It would be remiss of me not to know you, wouldn't it?'

'Er . . . s'pose,' was the man's best attempt at a riposte.

'You still haven't got a key to the door, I expect?' Crawford asked.

'Nah,' Lawrenson said. 'Didn't the other day. Haven't now.'

'Look away, then,' the policeman advised and fiddled with the lock. In seconds, the door swung open.

''Ere!' Lawrenson was astonished. 'How did you do that?'

'I used to be a conjuror,' Crawford said, 'but the magic went out of it. Thank you, Mr Lawrenson. We'll take it from here.'

Jacob Lawrenson had not got to where he was today by sticking his neck out too far. 'Thank you,' he replied politely, shuffling upstairs again. 'Close both doors on your way out.'

Crawford took in the sad little rooms. Nothing appeared to have changed, except for the absence of a dead girl on the bed. The CID had been less than thorough, he was sure, and he rummaged in every corner. Wherever he was, Margaret was elsewhere, although seeing much even with the aid of Crawford's single lantern beam was difficult. Time and again, Crawford came back to the bed. It was heavy, with brass and iron holding together a wooden frame. He lifted the mattress, pushing the horsehair to one side. And there it was. Or rather, there was where it had been. A drawer had been fitted under the springs, out of sight unless the mattress was removed. One piece of paper had become caught in the drawer's joints. At the top was a handwritten number 3 – and there were two names below that.

'Well, well.' Crawford held his bull's-eye close to the paper.

Margaret Murray almost clapped her hands together. 'A client list,' she said, 'or I'm a Dutchman. Can you make out the names?'

Crawford could. 'Reginald Glass and James Brisket,' he read aloud. 'It says "three" at the top. I assume the first two pages are missing.'

She smiled. 'Spoken like a true archaeologist,' she said. 'Remind me to let you look at the Habakkuk archives sometime. What do you make of this?'

The archaeologist was holding a box in her hands, carved deal if she wasn't mistaken, with a brass clasp and hinges. She put it on the bed and flicked it open. 'It was over there in the cupboard, alongside poor Helen's clothes.'

Crawford shone his torch inside. There was a screwed-up piece of wrapping paper that had been hastily handled and stuffed back in. A loop of coarse string was beneath it. Margaret carefully rolled the string and tucked it away in a corner of the box and then took out the paper carefully. 'Hold that light steady, Mr Crawford,' she said and smoothed the paper out on the bedside table. There were no markings of any kind but as she moved it another piece of paper fell out and she held it up to the light. 'A railway ticket,' she said. 'A return to Hampton-on-Sea, Kent. Dated the eighteenth of August.' She looked at him. 'Over two months ago. Term had not begun yet.'

'May I?' Crawford took the stub from her. 'A Summer Saturday Special,' he said, nodding and handing it back.

'A what?'

'My old dad worked on the railways,' Crawford smiled. 'There's nothing like sitting alongside the track on a balmy summer's evening writing down the numbers of the locos. I used to find it restful. And when I gravitated to a stopwatch my dad gave me . . . well, I was in heaven.'

Margaret smiled up at him; the huge constable was a little boy again, his eyes shining bright in the pistons and the rivets and the steam. Crawford came back to the here and now.

'The Kent and Thanet Railway,' he said. 'There's a time stamp. Two thirteen. This would be from Victoria. Let's see, it would get into Hampton at . . . allowing for crosswinds, leaves on the line . . . I wonder what the weather was, hmmm . . . overheating boiler and so on . . . depends on the size of the train, of course . . .' He looked at the low ceiling as he did his calculation and Margaret wanted to shake him but managed to control herself. 'Four thirty-eight, give or take a minute.'

'It's a return ticket,' Margaret Murray said.

'It is, and—'

'And why wasn't it handed in or punched?' she finished the thought for him. 'If the ticket collectors on the Kent and Thanet are as fastidious as I have found them to be on every other line.'

'The return wasn't used,' Crawford said. 'Whoever bought it came back by other means.'

'Or,' Margaret said, 'didn't come back at all.'

Crawford closed the box again. 'This lock's been tampered with. Look.' His bull's-eye beams gleamed on the brass of the lock. There were scratches all around the keyhole. He marched out of the dead woman's rooms and called up the stairs. 'Mr Lawrenson!'

The upstairs neighbour duly appeared. 'What is it now?' he asked.

'Has anybody been here, since last Friday, I mean? Apart from my colleagues in the police?'

'There may have been one or two,' the man said cagily.

'And you're sure you have no key to Miss Richardson's rooms?'

'I told you, no. And get it right, mate. Whatever they said at the inquest, her name was Alice Groves.'

* * *

It was a quiet Thursday at the Jeremy Bentham. Nobody knew quite why the place was less than packed on that particular day of the week; it just was. And that made it a perfect time for Margaret Murray to ask a favour of her favourite restaurateur. Thomas brought the Tetley's, as usual, to Margaret's perch in the far corner. It was not a generally known fact in the corridors of Gower, but the lecturer in Egyptology was addicted to American dime novels. And she, better than anyone, knew the insanity of sitting with your back to an open door or window. All right, the Jeremy Bentham was not exactly the Last Chance Saloon and Margaret didn't have the flowing moustachios of Wild Bill Hickok, but you couldn't be too careful. So here she was, in the innermost recess, barely visible behind the gleaming copper and hissing steam, but able to survey the entire room at a single glance.

Tom sat down opposite her. 'So,' he said, 'is this the item in question?'

'It is,' she said. 'What can you tell me?'

Tom whipped a pair of pince-nez from his waistcoat pocket. He didn't need them, but it gave him a gravitas he felt he needed in the heart of Academia as he was. 'Sorrento ware,' he said, looking at the box she had half-inched from Storey's Yard. 'Very nice. Notice the grain around the swallows. That'll get you three bob down Borough Market any day of the week; best part of two guineas in New Bond Street.'

'I'm not interested in its value, Thomas,' she said. 'Look at the lock – what do you see?'

Tom tilted the box. 'Oh, dear,' he said, leaning back. 'Work of a rank amateur. Somebody's tried to force it. See these scratches? Nail-file, probably. One of your stouter hatpins at the outside.'

Margaret nodded. She knew Thomas would know. 'Dree your weird, then.'

Tom had no idea what the Prof had just said, but he got the general gist – her Scottish accent had not been particularly convincing, but he assumed, rightly, that it was a saying from North of the Border. He tossed a teaspoon in his hand. 'You see, your Italian locksmith is no fool. Most people's inclination, if they're going to pick a lock, is to use something sharp, pointed. Whereas what we really need is something blunt, as much like a key as possible. Something like . . .' – and the lock clicked open – 'a spoon.'

Margaret clapped her hands together like the grown-up schoolgirl she was. 'Thomas, you're a marvel.'

'Thanks, Prof.' He got up and bowed. 'Praise indeed.' And he got up to go.

'Don't you want to know what was inside?' she asked. In her world, the packaging was important, yes, but the contents were the thing.

'No, thanks, Prof,' he chuckled. 'In my world, the less you know the less the esclops can get out of you, catch my drift.'

Margaret Murray had not been brought up with the backwards slang of the London rookeries, but she knew that 'esclops' were the boys in blue and she had no intention of prying into Thomas's past.

'Anyway,' he said, 'I've got a piece of Victoria sponge in the kitchen that's got your name all over it!'

The lights burned blue in Margaret Murray's inner sanctum in the darkest recesses of the Godless Institution. It was late and she'd long ago heard the click-click of the cleaners' brooms and their cheery 'goodnights' to each other. She didn't imbibe much – her uncle John, in whose rectory in Rugby she had spent some, at least, of her childhood, did not approve. Neither did the ayah who had brought her up in India – her religion forbade it. Even so, there were times, and tonight was one of them, when a little hair of the dog was definitely called for and Margaret reached into her desk, fumbling past the scarab amulet from Shepseskaph's tomb, and poured herself an averagely sized Dow's. She raised it to the stuffed owl in the corner.

'The fact is, Mrs Plinlimmon – and we have to face this – Helen Richardson was a woman of two worlds, a sort of Janus of our time, looking back to the old, looking ahead to the new. Although, come to think of it, both her faces looked backwards, didn't they? One peered into the past of archaeology; the other to what is, after all, the world's oldest profession. Or is that the Church?'

She sighed and sipped. 'Yes, I know Herne Bay is rather out of the way at the moment, but that railway ticket bothers me. If she bought it, why didn't she use it for the return journey? And what took her to Hampton-on-Sea in the first place? At the moment, we still have questions galore and not a single answer. Well' – she held up her glass to the lamplight – 'cheers,' she said. 'Who knows what tomorrow may bring?'

'How are you, George?' Professor Flinders Petrie had had the devil's own job getting to Gower Street that morning. There was a dray horse down in Gordon Square and a watermain had burst along Malet Street, threatening to drown the whole of Bloomsbury and beyond. As a result, the archaeologist was damp of foot and in a decidedly bad mood.

George Carey Foster's brandy helped with all that, except, perhaps, the damp feet and he offered a glass to his visitor now.

'God rot Arthur Evans,' Petrie toasted and Carey Foster sighed. Not of the archaeological persuasion himself, he could never understand the snipery that went on in the particularly murky corridors of that branch of academe. 'Now,' Petrie sat down in Foster's best Chesterfield and composed himself. 'I assume your summons involves the late Miss Richardson?'

'Hardly a summons, William,' Foster said, lolling back in his captain's swivel chair. 'You and I go back a long way.'

They did. George Carey Foster had been made principal of University College earlier that year, but he felt he had known Petrie all his life.

'Command, then,' Petrie corrected himself. 'Order. Decree from on high.'

'I don't think you should be so flippant, William,' Foster snapped. 'A woman is dead.'

'Sorry,' Petrie said. 'You're quite right, of course.'

'One of Margaret's, wasn't she?'

'Indirectly,' Petrie said. 'Attended the public classes, so I believe. Fridays.'

'And what's Margaret doing about it?'

Petrie guffawed. 'Why should Margaret be doing anything about it?'

'Because she's Margaret, William; you need no more than that. That's why I want you to step in.'

Petrie looked at the man, wide-eyed. 'Step in, George?' he echoed. 'Step in? You've just told me how precisely you know Margaret Murray. You must have some idea how ludicrous that suggestion is?'

The principal leaned forward in his chair and the springs groaned. 'See that filing cabinet?' He pointed to the furniture in question.

'I do,' Petrie said.

'Would it surprise you to learn that the entire top drawer – the locked one – contains a list of Margaret's delinquencies?'

'Delinquencies?' Petrie repeated. 'Oh, come, now . . .'

Foster didn't need to unlock the drawer. He knew the contents off by heart. 'The woman refers to herself as "Doctor", whereas she hasn't even, to my knowledge, got a bachelor's degree.'

'She has,' Petrie replied. 'I gave it to her myself.'

'You . . .? Such honours are not given out with the toilet paper, William.'

'The "Doctor" thing is a little outré, I'll grant you.' Petrie raised both hands. 'But again, Margaret and I agreed it would increase her standing in a world of men.'

'But we *are* in a world of men, Petrie!' Foster snapped. 'I was talking to Sidney Hartland the other day. The world's leading anthropologist doesn't even allow women into his lectures. And you can't just agree on a degree; the university has to confer it.'

'All in good time,' Petrie said.

But Foster hadn't finished. 'Then there's that business with Professor Virchow of Berlin.'

Petrie leaned back, cradling his left knee, perhaps for moral support. 'Never proven,' he said.

'And in Scottish law, as you know very well, that means as guilty as hell,' the principal reminded him. 'Then there was that wretched incident involving the Feuchtwanger diamonds.'

'*They* came to *her*,' Petrie reminded the principal.

'The theft of the King's College mascot?' Foster hadn't finished yet.

'Student pranks, George,' Petrie dismissed it. 'You're scraping the barrel.'

'Am I?' Foster thundered. 'I haven't got on to the Hissarlik controversy yet. Even you can't defend that one.'

As it turned out, Petrie couldn't. 'I'll grant you, she may have overstepped the mark there. But it was all in a good cause.'

'Good cause, my arse, Petrie.' Foster slammed his glass down on his desk. 'The only cause uppermost in my mind at the moment – as it should be in yours – is the reputation of this college. Bad enough that one of our students has lost her life, but for Margaret to poke her trowel into it all is unacceptable. I hear she attended the wretched girl's inquest the other day.'

'Well, what do you expect me to do about it?' Petrie felt obliged to ask.

'Rein her in, man,' Foster bellowed. 'Rein her in.' He jabbed his finger into the air. 'I warn you, if we have a repetition of that Abu Simbel nonsense, "Doctor" Murray will be looking for another job. Do I make myself clear, William?'

'As a bell, George,' Petrie sighed. 'As a bell.'

FOUR

The Hampton Pier Inn, it had to be said, had seen better days. So had the pier itself, swept away by the grey, surging sea and the collapse of the cliff. The Great Storm three years before had finished it off and the wind moaned in Margaret Murray's room on the hotel's first floor, making the curtains twitch and quiver. She sat by the dressing table, unpinning her hair and watching the breakers crash on the shingle as night fell. She turned up the lamp and, as she did so, caught sight of a figure wandering at the water's edge. It was a man, certainly, short and solid, with an Ulster around his shoulders which flapped in the wind. The warmth of an Indian Summer had gone now and it was cold on that beach, promising a grim autumn and winter to follow.

She wondered briefly who he was, the solitary soul on the edge of his world, standing foursquare against the wind. Then she reminisced on the day she had spent, making her enquiries. No one here had heard of Helen Richardson. Nor of Alice Groves. No one remembered seeing a mousey-haired girl wandering the old tramway track or digging in the dead oyster beds. A woman with a trowel in her hand, let alone a pick and shovel, would have merited notice; surely *somebody* would have seen her. Likewise, a London demi-monde would have raised eyebrows too. None of it, Margaret sighed, as she clambered into bed, made any sense at all. There had been no Helen or Alice staying at the Pier Inn and that was the only hotel in town. And she lay awake, listening to the moaning wind and the deadly hiss of the sea.

At breakfast, she saw him again; the solitary soul at the water's edge as night had fallen. But this time, he turned sharp right and was making his way to the hotel. More than that, he was coming into the restaurant, sweeping off an unfashionable wideawake and shaking the rain from the shoulders of his Ulster. He was a square-built man, with thinning hair and a waxed moustache, heavy hands and a thick neck. But his eyes were kind and twinkled in the reflection of the newly lit fire.

'Your usual, Inspector?' the waitress bobbed before him.

'Thank you, Elsie,' he said, and found himself a seat. To be fair, the Hampton Pier Inn wasn't exactly crowded. Apart from the waitress, Margaret Murray and the inspector were the only ones there. The archaeologist chose her moment and made eye contact.

'Good morning, Inspector Dier.'

A flicker of amusement swept briefly over the man's face as a pot of tea was placed in front of him. 'I think you must have mistaken me for somebody else, madam,' he said.

'Indeed I have,' she said, and transferred herself and her teacup to the man's table. 'You are actually Edmund Reid, late of Scotland Yard. You joined the Force in 1872 and the detective branch in P Division two years later. A series of promotions followed, as well as fifty commendations, I believe.

You set up J Division in 1886 and retired four years ago. Since then, I appear to have lost your spoor.'

'I'm very glad to hear it,' Reid said. 'And feel free to join me, by the way.'

'I'm so dreadfully sorry,' Margaret said, 'but I am a woman on something of a mission and you, Inspector, are a beacon on a stormy sea.'

'As you say, madam, I am retired. I rarely talk to the Press and you have the advantage of me.'

'How remiss,' she said as Reid's hearty full English arrived. 'Margaret Murray.'

'Miss Murray.' Reid shook the outstretched hand. '*Star*? *Sun*?'

'Doctor,' she corrected him, glancing down at his plate. 'Neither of the above – and those sausages are bad for you.'

'Er . . .'

She laughed. 'Just my idea of a little joke,' she said. 'I am a doctor of archaeology, not medicine. I followed your exploits in the Whitechapel murders on a daily basis during the autumn of terror, living in the sticks at Rugby as I was.'

Reid shook his head. 'Not my finest hour,' he muttered, buttering his toast. 'We never caught him.'

'Of course not,' she said. 'Once Fleet Street had invented Jack the Ripper, there wasn't the slightest chance of finding the actual killer.'

'You may have a point,' he said, sprinkling his salt liberally.

'May I be frank?' she asked.

'You may be anyone you like, Dr Murray,' he said.

'The Inspector Dier mysteries; I understand the author was a friend of yours.'

'Charlie Gibbon? Yes, he was. Alas, no longer with us.'

'That's a shame,' she said. 'I hoped later books would improve. They didn't do you justice. The *Weekly Despatch* called you – and I quote – "one of the most remarkable men of the century".'

'One of?' He raised an eyebrow. 'And that was *so* last century.'

They both laughed. 'Balloonist,' she said, 'conjuror, actor, a tenor of rare ability – how can all that be packed into one man of . . .'

'. . . only five foot six,' he finished the sentence for her. 'Just lucky, I suppose. Come to that, I was lucky to get into the Met at all, what with the height requirements back then. I wore thick socks on the day, that was my secret.'

'Ah,' she remembered, 'I was turned down for nursing for exactly the same reason, but since you loom over me, Mr Reid, I will have to bow to your experience. And it is that experience I need now.'

'You do?'

'Do you live here?' she asked.

'Not yet,' he said. 'But I hope to soon. I've got my eye on a little property not far away.'

'Lovely,' she said, finishing her tea. 'A cottage by the sea.'

'It was to have been a sort of retirement home for my wife and me.'

'Was to have been?'

A sudden sadness crossed his face. 'Emily died, Dr Murray, earlier in the year. In her memory, though, I thought I'd buy the house anyway.'

'I'm so sorry, Mr Reid,' she said. 'And good for you.'

He ferreted in his pocket and produced a card. 'This is how I spend my days now,' he said. 'In between the ballooning, of course, and the legerdemain and the singing . . .'

'A private detective,' she smiled. 'How exciting! I don't believe I've ever met one of those before.'

'Well, I've never met a doctor of archaeology before,' he told her.

Margaret clicked her fingers to summon the waitress for more tea. 'Well, that's the nub, actually,' she said, folding her arms on the table. 'I've lost one of my students.'

'Careless of you,' Reid said.

'I'm not sure careless is the word. She was murdered.'

Reid paused in mid-chew. 'Really?'

'Well, the papers said suicide. So did Inspector Blunt.'

'Athelgar Blunt?' Reid's eyes widened and he reached for more HP sauce. 'Last I heard of him he was on the horse troughs in Tooting, which I took to be the pinnacle of his ambition. Who was she?'

'Well, that's the curious thing,' Margaret said. 'I knew her as Helen Richardson, a part-time student of some promise. Alas, it appears that she was leading something of a double life, in a dingy apartment in Storey's Yard, Westminster.'

'By double life, you mean . . .?'

'She was, it seems, a prostitute, a scarlet sister, an unfortunate, a lady of the night. The world has many phrases to cover up tragedy, doesn't it?'

'Indeed it does. But what brings you to Hampton-on-Sea?'

'A railway ticket in a box in her rooms. A box that had been rifled before I got to it.'

'Yet, the ticket was still there?'

'Indeed, an oversight, I believe, by whoever had . . . jemmied it? Is that the phrase?'

Reid laughed. 'We'll make a trasseno of you yet, Dr Murray,' he said. Seeing incomprehension etched on her face, he added, 'Crook, in the East End.'

'Praise indeed.' She laughed too.

Margaret nipped back to her own table for her handbag. 'I don't have a photograph of Helen,' she said, 'but this is my rough sketch of her. It's not marvellous – the hair isn't quite right.'

'Not familiar, I'm afraid. The woman I saw was heavier, the hair dark.'

'You . . . you saw someone?'

'Yes. Four, perhaps five days ago. On the Reculver road near Swalecliffe, not far from the Lavender Brook.'

'Was she alone?'

'I believe so. Had a large canvas bag with her and was wearing rather shabby clothes. I took her to be a woman of the roads at first.'

'And later?'

Reid looked uncomfortable. 'Later, I thought she just might be one of the world's scarlet sisters. Her skirts were raised and buttoned up, showing a considerable amount of stocking for Hampton-on-Sea.'

Margaret laughed. 'That's female archaeologist attire, Mr Reid,' she said. 'It's to keep our skirts out of the mud. It's all right for you men – a pair of plus fours or a navvy's moleskins would be perfect for the job at hand. But if we ladies tried that, there'd be a national outcry. Mr Reid,' she looked at him solemnly, 'I have imposed upon you and ruined your breakfast, the most important meal of the day.'

Her second pot of tea arrived.

'Think nothing of it,' he smiled.

'I wonder, though, could I impose further? Could you, when you've finished your toast, show me exactly where you last saw this girl? I mean, what are the odds of *two* female archaeologists wandering the byways of Hampton-on-Sea?'

'And it was here you saw her?' Margaret Murray peered up at the private detective.

'Yes. Along this road. She said "Good morning", I said "Good morning". That was about it.'

The sea was still roaring along the shingle and the wind showed no sign of abating from the night before. Reid's Ulster snapped in the gusts and Margaret had to wrestle with her skirts. She had read only the other day that clothes for ladies were become more practical, but clearly, the *haute couture* of Paris had never considered the problems of the Kent coast.

'To the untutored eye,' she shouted over the wind, 'and I don't mean to offend, that looks like a disused building site.' She was pointing to the level ground above the beach.

'It does,' Reid conceded.

'Walk with me,' Margaret said and picked her way over the stones. Reid couldn't see it at first, but as the archaeologist talked him through it, all became a little clearer. 'This was the praetorium, the headquarters of a commanding officer. Oh, this is a smaller version of the real thing, of course. In legionary bases, the praetorium is about the size of a seaside villa, at the centre of a barracks. All Roman military camps were laid out in the same way, all very geometric and businesslike. How far is Reculver from here?'

'About three miles,' Reid told her. 'That way.' He pointed west, along the coast.

'It would be my guess,' Margaret said, 'that what we have here is an outpost of Reculver – Regulbium, the Romans called it. I am assuming, Mr Reid, that the woman you saw was not local.'

'I'd never seen her before and I haven't seen her since,' he said. 'But then, as you know, I'm not local myself. Have you asked around? The hotel? The golf clubs? Ah, I bet the Herne Bay Decorum Society could help.'

'The what?'

Reid laughed. 'A not-very-well-meaning clique of busybodies, largely female, saving your presence, who twitch curtains and look for outrage.'

'Ah, the perpetually offended,' Margaret smiled. 'You may remember, Inspector, that London has its fair share of those.'

'Indeed,' Reid nodded. 'Then, in the fullness of time, they retire and come to live in Herne Bay. Shall I introduce you?'

Ethelfleda Charlton had helped to put the 'bomb' into bombazine. That she was a stout lady could not be denied, but her corsets and various whalebone structures added to that concept appreciably and she reminded Margaret Murray of depictions of the Biblical juggernaut she had used when teaching Sunday School back in Rugby. That said, Ethefleda's drawing room was tasteful enough and her tea, particularly after a tramp along the beach, most welcome.

Inspector Reid was notable by his absence. Having effected introductions after a simple ring of the bell and an apology for the unlooked-for intrusion, he had remembered an important prior engagement and done, as the Underworld he knew all too well had it, a runner. More than that, he was away on his dancers.

'Archaeology,' Ethelfleda was saying, peering at Margaret through her lorgnette. 'How fascinating. Men's work, though, surely?'

Margaret smiled. Rising before her was another brick wall of chauvinism, built, no doubt, by generations of men of the Charlton family. 'I believe the distaff side can make an effective contribution,' she said.

'Oh, you sketch things, do you? Pots and so on?'

'Among other things,' Margaret said. 'I also translate hieroglyphs, working from Egyptian originals and the occasional
Greek. Latin, if I must.'

'Good Lord!' Ethelfleda had simply no idea.

'And, of course, field work.'

'You work in fields?' Ethelfleda was astonished.

'It's often where we find ancient remains,' Margaret
explained, 'which is, I believe, what the young lady I am
looking for was doing.'

'Ah.' Ethelfleda's face hardened and her lips twitched as
she sipped her Tetley's. 'Yes, I am afraid that the Society had
to send a Note.' The capital N rang down Ethelfleda Charlton's
nasal passages as through a carynx.

'A note?'

'Why, yes. My dear Dr Murray, what is the point of having
a Decorum Society unless decorum is rigorously observed? It
is our *raison d'être*, as the French have it.'

'Then you know the young lady's name?'

'Alas, no. One of our Society had seen her wandering the
beach and took her, at first, for an escapee from some asylum.'

'As indeed you would,' Margaret smiled, trying desperately
to see the world through the cock-eyed lens of Ethelfleda
Charlton.

'Quite. On one occasion, the wretched girl was seen with
a trowel in her hand and what looked like a paintbrush. Now,
picture the scene, doctor; a woman, alone, without a chaperone
of any kind, dressed, I have to say, indecently, carrying the
tools of a workman. It was all very odd and not a little discon-
certing. She was staying at the Customs House.'

'The . . .?' Margaret was reaching for her notepad.

'Oh, I shouldn't bother with that. It fell down last week.'

'Fell down?' The archaeologist wasn't sure she had heard
right. 'You mean it just . . .?'

'Fell down, yes. It happens all the time on this part of the
coast. Erosion, I believe it's called. I'm sure they'll find a cure
for it one day. The place was never very secure and it was *far*
too near the sea. It was a small cottage, really, rented out for
the summer months. I'm afraid I have no idea who actually
owned it. Apparently, this girl was staying there, though for

how long and exactly why, I have no idea. Well, obviously
. . .' Ethelfleda Charlton adjusted her rolltop bust as discreetly
as she could; whalebone did cut in so, as the afternoon wore
on. 'Obviously, the Note was dropped through the Customs
House letterbox, addressed to "The Occupier", demanding to
know who she was and what she was doing here. You must
realize, Dr Murray, that we live in dangerous times. Apart
from those wretched Boers, there are far too many deranged
women in the world. One of them, if you read your *Telegraph*,
threw an axe at the Kaiser the other day.'

Margaret tutted and shook her head. 'Did you receive a
reply, Miss Charlton?' she asked.

'No . . . well, yes, of sorts. Our Note was penned by dear
old Mabel Bickersteth, our secretary. Mabel *did* receive a
missive, but it was blank. As Chair, I have it here. All it has
is a letterhead. In Latin, I'm afraid.' She chuckled. 'And I
must concede, that was never my strong suit at the Hinchindale
Academy for Young Ladies, of which I am a graduate.'

Hooray for education, Margaret mused. 'May I see it?'

'Of course. The lack of reply, a calculated mark of contempt,
I'm sure you agree, is obviously the result of an appalling
upbringing.'

Ethelfleda rummaged in an escritoire on a nearby table and
produced a piece of paper. *Sancte et Sapienter* was printed at
the top. Margaret smiled. 'King's College,' she said, and stood
up. 'Thank you, Miss Charlton. You've been more helpful than
you know.'

'Well, at least the Note did the business. The wretched girl
hasn't been seen since. And of course, the collapse of
her house was just the final full stop; wouldn't you agree?'

'I would, Miss Charlton,' Margaret said, gathering up her
belongings to leave. 'If you were right.'

Edmund Reid had not been too pleased to be winkled out of
his seaside torpor by a bustling little body like Margaret
Murray. He had seen her off on the London train and had
never thought that he might become the clichéd grieving
widower shut away in a boarding house on the coast but
somehow – here he was. He had not enjoyed good health since

his wife had passed away – since before then, if he were to be scrupulously honest with himself – but what with one thing and another, he had soldiered on. Sitting looking out to sea with an occasional stroll along the Esplanade had suited him down to the ground. Until now. Now, he was sitting at his solitary tea, watching the sun gild the tips of the waves as the tide turned, and he felt his old detecting urges tapping at the back of his head, just like they had in the old days.

He sliced his Battenberg cake across, dividing the quarters into eighths, into sixteenths, into crumbs. His tea got cold, the tell-tale scum on the top denoting that the Girl Who Did at teatime had put the milk in second *again*. He sipped it and put the cup hurriedly back in the saucer. Cold. He glanced at the clock and round the room. Half past four – he was the only one left in the lounge. All the old biddies and the occasional old geezer had all gone upstairs for a lie down or a titivate, according to taste, before the dinner gong went.

Edmund Reid had not made Inspector at Scotland Yard by shilly-shallying, as he told his subordinates on a regular basis. He pushed the mangled Battenberg aside and marched across the hall on his way to his room on the first floor, turn left at the top of the stairs and then left again; he had a room with a view of the sea, one of the honoured few. Mrs Mulvahey the landlady liked to treat her single gentlemen well; as she told her friends at tea in her private sitting room, as a widow, one never knew where it might lead. He slung his Ulster over his shoulders, crammed the wideawake down on his head and clattered down the stairs and out through the revolving door into the sharp sting of an easterly. The sun on the waves had been a bit of a joke by the weather; it was bitter out and he did up every button, right to the chin, before bending his head into the wind and setting off, retracing the steps he and Dr Murray had already taken, out to the exposed site of Helen Richardson's abandoned dig. He didn't know why; but it was certainly better than sitting in the bay window crumbling cake.

Once upon a time, Edmund Reid had been more at home in the dark than in the light. He had had eyes like a cat and could see every nuanced shadow. He was pleased to discover that he hadn't lost the knack, at least not completely. He told himself to listen to his feet, to feel the ground beneath him, not to hurry because rushing got you nothing but grazed knees and, at the worst, a bloody nose. Despite the wind, he made good time and was soon at the site of the dig. Without an archaeologist at his elbow, it made even less sense now than it had before. Margaret Murray had pointed out various elements which meant something to her, but now, by the light of the rising moon, it looked like a few lines of stone which could almost be naturally occurring, so encrusted were they with lichen and impacted sand.

Reid had always been more involved in the here and now than the there and then, but he could see the draw of the past as he looked out at the site. The sea had engulfed this part of the coast many times, covering the remains deep in sand and shingle, only to uncover it all again. To his right, as he stood with his back to the sea, which had turned as he walked along the Esplanade and was going out, was a stand of dune, sculpted so that it almost looked like a wave frozen in flight. The under-edge was scooped out as though by a giant spoon and the surface was so smooth it looked like stone. Like a man drawn to walk under a ladder, Reid walked towards the dune and stopped under its lee, out of the wind. Without the whistle in his ears, the place was as silent as the grave. He fancied he could hear the tramp of sandalled feet, the cries of the parade ground, the slap of leather and metal as the ghostly Romans banked and wheeled on the square beyond the dune. He chuckled to himself; what would people think if they knew that Edmund Reid, Detective Dier, was so fanciful? He shrugged his Ulster back on to his shoulders and pressed down his hat as he turned back into the wind. Why he had come, he now scarcely knew. But whether it was the fresh sea air or the thought of getting back out and detecting, he felt ten years younger and twenty years healthier. He could almost hear his beloved wife chuckle with him, to see him so chipper.

It happened almost before he could draw another breath. With a soft whisper, the dune, hanging as it was through good luck and the compacted sand, salt and marram, collapsed over his head, knocking him on to his hands and knees. He braced his back against the weight of it, feeling his thighs and arms tremble with the effort. The fall seemed to go on for ever but finally, with a last susurration, the sand stopped moving and all was still.

Reid stayed still for a moment, waiting, as all policemen probably do, for the cosh on the back of the head, the knife between the ribs, the bullet through the skull. But nothing followed, just more silence and the whine of the wind. He had kept his head down and his eyes shut and as he clambered to his feet, he stayed that way. Being careful not to use his sandy fingers, he wiped his face on the cuff of his shirt, and blew through his moustache, cursing the wax which kept the sand thickly around his mouth. His beard was full of it too, but his eyes were clear and he looked around. There wasn't a soul to be seen and, with the moon full and high, anyone would be obvious running along either the beach or the ridge above.

He shook himself all over to dislodge as much sand as he could. He knew that he was not going to be popular at Mrs Mulvahey's establishment – the strictures against bringing sand into the premises were clearly written in very large capitals in the lobby. But he could cross that bridge when he came to it. He had stuck his head over this particular parapet and lived to tell the tale. And for now, that was enough.

Or, perhaps not. As he turned to walk away, there was another sigh from the remains of the dune and he turned to watch it under the moon. As he had got to know this coast, where he intended to make his home, he had watched the dunes and the beach change almost daily. Buildings tumbling to the power of the waves were not even newsworthy; as Ethelfleda Charlton knew only too well, it happened all the time. And yet, there was still something hypnotic about it, the sigh as the sand began to lose its adhesion, the inevitability of its slow descent to a lower level. He had never watched a collapse by moonlight and something about Margaret Murray had made him fanciful, so he stepped back to get the best effect. He also didn't fancy being engulfed again, not only because of what Mrs Mulvahey would have to say about it.

It was disappointing. He had expected a smooth slide of silvered sand but it seemed to be impeded by something. A branch of a tree appeared to be sticking out of the hanging dune, a bunch of twigs on the end pointing to the sky. Filaments of moss hung from the branch and swayed in the wind, whipping and flicking sand in small gobbets into the air. Then, the whole thing collapsed, not slowly as he had expected, but with a rush, the tree rolling and careening down the slope. Reid found that he was worrying about the Roman camp above. It would be a shame, after it had survived so much and for so long, for it all to tumble down on to the beach to be eaten by the tide. He took another step back, just in case.

And then, holding his breath and narrowing his eyes against the salt-laden, stinging wind and his natural short sight, he stepped forward and stared at the horror on the beach. Because there, one arm to the sky, the other clasped across her breast, her skirts kirtled up against the mud and the wet, lay the body of a woman. Young. Stocky. Dark-haired. And very, very dead.

FIVE

The first of the boys came home from Cape Town that Sunday. There were brass bands and fluttering bunting and cheering crowds. All the tunes of glory rang out over the city and the Fusiliers came back to their Tower barracks. Their ranks were thinner, it was true, but most of the tears shed that day were those of joy. The war was not yet over, but it was surely won, unless of course that idiot Kitchener buggered it up.

Constable Crawford was working a double shift as a result. All day, he had held back crowds, lifted little children on to his broad shoulders so that they could get a better view of their daddies. He helped old ladies cross roads without being run over by scorchers on their Chater-Lea Whippets, reconnected sobbing toddlers with their distraught mothers and now and then failed to act as a 'preventative police' by arresting pickpockets.

As night fell and drunks still wandered Westminster, toasting 'Bobs' with their porter and gin and kicking effigies of Cronjé around the gutters, Crawford found himself in Storey's Yard again, where he had found the dead body of a woman only days ago.

'Constable.' A female voice made him turn. A woman stood there, a stole around her shoulders and her bodice open at the top. He hadn't seen her before, but he knew her calling.

'If you're going to ask me if I'm "good-natured",' he warned her, 'don't. Because I'm not.'

The woman laughed. 'I'm a bit long in the tooth to try it on with a copper,' she said. 'Is this your beat?'

Crawford couldn't pinpoint the accent. The East, certainly, but Spitalfields? Stepney? Shoreditch, at a pinch? It was difficult. One of the sergeants at the nick was so good with accents, he made almost as much as his salary taking bets in the pub when he was off duty that he could guess anyone's accent to within a street. He was rarely wrong, but it seemed to Crawford to be a pretty useless skill. You would need to have already arrested the criminal to be able to use it. But everyone needs a hobby.

'It is,' he told her, shining his bull's-eye into her face. 'What of it?'

She held up her hand to avoid the glare of the flame. 'Did you know Roman Alice?'

Crawford blinked and lowered the lantern. 'Who?' he asked.

'Alice Groves. She lived hereabouts. Over there, if I remember right. Number fourteen.'

'Yes,' Crawford said. 'I knew her. Why do you ask?'

'She was a friend of mine,' the woman said, 'and she was done in.'

'The coroner said suicide,' Crawford told her.

'That coroner don't know his arse from a hole in the ground,' she said flatly and proceeded to light up a briar pipe she carried in her apron front.

'How did you know her?' Crawford asked.

'We used to work the same stretch,' the woman told him. 'Along the Wall, near the Tower.'

'The Roman wall?' Crawford wanted to be sure. There were an awful lot of walls in London.

The woman nodded, her hard face lit momentarily by the

flare of the vesta. 'That's how we come to call her Roman Alice. I'm Roman Lil, by the way.'

'And what's your last name, Roman Lil?' Crawford asked.

Lil shook her head. 'You don't need to know that,' she said. 'I come here looking for answers. What's the song say? "If you want to know the time, ask a p'liceman"?' It took Crawford a moment to realize she was singing; the briar had turned her voice to gravel. 'Well, I was hoping for an answer to a different problem.'

'When did you see Alice last?' Crawford checked the street. He knew all too well the old ruse of being worked over while in conversation. Most of these street girls had a bully somewhere, handy with a cosh and mean with it.

'Couple of weeks ago, I s'pose,' Lil said. 'Alice, she'd come on since the old Wall days. Had a brain in her head, did Alice. Had her own place up West, right here.'

She looked in awe at the respectable houses along Storey's Yard. Not for Alice the rough kiss of open brickwork grazing her arse. 'She said she'd show me her place more than once, but she never did.'

'What makes you think Alice was murdered, Lil?' Crawford asked.

'Goes with the territory,' the woman shrugged, drawing on her pipe. The red glow softened her features and for a moment, Crawford could see the girl who thought she would try it, just the once, just for the price of a bed. She could always stop it later, if it didn't suit. 'I was new to the trade when Jackie boy struck in Whitechapel. And he's still out there, you know; you boys never caught him, did you?'

'No,' Crawford had to admit. 'We didn't.'

'Alice and I'd meet up every month,' Lil said. 'Regular as clockwork. Talk over old times, new times. She'd come into money.'

'Really?' Crawford was all ears. He realized anew that he knew nothing about the dead woman at all. 'How? From whom?'

'She didn't say,' Lil told him. 'She just said – and it sounded strange coming from her – "Miracles do happen."'

'What do you think she meant by that?' Crawford asked.

'Don't know.' Lil's attention drifted suddenly to two soldiers loitering under the gas light at the end of the street. 'Got to go,' she said. 'Couple of lads over there who deserve a bit of a welcome, I shouldn't wonder. If Alice died on your beat, Mr Policeman, you see to it, all right?' Lil was staring Crawford in the face, albeit a head below him, but her eyes were burning and her mouth was set. 'You find the bastard who killed her.' She broke away, snuffing out her pipe and stuffing a violet cachou into her mouth.

'Hello, boys,' Crawford heard her call as she sauntered away, swinging her hips. 'Either of you feeling good-natured?'

Margaret Murray had many skills; some she shared widely, others she kept more or less to herself. One of her favourites and one which incidentally had got her into hot water more times than she could count as a child, was being able to retreat into a world of her own, where the here and now faded and disappeared and the past rose up to envelop her in a cloud of her own making. She couldn't feel the chair she was sitting on in her inner sanctum, she could no longer hear the sounds around her, smell the scents which wafted past her nose. On this particular Monday afternoon, she was no longer in a foggy London, where the sounds were muffled by the thickened air and the smell of burning coal and humanity tickled the nose. She was in the heat and dust of the Lower Nile, feeling the pull of the rope over her shoulder as she strained with her fellows to raise a pyramid to a man she would never even see, but who had ruled her life since birth. She could smell the dung of the labouring camels, feel the exhausted sun beat down on her shaved head. She could hear—

'Dr Murray?'

That made no sense. Who would be saying that to a slave?

'Dr Murray? If it's not too much trouble . . .'

The small bubble of Egypt popped with an audible sigh and Margaret turned round to see who had interrupted her train of thought. She had her scowl all ready.

'Inspector Reid!' She stood up, her hand out. 'I wasn't expecting to see you here.' She looked into his face. 'Has something happened?'

'Yes, indeed it has. I found a body.'

Margaret looked round wildly. 'Where?'

He chuckled. 'Not here, Dr Murray. Back in Hampton. On the beach. Well, I suppose more accurately . . .'

Before he could continue, her need for total accuracy in all things took precedence. 'Sit down, Inspector, please. And take things in *strict* chronological order and don't spare me the details. I have seen more dead bodies than you have had hot dinners.'

He raised a dubious eyebrow.

'No, I have,' she insisted. 'Deader than the ones you usually have . . . er . . . consorted with, if that is the word I am looking for . . .' She frowned. She wasn't at all sure it was.

Reid knew it wasn't. He had banged up several people for doing just that, and it wasn't pretty. But he knew what she meant and nodded for her to carry on.

'What happened? And when?'

Reid told her of his rather exciting Saturday night. He glossed over his less than satisfactory brush with the Kent Constabulary, except to say that had they been under him, back in the day, horse troughs would have been the apogee of their careers. Beyond the fact that it was the woman he had seen on the beach, judging by the clothes and the place of burial—

'Burial? You dug her up?' Margaret's eyes were wide. He had clearly caught more than a whiff of the call of archaeology.

'No, Dr Murray. She fell on me. Out of the dune. Someone else had buried her and nature had exhumed her. She had no papers on her and, as you know, her house has fallen into the sea taking everything with it. So as far as that goes, we are not much further forward.'

Margaret held up a finger and he stopped.

'Yes?' Many was the old lag whose blood would freeze at the sound of that gravelly voice, but archaeologists are made of sterner stuff than the average burglar.

'I think I may know where she was studying,' she said. 'Ethefleda Charlton had a letterheaded piece of paper from her. She went to King's College.'

'You didn't say.' Reid was huffy.

'You didn't ask. And I wasn't sure of the significance. I couldn't just go into King's and ask to speak to all their female students, could I?'

'There can't be many, surely?' Reid didn't see the trap until he had sprung it.

'Indeed there are not many, Inspector,' she said, drawing herself up to her full height, such as it was. 'There should be very many more. But even the small number can't be called to account by someone such as myself, with little reason given. Now, though, we can easily do it.'

'How can it be easier now she's dead?' Reid said and answered himself at once. 'Because now she's missing, so she is just one, rather than one of many.'

Margaret beamed on him as if her favourite student had just solved the riddle of the sands. 'Correct! I know that students can be a little . . . louche, these days. But even King's can surely only have one missing student!'

Reid picked up his hat, which he had deposited on a plaster head purporting to be a likeness of Alfred the Great. 'Shall we go?'

'Now? Don't we need to know a little more about your body first? Such as, how did she die?'

'The inquest was adjourned this morning. They called it with commendable speed, but I was expecting that. They just need to be able to investigate more, though from what I saw when I went to the police station to report finding the body, I don't expect them to get very far.'

Margaret was contrite. 'I should have asked . . . you weren't injured, were you, when the body fell on you?' She looked at him, her head cocked inquisitively. 'How did that happen, by the way? I can imagine falling into a grave. Indeed, I have done it several times myself. But having a grave fall on you . . .?'

'It's all to do with the lie of the land,' Reid dismissed it. 'The dune gave way. I hailed a passing fisherman on his way to the headland. There was a mackerel run and he was after sardines.'

'I suppose that makes sense to someone,' Margaret said.

'Ask anyone in your Biology department,' Reid suggested.

'He wasn't keen, but he stood by the body until I could come back with some of the local men. They brought the drunk cart – all they had to hand, apparently, at short notice – and loaded it up, and to be fair to them, they left a constable on watch overnight. I went back in the morning to make sure nothing was missed, and they were thorough. They sieved the sand and found nothing. Except a few stray finger bones.' He coughed gently to warn what he still tended to think of as a member of the weaker sex that something unpleasant was afoot. 'The . . . er . . . the crabs had been busy, you see.' He waggled his own fingers by way of illustration and Margaret almost expected a bunch of flowers or an ace of spades to spring forth.

'Was the cause of death apparent?' She leaned forward.

'Not at the time, but they did a post-mortem on her on the Sunday afternoon. The local quack wasn't keen either, but it isn't good for a genteel seaside place to have dead bodies scattered over its beaches, so they put a move on. Just as well it's not the season.'

'Hardly scattered,' Margaret murmured.

Reid coughed and then smiled. His smile transformed him and Margaret saw the naughty schoolboy he carried inside him peering out. 'There were rumours,' he said. 'Heaven only knows how these things begin.'

'Heaven only knows indeed.' She smiled back. 'So . . . cause of death?' She hoped it would be poison, but that seemed unlikely.

'Although . . . er . . . putrefaction had set in in the warmer months . . . I should have said, they estimate she had been dead for around two months or more . . . there was enough soft tissue to tell that she had died from strangulation. Well, that and the scarf tied tightly around her neck.' He arched an eyebrow. 'I did say their methods leave a little to be desired. I had to point it out to the idiot doing the autopsy.'

'You *attended*?' Margaret was impressed.

'Well,' the ex-inspector preened, 'I *am* Inspector Dier, when all is said and done.' He put his hat on his head and gave it a decisive tap. 'Now' – he extended an elbow – 'shall we?'

* * *

Edmund Reid didn't need telling about the rivalry between King's and University College. He had been in the thick of things – though latterly more in a role of looking on from an upstairs window – in various clashes over the years. University College had been set up with no nod in the direction of a particular denomination, hence the 'Godless Institution'. King's, on the other hand, was up to its academic neck in the Church of England and the Duke of Wellington, no less, had been a prime mover – as well as prime minister – when it was opened. University College had been gunning for them ever since. He and Margaret agreed without discussion that it would probably be better in the first instance if he did the talking. Margaret, loyal to her fingertips to the Godless Institution, turned her nose up at the rather dark and gloomy entranceway that led from the Strand and Reid nudged her and almost knocked her over when she ran a gloved finger over a balustrade to check for dust.

'Dr Murray,' he hissed. 'Any more of it and I am going to have to send you home.'

In any other mouth it would be an empty threat, but somehow from Reid it wasn't. Margaret duly fell into step behind him and tried to be good.

Reid tapped on an anonymous door and Margaret touched his sleeve.

'Are we in the right place? We need to see the Almoner or someone, don't we? How do you know . . .?'

He fixed her with a glare. 'Madam,' he said, drawing himself up to make what he could of his height, 'I know every building in London, outside *and* in. As well as the people.' He stopped and looked thoughtful. 'The people I am possibly a few months out of date on, but the interiors, no. The chapel, should you feel the need, is up the stairs to your right. The refectory, if required, is down the stairs, that way; but I wouldn't recommend it – too near the river.'

Margaret Murray was a kind woman, but she did feel a weasel of hope that he would have chosen the wrong door. She hugged it to her as they listened for a voice telling them to enter.

'Come in.' A contralto trill came through the mahogany and

Reid turned the handle, peering round the door. 'Edmund!' The trill went up the scale and Margaret Murray quietly strangled the weasel. 'How lovely! They didn't say it was you.' He pushed the door open and revealed Margaret from behind him, like, almost literally, a conjuror producing a rabbit from a hat. 'And Miss Murray! Well, this is a *wonderful* way to start a week, I must say!'

The woman who had risen from behind a palatial desk was a head taller than Reid and several taller than Margaret. She was, nonetheless, graceful, dressed from head to toe in elegantly cut fine tweed. Lace frothed at her neck, snowy and starched to within an inch of its life and a small fragment of it was wound into the curls at the nape of her neck. Margaret, never much bothered by the sartorial, felt the weasel stir.

Reid basked in the woman. Recently widowed or no, there wasn't a man alive who could not feel the warmth of her. Grasping her hand, Reid turned to his companion. 'Margaret, may I introduce Miss Rosa Stone, Almoner of King's. There is just *nothing* that this lady doesn't know about this college.'

'Rosa Stone?' Margaret raised an eyebrow.

'I *know*!' The Almoner released Reid's hand and grasped Margaret's. 'What *were* my parents thinking? Still, I suppose after a hundred and one years, the joke is a bit old by now.'

Damn the woman! She even had archaeological facts at her perfectly manicured fingertips.

'Do sit down, both of you.' Miss Stone resumed her place at the desk and pulled a clean piece of paper and a pencil towards her, ready to make notes. 'How may I help? I assume neither of you has come to enrol?' The laugh trilled up the scale again.

Margaret took a deep breath and Reid hacked her ankle with his highly polished shoe. 'We would like to ask a delicate question, Rosa, if we may. For reasons I can't divulge, we need to ask if you are missing any lady students at the moment.'

Rosa Stone tapped the desk with the end of her pencil. 'Rather a redundant question on a Monday, Edmund, if you don't mind my saying so. Until Tuesday, I could not claim to have a full complement of either sex, but the women do seem to like a lie-in rather more than somewhat on a Monday.

Especially when the weather is inclement. It makes their hair frizz, I suppose.' She shot a wry glance at Margaret, who prevented herself from patting her own hair only by a supreme act of will. There was something about this woman that made her feel like a guttersnipe.

'Not just missing today,' Reid specified. 'Missing since before the beginning of term.'

'Well, if she was missing from before the beginning of term, then she isn't a student here, is she?' Miss Stone was pernickety, you had to say that for her.

Reid bowed his head in acquiescence. 'She has been on your roll for a year or two, I would imagine. She may even be post-graduate.' He arched an eyebrow and looked hopeful.

Rosa Stone pushed her chair back and turned to reach a low filing cabinet behind her. 'I think I may be able . . .' She rummaged for a moment. 'Yes, here we are.' She pulled out a sheet of paper and spun round again, pulling herself back up to the desk. 'Miss . . . erm . . . Miss Emmeline . . . but I believe she went by Emma . . . Miss Emmeline Barker. She was indeed post-graduate. She was in the Archaeology faculty.'

She looked up at Margaret's indrawn breath.

'I see we have the right person. But she isn't missing. She has simply . . . well, she's given up, it seems. Not *everyone* has your tenacity, Miss Murray.'

'Given up?' Margaret couldn't see what harm a simple question could do but moved her ankles out of range even so.

'Yes.' Miss Stone pushed the sheet of paper across the table for them to read but kept her finger on it, so they had to lean forward.

They both scanned it. It was typewritten, by someone with little skill at the machine, if the oddly spaced rows and irregular spaces and pressure on certain letters were any guide.

'Read it out, Dr Murray,' Reid said. 'I have left my glasses in my other coat.'

'"Dear Miss Stone,"' Margaret read, and stopped. 'There doesn't seem to be a sender's address. Do you not find that odd?' She looked up and locked eyes with the Almoner.

'I assumed she had written it from her parents' home,' the woman said and pushed the paper forward just a touch. She didn't have all the time in the world, unlike a retired policeman and some kind of woman lecturer.

Margaret continued. "'I have been thinking things over through the summer vacation and have concluded that I do not wish to pursue an academic career any further. I have met a wonderful gentleman who has done me the honour of asking me to be his wife and I cannot do justice to that exalted position when also giving time to my research. My abject apologies for the short notice.'" Margaret sat upright. "'Yours, et cetera.'" She looked at the Almoner again. 'And you didn't query this?'

'Why should I? It is signed and all perfectly in order. Women students fall by the wayside every day, Miss Murray, you must know that. Why, this very year, when we mustered for the new term, one young flibbertigibbet walked in on the arm of some chinless wonder, took one look and turned tail and fled. She holds the record, actually; until this term, it stood at five hours.' She pulled the letter back towards her and folded it in half. 'Can I help you with anything else?'

'No,' Reid said, standing up and tapping Margaret on the shoulder to follow suit. 'I think that's all. I would like her family address, if you have it. So that the Kent police can let her parents know.'

'Know?' Rosa Stone's perfect eyebrow seemed poised for flight. 'Know what?'

'Why, that she's dead, of course.' He let the words hang in the air.

'Emma? Dead? I . . .' For one of the very few times in her life, Rosa Stone was lost for words.

'Obviously,' Reid said, tapping his hat in place in his usual decisive way, 'I can't go into any details. But I dare say I can get the Kent police to get in touch directly with you, Rosa, if you prefer . . .' He turned the statement into a question and looked at Margaret for direction. But before she could concur, Rosa Stone had an answer.

'My dear Edmund! There is absolutely no need for anything like that!' Having a celebrity like Reid in her office was one thing; a load of Kentish oafs lumbering about in their size twelves was quite another. 'I have a box of Emma's effects here.' She touched a bell on her desk and a door to her right immediately sprang open. 'Umm . . . Felicity. Could you bring Miss Barker's box through, please?' She turned to Reid. She had decided to wipe Margaret from her field of view. She found that she could do that to most women without turning a hair.

'I believe it's in the basement, Miss Stone.' The downtrodden little factotum could hardly raise the energy to speak. Living in Rosa Stone's shadow was a cold place to be.

Rosa sighed, her breasts heaving and struggling beneath the tweed and reminding Edmund Reid of the tide coming in over the humped sands of Margate. 'Then . . . then take this gentleman and . . . er . . . lady down with you, give them the box and show them the quickest way out. The river entrance, almost certainly.' She turned back to Reid and managed a ghost of a smile. 'So I can leave it all to you, can I, Edmund?'

'Indeed you can, Rosa. Indeed you can.' He tapped the brim of his hat and turned to Felicity. 'Shall we?' he said, extending his elbow.

Margaret tapped the weasel sharply on the nose. She now had the moral high ground, as well as a box which might solve the problem. Magnanimity could now be her middle name for a while. She smiled at Rosa Stone and swept out, leaving the Almoner reaching for the Amontillado. With a dash of gin, to give it body.

The box had held very little, some papers which looked as though they had been bundled in in some haste, as indeed they had been, and a more formal letter, which was addressed to 'Miss E. Barker, The Limes, Canterbury' and which told her in a few lines that she had gained a place at King's College. The letter was, by definition, several years old, but Reid and Margaret hoped that might still be the parental address. Margaret had taken a glance at the clock on the tower of St Clement Danes and dashed off with a squawk; she was late for a tutorial. She didn't add 'again' but would have been well within her rights had she done so. Reid raised his hat, pocketed the letter and strolled off back to his hotel.

Edmund Reid had given parents and other sundry loved ones bad news more times than he could remember. It was never easy, but some were easier than others. One widow always stood out for him. Her husband had been cut in half by the 2.23 to Penge and the news had travelled faster than the train. When he got to the dead man's house, his widow was already in the throes of selling his clothes to three Jewish dealers from Petticoat Lane and her only regret, it seemed, was that he had been wearing his best trousers when he caught the train, making her profit somewhat smaller. But she was unusual, a vanishingly small minority. When he and Margaret had discovered Emma Barker's name and address from Rosa Stone at King's, he had telephoned the Kent Constabulary, as represented in Herne Bay.

'Herne Bay police.' The voice was deep and rumbling and belonged to someone who very much did not want to be stuck on the front desk answering the telephone.

'Hello.' Reid could tell this was a time to keep things simple. 'I found a body on the beach at the weekend . . .'

'I must remonstrate with you, sir.' Reid was staggered to find that the owner of the voice knew a word that long. 'Bodies are no joking matter. When you find one, you must report it at once.' The noise of a wet constabulary tongue licking a pencil came clearly down the line. 'Now, when and where did you find this alleged body?'

'No, no,' Reid sighed, and ran a hand through his hair, what was left of it. 'I already have reported it. I'm—'

'I see.' The voice was cold. 'One of them ghouls, are you? Well, all I can say, sir, is . . .'

'Can we start again?' So much for keeping it simple. 'I am Edmund Reid. Late of Scotland Yard. And I came in and reported the body. It was along by the dunes, if you recall. The inquest was on Monday. Adjourned.'

There was a huge silence.

'Hello? Are you still there?'

'I'm here, sir. I was just wondering why you are calling.'

Reid sensed that the man was no longer alone and could imagine his wild gesticulations as he called over someone more senior who could deal with prank callers.

'I'm calling because I know who she is.'

The voice became smug. The whole police station had been

sure that the ex-copper had known more than he was letting on. Found it by accident; in a pig's ear. 'You didn't say, sir.'

'I didn't know then. I have found out this afternoon. She was Emmeline Barker, a student at King's College in London.'

There were noises off now, including a snatch of whispered conversation and the next voice was a new one.

'Inspector Reid. Inspector Morrison here. Now, how may I help you?'

Reid sighed. 'Good afternoon, Inspector. I'm just calling to let you know I have identified the poor unfortunate girl whose body I found on the beach.'

'Ah. May I ask how?'

'A friend of mine had been making enquiries about her – before the finding of her body, of course – and had discovered she may have been a student at King's College. I happen to know the Almoner there.' Reid waited for the sound of a knowing tut and was not disappointed. 'She was able to identify the girl. The circumstances are rather unusual and I will write them all down and let you have them in due course, but I thought that perhaps you might like to inform her parents.'

'What of?'

'Um . . . that their daughter is dead.'

'You can't be sure, though, can you?' Morrison was being pedantic.

'Of course not,' Reid snapped. 'Without a proper identification, of course not. But unless we tell the – let's call them putative parents, we'll never get that, will we? And we'll go round in circles for ever.'

'No point in upsetting good folks for nothing.' Morrison was feeling altruistic.

'No point in letting her lie in an unmarked grave either.' Reid was feeling caustic.

'I still think—'

'Really?' Reid was at the end of his tether. It hadn't been Morrison's head that Emmeline Barker's mortal remains had landed on, when all was said and done.

'There's no need to be like that, Inspector,' Morrison complained. 'We're very busy here, as you well know. I can't go chasing all over the country on wild goose chases just because you think you might have identified a body.'

Reid was staggered that Morrison couldn't hear how wrong that sounded, but it took all sorts to make a world. 'The parents live in Canterbury.'

'Very pleasant little town, or so I understand. Never been there, myself.'

'It's nine miles.'

'As much as that?' Morrison was vindicated. Who would want to make that sort of journey? After all, there was a war on.

Reid tapped his fingers restlessly on the table. The telephone at the Tambour House Hotel was in a discreet ante-room off the lobby and he could have screamed with frustration had he been so inclined, but he settled for a tap. 'Could you send someone, perhaps? If you don't want to go yourself?'

'Very busy, here, Inspector, as I think I may have mentioned. So . . .'

'Would you like me to go?' The Tambour House Hotel thought of everything and there was a Bradshaw's on the shelf above the apparatus. Reid pulled it down and flicked through it. It was too late today, but tomorrow would work very well.

'Oh, I don't know, sir.' Morrison was suddenly on his mettle. 'You being a member of the public and all.'

'A member of the public who found their daughter's body.'

'Alleged.'

'What?' Reid was getting confused.

'Their alleged daughter's body.'

'All right, if you insist. Alleged. But I will be able to tell when I get there. She sent a letter to the college about having gone home to get married. If she isn't there, or isn't married, then surely . . .' Reid had no idea how much this long conversation would have added to his bill, but he was sure he could have eaten in the dining room quite royally several times for the same money.

Morrison came to a decision. After all, when it turned out that this student woman – something with which he heartily disagreed anyway – was alive and well, then it wasn't him who would look an idiot. 'If you are willing to shoulder the responsibility for any complaints, Inspector Reid, then I don't see why you can't visit these people. But in my opinion . . .'

Pitching his voice high and holding his nose, Reid said, 'Sorry, caller, this line is needed for an urgent call. Sorry for any inconvenience.' He rattled the mouthpiece against the table and made whistling noises out of the corner of his mouth. 'Sorry, Morrison,' he said in his normal voice, but holding the mouthpiece as far away as his arms would allow. 'This line seems to . . .'

Smiling, he reached for his reading glasses and pulled out his notepad and pen. Bradshaw's was a start, but this journey would need planning and if there was one thing that Edmund Reid enjoyed, it was a plan.

SIX

Abel Turner had had a good night when the lads came home. He had another one the following night when everybody was still in a party mood, and free drinks were on offer. There was one old Temperance killjoy who carried a placard and warned everybody about the pitfalls of the demon drink but he was hopelessly outnumbered by the contingent in khaki and gave up a little before midnight.

It was a little after that that Turner became aware of a shadow following him. The rent collector was used to this. Any number of wide-shouldered trassenos knew his calling and knew that the little man often carried cash. Because of that, and because he was little, Turner also carried a cudgel, studded with lead at one end, tucked into a special pocket in his long coat. The party spirit was drifting away from him and by the time he'd crossed Ludgate Circus and was making his way up the hill towards Paul's, he felt decidedly alone. Whoever was behind him had followed him from the Queen's Head, via the Cornucopia and the Old Lud, and was now just out of sight behind his left shoulder.

Turner toyed with cutting northwards, to the tangle of alleys around Amen Corner, but he knew those streets to be dark and narrow; better stick to the light. He wasn't as young as he was and he couldn't be sure of out-running anybody these days. On the other hand, he only had one and three ha'pence on him, so what was worth stealing? On the *other* hand, did his shadow know that, or even care?

Suddenly, there were no other hands left and Turner felt a large fist grab his collar and spin him round. The cosh was in his hand and immediately out of it again as a hard rap cracked his knuckles and sent it flying. A wooden truncheon, Metropolitan Police, for the use of, was jabbed under his chin and pushing him on to his tiptoes.

'Now you could,' said his assailant, 'take this opportunity to knee me in the balls and do a runner. If you don't mind being unable to walk for a couple of weeks, that is.'

Turner let out a half-strangled cry. 'It's Constable Crawford, isn't it?' he managed.

Crawford released his grip, but only slightly. 'I'm flattered you recognize me without the helmet,' he said. 'Sorry to bother you, Mr Turner, but I wasn't up to playing cat and mouse *all* over London.'

'Indeed.' Turner's smile had turned to a rictus grin. 'To what do I owe the pleasure?'

'I didn't have a chance, the other night, to enquire too much into the affairs of the deceased, Alice Groves.'

'Dear Alice,' Turner said. 'I was always very fond.' He *should* have felt easier now he knew his shadow was a police officer but there was something in Constable Crawford's face and Constable Crawford's truncheon that made that impossible.

'I'm sure.' Crawford smiled. 'You knew she was on the game, of course.'

'Er . . . yes.' Turner shrugged. 'I try not to judge, Constable Crawford. We all have to earn our crust, don't we? These are hard times.'

'Aren't they, though? Who's your boss?'

'Eh?'

Crawford notched the truncheon a little higher. 'The man you work for,' he translated for Turner's benefit. 'The man who owns the premises at fourteen, Storey's Yard.'

'What about him?'

'In British law, Mr Turner,' Crawford said, 'ignorance is no defence. There can't be many people in this fair city of ours who are more ignorant than you, but, you see, it's not going to save you from me taking your knee-caps out.'

'Jack Daventry,' Turner squawked above the truncheon.

'Address?'

'Thirty-six, Firtree Road, Isleworth.'

'Isleworth.' Crawford smiled. 'Delightful suburb.' He let the truncheon fall. 'Well, don't look so worried, Mr Turner; as you see from my civilian attire, I'm off duty tonight. Oh,' he paused as he turned away. 'I should try to find that cosh of yours if I were you. You can't be too careful. There are some really unpleasant people about at this time of night. Mind how you go.'

Adam Crawford knocked on the door at thirty-six, Firtree Road, Isleworth as early as he thought decent the next day. He suspected that Mr Daventry was not a working man as most people would understand it, but even so, it seemed churlish to knock him up betimes. After a short wait, he heard footsteps on the linoleum of the hall and a moustachioed face appeared as the door creaked open an inch or two.

'Yes?'

'Mr Daventry?' Crawford tipped his hat. 'Mr Jack Daventry?'

Jack Daventry took in the stranger – tall, broad, shoulders like wardrobes. He hadn't seen him before but that hardly mattered; new muscle was turning up on doorsteps all the time. 'That depends,' he said, cagily.

'On what?' Crawford pushed the door open and barged his way in.

''Ere,' Daventry shouted. 'I'll have the law on you!'

'Oh, the law's already here, Mr Daventry. But I can call for reinforcements, if you like.'

'What?' All Daventry could do was to follow Crawford into the living room. 'Look. What the bloody 'ell's going on?'

Crawford took in the surroundings. Rich without being tasteful, heavy on the chintz and the candelabra. 'Nice,' he said, 'but how much of it comes from immoral earnings, I wonder?'

'Immoral . . .? How dare you? Are you a copper?'

Crawford clicked his fingers. 'I hoped it wouldn't show,' he said. Daventry's eyes swivelled to his rolltop desk. 'And if there's a gun or a chiv in there, I really wouldn't recommend it. Fourteen inches of hardwood wins every time.' He patted the truncheon discreetly tucked into his trousers. Then he sat down, wincing. 'Of course,' he said, 'such weaponry does have its down side.'

'What do you want?' Daventry narrowed his eyes at his visitor.

'It doesn't look like I'm going to be offered any tea, so I'll come to the point,' Crawford said. 'A number of apartments at number fourteen, Storey's Yard, Westminster.'

'What about them?'

'You own them, I believe.'

'I do.' Daventry sat down too, facing the uniform-man-turned-detective. 'What of it?'

'The ground floor apartment, to the right as you go in.'

'Yes?'

'The tenant was one Alice Groves.'

'If you say so.' Daventry leaned back, a little more relaxed now. 'I can't say I actually know my tenants. I have people for that.'

'Abel Turner,' Crawford nodded, noting Daventry's reaction. If he had landed the rent collector in any hot water, he really couldn't care less. 'Miss Groves is dead.'

'Oh, yes,' the landlord said. 'I had heard something along those lines. Suicide, wasn't it?'

'Murder,' Crawford corrected him.

'Murder?' Daventry didn't like the direction this conversation was taking.

'You knew that Alice was on the game,' Crawford said. It was a statement, not a question.

'No.' Daventry spread his arms and did his best to look innocent. 'No, I wouldn't allow that. All my tenants have the very best bona fides.'

Crawford chuckled. 'I'm sure they do,' he said. 'Ready to go?' He stood up.

'Go where?' Daventry asked.

'The nick.'

'The nick?' Daventry's eyebrows threatened his hairline.

'I have to caution you,' Crawford said, 'in connection with the unnatural death of Alice Groves.'

'I don't know what the bloody 'ell—' but Jack Daventry's planned list of expletives never got off the ground because the door to the living room swung open and a stoutish woman stood there, unpinning her second-best marketing hat.

'I don't know why we pay a cook,' she was muttering as she came in. 'That butcher robs us blind . . . Oh!' She stopped when she saw Crawford standing there. 'I beg your pardon; I didn't know we had company.'

Daventry blustered. 'This isn't company, Ada, it's Mr . . .' he looked at Crawford wild-eyed.

'Crawford,' Crawford obliged.

'Crawford, yes. He's here to discuss the rents at . . . at Storey's Yard.'

Ada narrowed her eyes at her husband. She knew what side her bread was buttered so she seldom rocked the marital boat, but she hated being taken for a fool, by her husband, the butcher or the cook. 'I thought it was Mr Turner who collected those rents,' she said.

Crawford clicked his tongue. 'Old Abel, eh?' he said, with a chuckle. 'He's a card. He asked me to pop in for him; he's a bit busy at the moment and didn't have time to come all this way.'

Ada Daventry's face softened. What a kind young man; and not hard on the eyes, either. 'How thoughtful,' she said, looking around and noticing a dearth of teacups. 'Jack! Why haven't you got Mr Crawford a cup of tea?'

'No, really, Mrs Daventry,' Crawford said. 'I was just going.'

'Are you sure? Because it's no trouble. I need to see Cook about something else, anyway.' She smiled at him but the way she jabbed her hatpin into the holder on the sideboard made Crawford wince.

'No, really.' Jack Daventry was quick to intervene. 'I'll just see Mr Crawford out, dear. I wouldn't mind a cuppa, though.'

Ada Daventry looked her husband up and down. She had

thought him quite a catch when she married him; she had, after all, buried two husbands who hadn't quite come up to snuff, so she thought she knew what was what. But, money or no money, he looked a poor thing next to Crawford, pigeon-chested, belly out to who-knew-where. But still, at least no one else would want him. She made up her mind. 'I'll get the kettle put on,' she announced and swept out of the room.

Crawford loomed over Daventry, taking advantage of the man's naturally cowed condition after the arrival of his wife. 'You have a lovely wife, there, Mr Daventry. A nice armful. I don't expect you would ever need to look elsewhere.'

Daventry gulped and eased his collar.

'So I don't expect that you ever had to visit Alice Groves or any of her fallen sisters in a . . . professional capacity. So you wouldn't know if she had a client list or anything similar.'

'Client list?' Daventry shook his head. 'What's one of those?'

Crawford smiled and patted the man's arm in a friendly fashion and almost knocked him flying. 'I'm sure I can't imagine,' he said.

Daventry ushered him down the hall and opened the front door. He looked over his shoulder but there was no sign of his wife, just the muffled sound of a good haranguing coming from beyond the baize door. He lowered his voice even so. 'I should talk to that bloke upstairs at number fourteen,' he said. 'I have reason to believe he was getting a free one out of Alice.' He looked startled as he realized what he had said. 'Not that I have any way of knowing it was free . . . or whether she . . .'

Crawford looked at him with his head on one side. It was a similar view to the last one a worm has when the blackbird has it in its sights.

The door slammed and, chuckling, Adam Crawford walked down Firtree Road, heading for Storey's Yard.

Edmund Reid rather enjoyed trains. So much of his life had been lived at the pitch of high drama, whether it was a ballooning escapade, a magic show or a solo performance as a tenor – only once, on a very memorable occasion, all three at once – or the cut and thrust of being a senior policeman in the largest and arguably most crime-ridden city in the world. Being taken somewhere by a snorting, steam-belching behemoth at the engine's own pace and on a route he couldn't change was really rather soothing. He disliked Victoria station and had arrived almost at the moment of his train's departure. He had balanced the spending time at the building site which Victoria always seemed to be but with a smooth journey, against the airy delights of St Pancras and the journey from hell with a change at Tilbury and Victoria, and speed won hands down. And he had made the right choice. Apart from a drop in steam pressure at Faversham, the journey was faultless and he was ready for anything when he alighted at Canterbury East.

The station was surprisingly busy for a mid-morning, but he quickly learned from the lugubrious porter that it was Market Day, and to be expected. This also, for reasons which Reid could not quite fathom, explained the complete lack of any cabs for hire. And in any event, the porter told him, there were at least six houses called The Limes in Canterbury; didn't he have a street as well?

'I just have "The Limes",' Reid said. 'The name of the family is Barker, if that helps.'

'Oh, glory be!' The porter actually smiled and it looked as if it hurt him. 'That bastard. Well, good luck to you, sir, that's all I can say.' He suddenly looked perturbed, far closer to his normal expression. 'I'm assuming you're not a friend of his, as you don't know where he lives, and all.'

'I just have some business,' Reid said cagily.

'Lor' love you,' the porter said. 'Count your fingers when you've shook hands with that one. As crooked a man as ever walked, is Mr William Barker.' He sucked his teeth and looked thoughtful. 'Wife's a nice woman, though. Daughter is a bit of an eyeful an' all, but she's not been seen round here a good while. They say there's a scandal there, but I wouldn't know anything about it.'

Reid loved to hear that phrase. It usually meant he was about to hear everything, with knobs on. It was just a case of deciding which knobs were genuine and which were embroidery.

'Scandal? I hadn't heard that.' He extracted a half crown from the watch pocket of his waistcoat and twirled it in his fingers.

'I got this from my missus, mind,' the porter said, upending his trolley and leaning on the handles, ready for a chinwag. 'She goes to the Mothers' Meeting at the Methodists once a week. Not that we're Methodists, mind.' He was anxious to make sure Reid made no judgements which might cause the coin to dive back into his pocket. 'But they do the best cake.'

Reid nodded, smiling. Cake was important.

'Anyway, according to the missus, who got it off the sister of the woman who does for Mrs Barker's next-door neighbour . . .'

Reid held up his hand while he processed the information, then nodded for the man to continue.

'According to her, there was an almighty bust-up, ooh, when would it be? Years ago, anyway, when the girl was about eighteen, just back from school in Switzerland.'

Reid was impressed. 'I didn't realize that the Barkers were in that league, financially,' he said.

'Lor', yes,' the porter said. 'Like I say, crooked as a . . .' He couldn't think of a metaphor, so coughed and changed tack. 'Been in Switzerland four years, she had, or thereabouts. Come home and I reckon she were up the spout.'

Reid's eyebrows almost dislodged his hat.

'What else would make her take off like that? Her ma, she was in a taking on, didn't come out of the house for munfs, then she come out bit by bit and now, you'd hardly think they ever had a daughter.'

'So, the girl has never been back?' Reid checked.

'Well, I never seen her and I see most people what come into town. But that don't mean to say that she hasn't come back some uvver way.' The porter spoke in the tones of one who could imagine no other way.

'Where is their house?' It was the final piece of information that he needed.

'Not far,' said the porter. 'Out of here, turn left and it's about the fifth or sixth on the right. Big place. Trees in the front.'

'Limes?' Reid liked precision in his directions.

'Monkey puzzles, mainly,' the porter said. 'But you can't call a house Monkey Puzzle, could ya? Be stupid, that.'

'Well, thank you very much,' Reid said, and flipped the coin in the air. The porter held out his hand to catch it, but it never arrived in his palm. He looked up, wonderingly, into the sky as Reid went out of there and turned left.

The Limes was easy to pick out from among its fellows. It had been a large house to start with, built in that most elegant of times, the Georgian period. Since then, many hands had wrought havoc to its beautiful lines, with gargoyles, dragon finials and extended wings aplenty. Edmund Reid judged homes by their comfort as a rule and not by their appearance, but The Limes had jangled his nerves even before he rang the doorbell.

A neat little maid with a smart white cap on her smoothed-back hair opened the door and stood there, looking helpful.

'I would like to speak to Mr and Mrs Barker, if I may?' Reid doffed his hat and gave her his best smile.

She gave him her best smile back. 'Who should I say is calling?' she asked politely.

Reid hesitated. He had always disliked people who clung to ranks and prefixes long after the event, but he sensed that in this case, it wouldn't hurt. 'Tell them Inspector Reid, Scotland Yard,' he said.

The girl's eyes widened and she looked alarmed but she collected herself enough to ask him in. 'If you'll just wait in here, sir,' she said, opening a door immediately inside the front porch. It was clearly a room for putting visitors of dubious standing in, neat but not too comfortable, the chairs just one step up from the arse-numbing wooden ones in the hall. Reid walked around the room, looking at the pictures hanging on cords from the rail. They were all fakes of one kind or another – they might fool some people, but Reid knew that a businessman in a dodgy mucked-up house near a station had never had an ancestor painted by Gainsborough, no matter what the signature said.

He had his head on one side trying to work out which of the many forgers he had collared over the years had turned it out when the door behind him opened and a man stood there, looking aggressive.

Reid doffed his hat once more. 'Mr Barker?' he asked.

'Who's asking?' The tone was cultured, but it overlaid something Reid struggled for a moment to place; then it came to him. Mile End Waste, or he was a Dutchman.

'My name is Edmund Reid. I used to be a police inspector at Scotland Yard and I have been asked by the Herne Bay police to come and speak to you about your daughter.'

Barker was making popping noises, like a saucepan coming to the boil, but Reid talked over him; it was the only way. Barker finally got his tongue under control and rapped out, 'I have no daughter.'

'I do understand that there was a falling out of some kind,' Reid said, again speaking a little louder than normal to cover Barker's fury. 'I am not here to judge. Sadly, I believe that your daughter was found dead last Saturday – I found her, in fact, on the beach – and I don't think you would like her to have a pauper's unmarked grave, surely, would you, Mr Barker?'

If Barker cared, it was hard to tell. 'Dead?' he asked. He might as well have been speaking of the rather seedy-looking aspidistra in the window. 'How do you know it is Emmeline? And why are you working for the Herne Bay police?' The man took a step forward and raised a finger, pointing it in Reid's face. 'I think you are a blackguard, sir, that's what I think.'

Reid kept his composure; it was what he did, whatever the circumstances. 'I'm not sure what you think I have to gain by any imposture,' he said coolly. 'I believe that your daughter is dead because of investigations I have carried out, but more especially because that picture over there . . .'

Barker spun round. He had *specifically* told his wife to remove all images of Emmeline, but she had clearly disobeyed. He would take that up with her later.

'. . . is, allowing for the ravages of time, sand, weather and – I hesitate to mention it, but you are clearly a man who speaks his mind – crustacea, the same woman who I saw on the beach. Dead.'

The door behind him opened and a little woman bustled in, smiling. They didn't have many visitors these days and she had heard voices. She advanced with her hand outstretched.

'Good morning,' she said, beaming. 'I am Mrs Barker. Did I hear you say "dead"? Are you collecting for something? Cavalry horses? Something of that nature. Because I must tell you that Mr Barker and I don't believe in giving to charity.'

The smile tightened a little as she spoke and Reid, from having been surprised to find her so jolly bearing in mind that she lived with Mr Barker, saw that she was hanging on to her persona by an unravelling thread. He bit back his retort and prepared to break it to her gently, but her husband had no such qualms.

'This gentleman was just going,' he snapped. 'He's just dropped by to tell us Emmeline is dead, so he can leave now. He has told us all we need to know.'

The woman's face crumpled and she turned to Reid, the tears spilling over the reddened lids and falling down her cheeks. They were not the first tears she had cried that day, Reid could tell, and they wouldn't be the last. She grabbed his arm with both hands and sagged towards him.

'Dead?' she whispered. 'Dead? Emmeline? How can that be? She was so . . . so young.'

Barker stepped forward and pulled her away from Reid's sheltering arm, giving her a shake as one would a recalcitrant child. 'She was found on a beach,' he said. 'As I think I told you when I showed her the door, she was no better than she should be and would come to a bad end. And now she has, so I don't see how our situation is any different now than how it was then.' He shook her again. 'Stop crying, woman. I thought I had forbidden it.'

'But . . . but William.' She turned and clawed at his coat. 'Our baby. Emmeline. She's dead. How can you not care?'

'Take hold of yourself, woman,' Barker snarled. 'Compose yourself while I see this gentleman out.' He pushed her on to one of the only semi-padded chairs and stepped round Reid to the door, opening it wide. 'This way, please, Mr Reid, if that is indeed your name.'

Reid looked at him as he would look at dogshit on his shoe. 'You will be sorry you behaved like that, Mr Barker,' he said in a tight monotone. 'I don't know what your business is, but I will find out. You will see your clients drop away, your income dwindle, your standing in this town drop lower than even you deserve. You are a pig, sir, and nothing will change that. I came here today ready to comfort grieving parents. Instead, what I have seen has sickened me more than I can say.' He sighed. 'I know that you will now proceed to take your anger out on your wife. But I would like you to know that if your wife is not seen, safe and well, on the streets of Canterbury at least once a day from now on, you will have police on your doorstep day and night. If she has anywhere to go, I hope she goes there.' He took a deep breath, because he was not usually a profane man. 'I hope to God that you rot in hell.' And he swept out.

In the garden, he found he was trembling. Edmund Reid had faced down gangs outnumbering him six to one, each one of them seeming to be twice his height and girth and half his age. But no confrontation had upset him as much as this one with William Barker. Since his wife had died, he had never really known what he thought about God, heaven and man's immortal soul. But he knew that in William Barker, he had smelt the stench of sulphur; the man was evil, through and through.

'Mr Reid?' A small voice cut through his thoughts. 'Mr Reid? Are you quite well?'

He turned and, coming across the lawn, throwing a shawl around her shoulders, came Mrs Barker, with tear streaks on her cheeks. She was looking behind her as if the hounds of hell were baying at her heels, as indeed, in a way, they were.

'Mrs Barker!' He hurried towards her. 'Should you . . . should you be out here?'

'Mr Reid,' she said, with a sad smile. 'I shouldn't be here, in this house, at all. My husband hates me; I gave birth to Emmeline, you see, and that makes me complicit in her wrong-doing.' She patted his hand as if he needed comfort. 'He alienated all my friends and family within months of our marriage, so I have nowhere else to go. Don't worry, Mr Reid; he doesn't often use physical violence. It is usually as you saw it today, a little rough handling, some rough speech.'

'But that's too much,' Reid said. 'There should be none of either.' He remembered his wife, the quiet evenings they had spent, the companionable walks, the little holidays, their plans to retire to Kent. He looked down at the little woman, standing there so resigned and could have wept.

'William was brought up in poverty in the East End, Mr Reid,' she said. 'He thinks that money is enough for anyone. He has forgotten that people matter. Even himself.'

Reid patted himself on the back. He hadn't lost his touch.

'He sent Emmeline to all the best schools, then was surprised when she wanted to go on learning. She applied to King's College and was so excited when she heard she had got in.' She clasped her hands and looked down, telling the story to herself as much as to Reid. 'She came running into the breakfast room with the letter, waving it in the air and twirling round and round. I remember her curls flying, her feet dancing. Even William had to smile.'

Her face glowed beneath the tears, then crumpled again.

'That was the last day she spent under our roof. As soon as William discovered what she was planning, he threw her out, with just the clothes on her back.'

Reid frowned. 'The rumour in town . . .' Then he decided to not share the rest of the gossip.

'Oh, don't worry about that, Mr Reid,' she said. 'I started that rumour myself. Everyone could understand that, you see. A daughter in the family way being shown the door; well, there is more than one very respectable house in this very street where that happened. No, God forgive me, but I didn't want people to look down on William, for his arrant stupidity and pigheadedness. He should have been proud of our girl.' She buried her head in her hands and Reid let her cry. He knew that the slightest touch, a note of sympathy in his voice and she would be lost in her misery, perhaps for ever. He waited patiently and in a while, she drew a huge breath and carried on.

'I managed to see her twice. Once when I said I was going up to town to see my dentist, the other to see my doctor.'

'Are you ill?' Reid was concerned.

'No, amazingly, not. But William chooses my clothes, so shopping was not something I could claim to be the reason. He would accompany me to the doctor if he could, to make sure . . . well, he made sure there were no marks when I said where I was going, so that was good for two reasons, not only because I was seeing Emmeline.' She sniffed. 'She was so happy. I had managed to get some money to her and she lived frugally. She was doing research into somesuch thing I didn't really understand. But . . .' – she turned back to the house, anxious to be gone – 'but she *was* happy, Mr Reid. She wasn't . . . well, she hadn't *fallen*, had she? She wasn't dead on the beach because she had *fallen*?'

Reid patted her arm. 'No, Mrs Barker. She was still doing her research. We don't know who killed her, or why. But we will. I promise you. Just one more thing. I can tell you want to go back inside.'

'*Need* to, Mr Reid, not want.' She was resigned, and that was more heartbreaking than the tears.

'But before you go, do you know if she had a friend in London, a special friend?'

'A man, you mean?' Mrs Barker had not wanted a man for her daughter. She had fallen in love, and look where that had landed her.

'Or a woman. Just someone we can talk to.'

'She lived . . . the last time we spoke, she lived in a mews, just off the Strand. I can't remember the name . . .' She put a hand to her forehead. 'You will think badly of me, Mr Reid, but I say I can scarcely remember my name some days. It was . . . umm . . . something to do with trees . . . and for some reason, I remember it was number fifteen; it was my mother's birthday, that's probably why.' She twisted her hands together and looked up at him desperately.

Reid racked his encyclopaedic knowledge of minor London streets. 'Not Walnut Mews?' he asked hopefully.

'That's the *one*! Goodness, Mr Reid, that is quite extraordinary.'

'I know it,' he said. He didn't tell her it was because it had been the scene of more violence and robbery than virtually any other street in the area, though it was too late to worry her now. 'The friend's name, can you remember?'

'Oh, yes! What a sweet girl. Her name is Marjy.'

Reid looked at her, eyebrows raised, waiting for the rest.

'I'm afraid I don't remember the rest.'

'Never mind, Mrs Barker,' he said softly. She turned to go. 'Keep safe,' he whispered, as he always whispered forlorn hopes.

Jacob Lawrenson was at home that Tuesday afternoon, which told Adam Crawford a lot. On questioning, it turned out he was a gas mantle repairer, currently not employed as there had been an unprecedented lull in breakages of gas mantles in the immediate area. For medical reasons which he preferred not to specify, he couldn't travel.

'You could travel downstairs, though, or so I understand?' Crawford remarked.

'Downstairs?' Lawrenson looked furtive.

'Downstairs as far as Alice Groves's apartment, perhaps.'

Lawrenson drew himself up and looked pompous. 'I scarcely knew the woman,' he said. 'Anyone will tell you that.' He dropped his voice, though there was no one else there. 'She was on the game, you know. No better than she should be. Brought the neighbourhood down, in my opinion.'

'I do know that, Mr Lawrenson, and you know that I do. But please, don't come the injured neighbour with me. I have it on good authority that you and Alice were more than passing acquaintances. In fact, I have it on *very* good authority that you were indulging in what we could call her stock-in-trade – and for nothing. Is that so?' Crawford smiled. 'Is there a *Mrs* Lawrenson, by the way?'

'Yes, there certainly is!' Lawrenson was outraged. 'And I will have you know, we are very active in that department. Anyone will tell you that.'

'Good grief!' Crawford stepped back. 'Wherever do you do it, Mr Lawrenson, that anyone will tell me that?'

'Well.' Lawrenson was deflated. 'Not literally. But everyone knows that me and my Tilly get on like a house on fire.'

'I know that kind of marriage,' Crawford said knowingly. 'Lots of heat and flames and people running about screaming. I hope we didn't disturb her the other night, what with the shouting and such.' He sighed and plumped down into an armchair, to the surprise of a sleeping cat. 'Sorry.' Crawford was fond of animals. 'I'm sure she will be all right.' The cat sat on the table, looking balefully at Crawford, its tail in the butter.

Lawrenson seemed to run out of steam. 'All right, all right,' he said. 'Tilly left me about a year ago. I have . . . I have rather special needs, if you must know, which Tilly was not willing to provide. Alice was good enough to . . .' He stared at Crawford, not knowing how to go on.

'Step into the breach?' Crawford offered.

'If you like.' Lawrenson relaxed. This copper might look wet behind the ears, but he seemed to understand life. 'She didn't mind it when I asked her to—'

Crawford held up his hand. 'No need for details, Mr Lawrenson, really there isn't. I was wondering, though, whether you knew any of her other clients? Whether you ever met one of them, for instance, in the doorway or perhaps when you were even in her room.'

''Ere!' Lawrenson was outraged. 'There was none of that muck going on, if you please! It was strictly her and me, in the dark for preference.' He folded his arms and looked aggrieved. 'I was brought up a Methodist, you know. The idea!'

'I wasn't suggesting anything untoward, Mr Lawrenson,' Crawford said, trying not to smile. He couldn't blame the man for wanting to keep his peccadilloes to himself. What he could see of them through his clothes was unpleasant enough. 'I simply wondered whether . . . well, for the sake of an example, did you ever happen to be looking out of your window when Alice had visitors?'

Lawrenson was sulking. 'I might of.'

'And?'

'No good asking me who they were. You can see for yourself. All you get from up here is the top of folks' heads. A few bald ones. The rest had hair. And that's all I can tell you.'

And indeed it was. Lawrenson shut his mouth like a trap, the cat rolled over and licked its bum and Adam Crawford saw himself out.

SEVEN

'This morning's tutorial will be a little different,' Margaret Murray told her assembled students. They were crowded into Flinders Petrie's study on the shady side of the college, mainly because his room was larger than hers. 'We will be focusing on Rome.'

An involuntary groan escaped from the lips of Ben Crouch and he immediately turned it into a cough.

'No, it's too late for that, Mr Crouch,' Margaret smiled. 'I recognize a tone of disapproval when I hear one.'

'No, no, Dr Murray.' The man held up a guilty hand, anxious to placate. 'It's just that I am, as you know, a Greek, with perhaps a hint of Egyptian.'

'How very cosmopolitan,' she said. 'Perhaps, however, you'd begin.' She passed him a heavy globular object which once clearly had been part of something else. 'What's this?' she asked.

'Oh, that's easy.' Crouch smiled broadly. He hated these tutorials when everyone was put on the spot, but he sensed that, this morning, he'd got off lightly. 'It's the pommel of a gladius,' he told the assembly, 'a legionary sword.'

'Period, Miss Bairnsfather?' Margaret had switched her gaze to the little Scots girl and Crouch had passed the pommel to her.

'Umm . . .' Janet had never faced one of Margaret Murray's tutorials before. She felt like a rabbit facing a stoat.

'Unfair question, Janet, my dear,' Margaret smiled. 'Mr Sheringham, you've been around the triforium a few times. Period?'

Will Sheringham was not one of Margaret's gang. Secretly, he was of the old school, not at all sure that archaeology, anthropology or indeed any academic discipline was a suitable topic for female discussion. But he wasn't about to let that show this morning. 'First century,' he said. 'Give or take.'

Margaret pursed her lips. 'Well, we can't allow too much

of that in archaeology, can we? Professor Petrie will have discussed with you whether our chosen field is a science or an art. I, of course, contend that it is both. Miss Crossley' – she half turned to Anthea – 'put these men out of their misery, would you?'

Anthea took the pommel and cradled it in her hand for a moment. 'First century,' she agreed, 'but it's not from a gladius; it's from a pugio.'

'A dagger?' Andrew Rose could not let that go. 'How the hell . . . oh, begging your pardon, Dr Murray . . . do you know that?'

Anthea all but threw the brass weight at him. 'Hold it, Andrew,' she said. 'Pretend you're holding the hilt it was attached to.' He did. 'Well?' She gave him a moment.

'Oh, all right,' he conceded. 'Pugio it is.'

'Explain, Mr Baxter.'

George Baxter had not joined to become an archaeologist. He had signed on for engineering, but the mathematics defeated him. Then he opted for linguistics, but translations were not for him. This was his second year in the faculty of Archaeology, though he was by now more than old enough to have graduated. Pompous, however, was his middle name. He flared his nostrils and with great gravitas said, 'Contrary to popular opinion, Roman hands of nineteen hundred years ago were roughly the same size as ours today. This is altogether too small for a sword hilt. Ergo . . .' – and he looked around smugly to see who was impressed with his Latin – 'it has to be a dagger.'

Margaret nodded. 'Carried by the legionaries on the right or the left, Miss Halifax?' she asked.

'The left, Dr Murray.' The girl was sure.

Andrew Rose snorted. Veronica had, after all, a fifty-fifty chance of being correct.

'Now,' Margaret said. 'We are sitting in more or less a circle. I want you all to close your eyes.'

They all did, except for Janet, Veronica and Piers Gibbs, whose first tutorial this was.

'It's all right,' Margaret assured them. 'All will become clear.'

They closed their eyes. 'Now,' she said, 'Anthea, pass the pommel to your left – that's Mr Swinscombe, who will take it . . . that's right. Hold it, Mr Swinscombe, feel the weight in your hand, the smoothness of it. Now, let your mind wander, back, back through time. You are standing on a shingle beach. It's cold. Colder than the weather you're used to. The sea is to your right. You've crossed that sea recently. And you're quite relieved because the land you're standing on isn't actually at the end of the world after all, despite the rumours. But then, it's not very welcoming, either. Take it, Miss Friend.'

Angela did so.

'All around you is the camp. It's an outpost. Smaller than most. Ahead is a trackway – there are no roads yet, unlike the Gaul that you probably know well. To your left, forest, dark, tangled, impenetrable. There aren't even any trackways there. But you know you have to go forward, because that's the Roman way. Mr Baxter, take the pommel. Your officers have told you this was the way the divine Julius came, making for a fording place on the river he called Thamesis. You know the fleet is to your right, Mr Baxter – floating on what we call the Medway – so what have you to fear? Pass the pommel.'

Still, all eyes were shut tight, the only sound in the room the hypnotic roll of Margaret Murray's voice. 'Mr Sheringham, you have everything to fear. There are madmen here and wild, shrieking women who worship the tree and the mistletoe and the stone. They crouch in sacred groves and they bury heads in holy water. Be afraid, Mr Sheringham, as you pass the pommel, because there are things that lie ahead that you cannot know, cannot understand. The wicker men, for example, and your comrades burning. No one here . . . take the pommel, Mr Rose . . . no one here speaks your language. No one cares whether you live or die. You are the enemy. There are the painted men to the far north; the Attacotti who eat the bodies of the men they have killed. Listen . . . listen, Miss Halifax, as you take the pommel, feel it bouncing on your left hip as you march . . . you can hear the moaning of the sea and the creak of leather; the tramp of the caligae and the shouts of the optio at your back. "Keep those lines straight. Where do you think you are, man? Fasten that strap, soldier. Or Teutates will get you!'"

Veronica couldn't help herself. Her eyes flickered open and she expected to see a gruff centurion in front of her, grim-faced, the weak British sun glinting off the falerae on his chest, the cruel wind ruffling the horsehair of his helmet. Instead, all she saw was a little lecturer in archaeology, smiling at her.

'And . . .' Margaret paused as the pommel came full circle, 'We're back.'

All eyes opened and everybody fidgeted, slightly embar-rassed at the places that their lecturer's voice had taken them to. Some of the old hands remembered other days like this; how, indeed, could you forget the time that Archie Mulholland had abandoned all decency and stripped off, running out into Gower Street before he could be prevented? Telling the policeman on point duty that he was a Viking berserker had cut no ice at all.

'Now, I think,' Margaret said, 'we're ready for Rome. Essential to get into the mood, don't you think?' She was passing out slips of paper in all directions. 'I wouldn't presume to put anyone on the spot,' she said, and Rose and Crouch exchanged glances with a simultaneous roll of the eyes. 'So I'd like you to work in pairs and do some translations for me. I'll give you . . . ooh, ten minutes.'

She bustled away along the corridor to coax that wretched kettle, the one with the mind of its own, into action. She hated not being able to offer tea to her class, but that was hospitality taken too far and the university in general frowned on such things. She heard the silence in Petrie's study rise to whispered mutterings, then audible discussion and finally, Anthea Crossley at her best.

'Don't talk utter bilge, Crouch. That's the subjunctive there or General Baden-Powell wears women's frocks!'

'Come off it, Anthea,' Crouch came back. 'You're supposed to have gone to a good school . . .'

The arrival of Margaret Murray put an end to the usual verbal brawl but no sooner had she come back into the room than an older, altogether more male, figure followed.

'Oh, Margaret . . . er . . . Miss . . . er, Dr Murray, I'm sorry.

I'd forgotten you were holding court today. I can't find my copy of Westropp anywhere and I know Flinders has one. Morning, gentlemen.'

There were murmurs of reply from the men in the room. The women sat there open-mouthed. Margaret Murray knew the spine of every book in Flinders Petrie's inner sanctum by heart and she reached instinctively for the tome in question. 'Here we are, Norman . . . er . . . Mr . . . Professor Minton.' Then she held it just out of his reach. 'But, now you're here,' she said, 'as our resident Roman expert; sit yourself down and help us with our Latin, will you?'

'Oh, now, Dr Murray . . .' Minton blustered.

'Oh, please, Professor,' Andrew Rose said. 'We'd *so* value your expertise.'

For a moment, Minton looked unsure. Then he folded. 'Oh, very well,' he said. 'But I usually like a *little* more notice than this. What do we have?'

'Well' – Margaret resumed her seat – 'as I said to these people when we started this morning, this tutorial will not be the usual fare. The pieces of paper you have before you, ladies and gentlemen, are copies of those taken from a box belonging to another student, not of this college. I regret to have to inform you all that that student's body was recently found on a beach in Kent.'

There was a stunned silence. Angela Friend found her voice first. 'May I ask how it came into your possession, Dr Murray?'

'You may.' Margaret smiled at her and moved on. 'I have, of course, already perused these papers myself and I must confess to being, on the whole, baffled by them.'

There were mutterings of dissent all round. Em-em might have her shortcomings – she could not, for example, see over the rail at Goodwood – but bafflement? Never.

'Which is why Professor Minton's arrival is so timely.' She turned to him, hands in her lap, waiting for the great man to explain the origins of the universe.

'So,' Minton said, 'let me see if I've got this straight. These papers, whatever they are, are a sort of last will and testimony to this poor girl?'

'In a way,' Margaret said.

'She was, I assume, an archaeologist?' Minton probed, fumbling in an inside pocket for his spectacles.

'She was; from King's.'

Minton looked aghast and crossed himself.

'Quite,' Margaret said solemnly.

'Was she working on a project? I know we have that system, but do they?'

'They do,' Margaret told him. 'The dead girl was based at Hampton-on-Sea, Herne Bay. She was working on what may have been an outpost of Reculver.'

'Ah, Regulbium' – Minton gave it its Roman name – 'the most northerly of the Saxon Shore forts. Anything about the Baetasians here?' He looked around him and met blank stares, even from Margaret, whose field, it must be said in all fairness, this was not.

'Chaps from Denmark,' Minton explained. 'Auxiliary cohorts, following the eagle.'

Piers Gibbs and Janet Bairnsfather at least had no idea what the eminence before them was talking about; and the sheer immensity of arcane archaeology rose up before them like a brick wall.

'Let me see.' Minton helped himself to the nearest piece of paper. There were doodles all over it. He'd seen such hieroglyphs before, mostly signs of boredom from the pens of students attending his lectures – especially, had he ever cared to look closely enough, the pen of Andrew Rose. 'Ah, yes, here we are. Oh, this is interesting; "*II Aug* . . .", "*Vesp* . . .", "*alae auxiliae*". Yes, yes, all good stuff. Are these fragments the originals, Dr Murray? From the . . . erm . . . horse's mouth, so to speak?'

'No,' Margaret said. 'Copies, but good ones, I venture to say, with all due modesty! Could you translate, Professor? We have some freshmen here.'

'Oh, certainly, certainly. Well, this is actually quite rare. Ground-breaking, in fact. "*II Aug*" is the Second Augusta Legion, one of four who invaded under Aulus Plautius in 43. Regulbium would have been a base for them before they moved west. "*Vesp*" is of course Vespasianus. I suppose you'd call him a colonel today; commanded the II Augusta.'

'Was he the one who became emperor later, Professor?'
Veronica asked.

'That's right, my dear,' Minton beamed, glad that *somebody* was paying attention. 'He was also the first man in
recorded history to invent the penny a pee machine for public
toilets . . .'

Janet Bairnsfather blushed to her Presbyterian roots.

'. . . Oh, not literally, of course, but he did place a tax on
urine. The Romans were nothing if not earthy. And pretty good
at making money, too. "*Alae auxiliae*" – Mr Crouch, you're
a graduate, for God's sake. Have a stab, man.'

'Er . . . auxiliary cavalry, Professor,' Crouch came back at
him.

'Good. Good. Now, what have we here?' Minton took
up another of the scattered sheets and read aloud. "*Me
salutatium* . . ." No, that can't be right.' He was frowning
now. 'And what's this? "*Non saxus in me* . . ." Margaret,
this is gibberish. You must have copied it wrongly.'

'Indeed I did not do any such thing.' Margaret didn't say
what she really felt, for fear of distressing the gentlemen
present. 'But that is more or less what I thought,' she said. 'I
was hoping wiser eyes could see what I could not.'

'"*Me salutatium*" is "my bow down". *My* bow down?
Doesn't make sense.' He took up another sheet. 'Ah, now, here
we go. "*Regulbium* . . ." Yes. Messengers have been sent to
Reculver. Urgent. Oh.' And he stopped dead.

'What is it, Norman?' Margaret asked.

'Oh, it's nothing,' the professor said. 'I must . . . This' – he
switched back to the earlier sheet – 'this is a poem of sorts.
Look, caesura, pes. It's supposed to be declaimed, recited,
sung, even.'

'Is it a soldier's song?' Sheringham asked.

'Well, it might be,' Minton nodded, 'but this is very defin-
itely reference to the first century – and soon after the conquest.
Is there anything else, Margaret? Inscriptions? Tablets?
Anything of that sort?'

'King's didn't seem to have anything else,' she told him,
'and I've been to the site itself, the one the poor girl was
working on. Nothing.'

'There's erosion, though, isn't there?' Rose asked, 'along that part of the coast?'

'There is indeed,' Minton said. 'Who knows what's been lost over time?'

'Ah, the archaeologist's dilemma,' Margaret said.

'This, though . . .' Minton had gone back to the third sheet. '"*Turbator Josephus* . . ."' and his voice trailed away. 'I shall need more time, Margaret,' he said stiffly, standing up. 'Look, could I take these papers away? They're probably the inconsequential ramblings of an undergraduate . . . oh, no offence to anyone.'

There were uneasy grins all round and someone muttered, 'None taken.'

'Feel free, Professor Minton,' Margaret said. 'We know, after all, where to find you. Here.' She opened her bag, which was tucked under her chair, and took out a large, thick envelope. 'Take the originals. I copied everything as I thought it should look, but perhaps something in the background I took to be dirt may have a bearing.'

'Thank you,' he said, taking the envelope and waiting by her chair.

'Yes?' She looked up.

'Westropp?'

'Oh, I am so sorry.' She handed the book over and he tucked the envelope inside. 'As you say, you know where to find me, so pop in at any time, see how I'm getting on.' He looked round the room and tried not to see any women. 'Yes, yes, indeed.' And he left, humming to himself.

'Next week,' Margaret said, when the door had closed behind Minton, 'we'll be looking at the *Iliad*, Mr Crouch, so we'll be back in your beloved Greece at last.'

'Thank you, Dr Murray.' Crouch half bowed and they stashed away their notebooks and made for the door.

'Boss wants a word with you, Crawford.' Sergeant Sadler, on the desk that morning, was a difficult man to read. That could mean 'You've been promoted, son, and you're probably in line for Commissioner' or it could mean 'Pack your waders, mate; it's the horse troughs for you'. In the event, it was neither of the above . . . quite.

'I'm afraid you've been over-zealous, lad.' Athelgar Blunt was wreathed in pipe smoke, in his office on the first floor.

'In what way, sir?' Crawford felt obliged to ask.

'In the way of getting right up the nose of a member of the public.'

'Anybody in particular?' It had to be said that Adam Crawford didn't like Athelgar Blunt. Technically, he wasn't even his boss, despite what Sergeant Sadler had said.

Blunt slammed his spare hand down on his desk so that the pens jumped and the inkwells rattled. 'I wouldn't be so flippant if I were you,' he snarled. 'For your information, the complainant is a Mr John Daventry, of . . .'

'. . . Firtree Road, Isleworth. Yes, sir; I thought it might be.'

'Mr Daventry is a property owner of some standing in this city,' Blunt told him. He narrowed his eyes at the constable. 'You're not one of those Socialists, are you?'

'No, I . . .'

'One of the lumpenproletariat trying to lose their chains?'

'No, I . . .'

'Sneering at men like Mr Daventry because he has money and a bit of class?'

Crawford had had enough. 'Mr Daventry,' he told the detective levelly, 'is an extortionist who charges obscene rents for slum properties. He is also – although I haven't got hard evidence yet – a pimp, renting out his premises to prostitutes.'

'Well, that's it!' Blunt screamed. 'I *was* going to be generous, Crawford, and let this go. Now, I'm not. Let me remind you, once and for all, that you are uniform. You do not detect, in any shape or form. Leave that to the big boys. From now on, until hell freezes over, you are on traffic duty in Bloomsbury. I want you as far away from the Yard as I can put you without embarrassing the Force. And you step out of line there – if you so much as help an old lady across the road – your feet won't touch, son. Do I make myself clear?'

'Abundantly, Detective Inspector.'

Norman Minton was not an imaginative man, and that was a shame. He worked, and lived, and had his being amongst perhaps the most romantic men the world had ever seen; even the humblest of pedes two thousand years ago had a story to tell to freeze the blood, but Norman never heard them. Rome and its empire was facts, figures, rules, regulations to Norman Minton. It was stone. It was sometimes wood. It was, even more rarely than wood, fabric or parchment. But it had no voice.

Even so, his Latin was immaculate. He had gone to the sort of school where every declension was beaten into his head with a swipe of the ruler or the master's palm. *Amo.* Smack! *Amas.* Thwack. *Amat.* Slap. *Amamus*, *Amatis*, *Amant*, gabbled quickly to cut down on blows. At first, it was just by rote. Then, one morning – he remembered it as if it were yesterday – the lines on the page had stopped being a code and begun to be words, a language he could hide in when the world got a bit much, when the chant of 'Minty, Minty, Minty, Slow and Fat and Squinty' had made him want to cry. It was good to be able to shout, '*Es porcos et adipem totum olfacies.*' Calling them fat smelly pigs wasn't high wit, but they didn't know what he had said. That it got him beaten up more than once scarcely mattered. It was just good to know that he knew more than them. And while they were giggling over the silly translation for eleven-year-olds – 'Caesar had some jam for tea; Pompey had a rat' – Norman Minton overtook them all.

And yet again – he took a slurp of tea long gone cold and hardly noticed – he knew more than the others here at the college too. Margaret Murray was clever enough – for a woman, at any rate. The students. Well, perhaps one or two had a brain in their heads. But they had to ask him what it was all about. For years he had been a professor, and yet he was still Minty, slow and fat and squinty, even if he exercised religiously and the eye had been sorted out years ago, by the simple expedient of sticking plaster over his glasses.

He laid out the papers in any order, then looked at them, narrowing his eyes in thought, not because he was squinting. He hummed a little to himself and moved two papers, swapping them over. Then two more. And then two more. He smiled again and rubbed his hands. He was just *too* clever, sometimes.

He didn't hear it coming. He certainly didn't see it coming. But from behind, wingèd Mercury, messenger of the gods, swept through the air and struck him around the side of the head. In an involuntary movement, his arms swung up, then out and down, scattering the papers across the desk, spattering them with his blood. His head fell forward on to the desk and he looked at the small arc of his study that he could see from there. His books. His statuary. All his lovely things. He drew air into his lungs with an effort almost too much for his dying brain and breathed it out softly.

Only his murderer heard his dying words. And he didn't understand them.

'*Vale*,' Norman Minton said. '*Vale in sempiternum*.'

Annie Scroggins had been a sweeper all her adult life. And for much of her childhood, come to that. She was nearing fifty now and, truth be told, the years of handling polished wood and lifting buckets had taken their toll. Her back clicked most mornings when she got up and there was an occasional numbness in her left leg. By evening, as it was now, her shoulders ached and she had to force her rheumatic fingers to pick up the screwed-up papers the students left behind.

Annie would never understand students, not if she lived to be fifty-one. Overgrown children, they were, entitled and with smells under their noses. Annie could read just like them and she knew what they, apparently, didn't; the world was going to change soon – that nice Mr Keir Hardie said so. So did the Reverend Cadwallader. He had told Annie to her face that the weak, of which she was definitely one, would one day inherit the earth. So it was written in the scriptures – Annie Scroggins, sweeper of the vestibule and main staircases of the University College of London, was about to be as good as her masters. *Then* let the students look down their noses at her, if they dare.

Darkness was coming to Gower Street, the gas lamps on the vestibule walls sending flickering shadows over the plaster. Lectures had long ago ended and the staff had gone home. The only people in the huge, echoing building were the cleaners. And, in the vestibule, only Annie. Old Jenkins, the nightwatchman, wouldn't be on until eight and Annie would have gone by then; doubly so, because the filthy old man couldn't keep his hands to himself.

But the moment had come. As it came every evening. It wasn't too bad in the summer when the street outside was still busy with gigs and broughams and, every now and again, one of those loud, terrifying motor carriages, the ones that would never catch on. At that time of year the sun shone, gilding the brass fittings of the vestibule, flooding the worn carpet with light. But now, in October, the shadows lengthened and the stairs hung heavy in the semi-dark. The only sound was the swish of Annie's broom. She looked up at the marble busts on the pedestals, the great and good who had presided over the college for three quarters of a century, pale patricians with chiselled features and side-whiskers to die for. Them, Annie could handle. Their faces were hard, unreal, their eyes as empty as the flask in Annie's apron pocket. Bugger! She thought she'd filled that up yesterday. Now she'd have to face the moment, not only alone as always, but stone cold sober.

At the far end of the corridor, she saw him, sitting, as always, on his chair, looking at her. He was always looking at her. And yet, he never said a word, nor raised a hand in greeting. Not to her, not to anyone. She busied herself with a cobweb in a tricky corner, bent to scoop it up into her pan. She flicked her duster along the skirting board, listening to the invisible rats behind the timbers stir themselves before they came out to hunt when the building was silent and empty. And all the time, she felt his eyes on her. Her heart was pounding, her throat tight with fear. Bugger again. She did this every day except the Sabbath; why wasn't she used to it? He never moved; never spoke; never did her any harm. So why . . .? She kept her eyes averted, hurtling around his glass case like a thing possessed, her broom rattling and clattering on the skirting board and hissing over the marble floor.

She'd done it! Thank God! It was over again for another day. She turned her back on him, sitting silently in his glass case, and she glanced up, broom in one hand, pan in the other. Then she saw it – a shadow, a blur, a darker shape in the darkness dashed across her view, coming from the stairs that led to the Archaeology department. Annie never went up there; she knew it was full of dead things that once had crawled the earth and would never do so again; people with sightless eyes and grey, leather skin. Who *was* that? *What* was that? There were no cleaners but her in this part of the building. Had it been one of them, she would have called 'Hello'. It couldn't be old Jenkins; he'd have made an excuse to come over to her and try to pat her bum. Anyway, she could count on the fingers of one hand the times he had approached from any direction but from behind. So . . . who?

She turned. And 'til her dying day, she didn't know why she did. She turned and looked at the dead man in his glass case. She saw his thigh bone jutting through his faded, moth-eaten breeches; she saw his toe bones under the collapsing leather of his boots. She saw the pale green frock coat and the tambour-sprigged vest, the wideawake hat. And she saw the square, shiny face and the grey glass eyes. And she knew, that in the tin hat box between his feet was the man's own head, a skull as grim and ghastly as anything kept upstairs in the Archaeology department. She forced herself away, the dustpan clattering to the floor, the broom following it with a crash that echoed and re-echoed through the whole building.

And Annie ran. She ran as she hadn't run for years, faster than she had ever run away from old Jenkins. Tears ran too, down her cheeks and into the corners of her open mouth, too terrified, as it was, to let out a scream. Because Annie had seen him. She had seen what she had always known lurked in this part of University College, the reason that men called it the Godless Institution. She had seen the ghost of the man in the glass case. She had seen the ghost of Jeremy Bentham. On the stairs, coming from where the dead things lay.

'Margaret.' Flinders Petrie stopped shuffling the papers he was working on and looked into those bright, grey eyes. 'Good of you to call. Er . . . what's going on?'

'Going on, Flinders? Whatever do you mean?' Hope sprang eternal in the breast of Margaret Murray but she knew perfectly well that there was little chance of getting anything past this man. Whether digging in some corner of a foreign field or ferreting out secrets nearer home, there was no one to touch him.

The lamps were glowing out all over Petrie's museum that evening, where things in jars sat elbow to elbow with papyri and amphorae and all things ancient. It was a second home to both of them.

Petrie got up from behind his desk and smoothed down his moustache. This one would take some careful timing. 'You're making quite a name for yourself in the university,' he said, smiling at his protégée.

'Thank you, Flinders.' She smiled back.

'But . . . and I don't quite know how to say this . . .'

'You aren't usually so tongue-tied.' She reached up to straighten his bow tie.

'I am, to put it bluntly, a little concerned.'

'Really?' She widened her eyes again. 'Why, pray?'

'Well,' he said, moving away from her, 'this whole wretched Helen Richardson business, of course. It's highly distasteful, Margaret.'

'Indeed it is,' she agreed. 'But you have known worse in the back streets of Cairo, surely . . .'

'Cairo be buggered, Margaret!' he stormed. 'Oh, saving your presence. Helen Richardson wasn't one of the fellaheen. I understand you've been talking to Scotland Yard.'

'They *do* have experience of sudden death in the Metropolis, Flinders,' she reminded him.

'And the tabloid newspapers, viz. and to wit, the *Illustrated Police News*. George Carey Foster is very concerned.'

'Oh, Flinders.' She waved her hands about. 'That was *days* ago! I have also consulted a private detective.'

'What?' Flinders Petrie's eyeballs looked ready to bounce out of their sockets.

'Flinders.' She crossed the study to him and led him gently back to his chair. 'As you know, discretion is my middle name. Now, let me put the kettle on and we'll talk about it over a Tetley's, shall we?'

Margaret Murray didn't hate many things in the world, but she did hate wasting time. So she walked along Gower Street one morning with even more than her usual vim and vigour. She was just about to turn into the University building when a familiar pair of shoulders caught her eye. She went to the edge of the pavement and peered through the morning traffic to make sure, then stepped off to cross the road.

'Watch it, lady!' The driver of a dray pulled up in the nick of time. 'Got a bleeding deaf wish, 'ave ya?'

Margaret waved insouciantly at him. 'Sorry,' she mouthed. 'I need this policeman.'

The drayman clicked his tongue and his horse moved off. The lad was well set up, he wouldn't deny, but surely even he wasn't worth dying for.

Margaret got to the middle of the road without further incident and stood as close to Adam Crawford as common decency would allow, then moved even closer to avoid being run over.

'Whatever are you doing here, Constable Crawford?' she said, raising her voice over the rumble of wheels.

He didn't look down, but stared straight ahead, his left hand raised in an admonitory gesture, his right elbow loose as his hand spun round to tell the waiting multitude it was finally their turn. It had been a tough morning thus far, and so he was a little terse.

'Directing traffic,' he said, through gritted teeth. An omnibus was heading straight for him and he knew the drivers did not take prisoners.

'But why?' Margaret was appalled.

'Just because, Dr Murray,' he said, counting cars on Gower Street from his left. If he let one too many through, there would be a riot. 'Just because.'

'Can I do anything?' Margaret couldn't help but worry whether perhaps at least a little of this was her fault.

'You can get back on the pavement without getting mown down and then go and do what you do all day,' he said. 'I don't always know what that is, to be frank. But what I do all day is easy to explain. It's this.' He waved an eloquent hand in a sweeping gesture and two milk carts collided with a crash of churns. He stepped back. '*Now* look what you've made me do. Goodbye, Dr Murray.' He hurried over and started helping to extricate the milkmen from their milk. Taking advantage of the stopped traffic, Margaret slunk back to the kerb. It had put a dent in her mood, that was certain. Perhaps Norman would have news to cheer her up.

Universities wake up slowly. So although it was bedlam outside in Gower Street, with the world and his wife going to work or sauntering home after working all night, inside the Godless Institution it was as quiet as death. Margaret made her way across the lobby and up the stairs towards the Archaeology faculty.

As was her habit, she bobbed a curtsy to the man in the glass case and Skinner the day porter wished, as he did every time, that he had the barefaced cheek to rumble 'Good morning, Dr Murray' and see how she liked them apples. But he didn't have the cheek, so the joke, as ever, could keep for another day.

On the top landing it was, as usual, quiet. Margaret could tell that Flinders Petrie wasn't in his rooms, as there was no fug of pipe smoke curling under the door. Her own room was, by definition, silent and dark – exactly as Mrs Plinlimmon the owl liked it. The kitchenette where the kettle sulked was similarly empty and dark. Margaret, through spending much of her time alone, didn't like silence, so she was humming a little tune – 'Goodbye, Dolly Grey', as it happened – as she pushed open the door to the Roman faculty.

Which was also dark. This surprised her, as she would have bet good money – indeed, she had a small wager on with Mrs Plinlimmon – that Norman Minton would have burned the candle at both ends to get to the bottom of her little conundrum. Propping the door open, she felt her way across the room to the high window in the end wall. Her feet kicked against cushions and books as she picked her way; Norman had never been the tidiest of men, but she didn't want to be so archetypally female as to remonstrate with him. She had always put it off, but really, he should—

She turned round and her hand flew to her mouth. For a moment, she couldn't make out what she was looking at. In the centre of Norman Minton's desk, there seemed to be something resembling a bunch of roses, red and glossy, with uneven edges. They were sitting in a pool of dark red ink, which dripped silently on to the carpet, and on to Norman's legs, tucked neatly below it. Norman's legs, yes; but where was Norman's head? Her brain then confirmed what her eyes had refused to see. That broken, battered thing in the middle of the mahogany desert *was* Norman's head. Cracked open like a walnut, spilling brain and blood out as if there was no room for them inside the skull any more.

Margaret knew what she should do. She should check to see if life was extinct, whether she should call for an ambulance or an undertaker. But she could tell there was no decision to be made. Norman Minton, Professor Norman Minton, as he had always reminded everyone, was quite, quite dead.

EIGHT

Margaret closed the door of the Roman department with due ceremony. She was not a religious woman, but she had a strong sense of what the dead were due and above all other things was reverence and ceremony; she had a horrible feeling, though, that Norman Minton's mortal remains were about to get precious little of either.

She waited for a moment outside the door, leaning against the wall, with her face raised to heaven and her eyes closed. She needed to compose herself before she unleashed the gods of the establishment; police, doctors and without doubt the Press. The principal would doubtless get himself involved. Flinders, inevitably. The university cat and Jeremy himself, of course. He hadn't missed a meeting, after all, in the sixty-eight years since he had died, so why start now?

She walked sedately down the stairs and no one but she could see how white her knuckles were on the railing. She walked up to the porter's booth and knocked demurely on his door.

'Morning, Dr Murray.' The porter gave her an old-fashioned look. 'Are you ill, miss?'

'No.' Margaret found she was having to swallow hard. Her mouth was full of saliva and not being sick became her new main objective. 'Can you stop anyone going upstairs until I get back, please, Skinner?'

'Why, miss?'

'Just do it!' She didn't want to use her teacher voice on this harmless chap, but there was no time for niceties. 'I'll be back in a moment, with a policeman. Until then, simply do as I say.'

Still calm, she walked outside and crossed the road to where Adam Crawford stood, a little less frazzled now the rush had begun to get less. She stood there until he noticed her.

'Dr Murray!' he hissed through his teeth. 'I mean it! Leave me alone.'

She stood there, silent, swaying a little. He noticed that she was very pale, rather green around the gills, you might almost have said.

'Dr Murray?'

She looked at him. 'Hmm?' she said, as if he had interrupted a train of thought.

'Dr Murray? What's wrong?' A cold hand of fear gripped him as he noticed the blood on the hem of her grey skirt and spattered on her shoes. 'It . . . it isn't *Angela*?'

She shook herself. 'No, no, of course it isn't Angela,' she said, almost like her usual self. 'It's . . . well,' she looked down at her feet and realized the grey smudge on the toe of her shoe was part of Norman Minton's brain, a part that would never think again. 'No, Adam, it's . . . well, it's murder.'

And then, for the first and she hoped the last time in her life, Margaret Murray, with a little sigh, fainted.

Margaret Murray had woken up in more unusual places than most women of her age and class but it took her a moment on this occasion to work out where she was. The view of the ceiling gave her no clues, being off-white and crazed with faint lines, like most ceilings in the building. She sniffed. No pipe smoke, so not a man's room, in all probability. No perfume either, so not the principal's secretary's room; a lovely woman in many ways, but addicted to Attar of Roses to an almost unhealthy extent. The smell was of . . . no smell at all; it was the smell of Clean.

She heard voices off to her left and turned her head, gingerly. She didn't feel giddy, so that was a relief, but she couldn't see the speakers either. Then, a face swam into view.

'She's awake,' the face said over its shoulder. 'How are you, Dr Murray?'

She started to get up but was prevented by kind hands. 'Don't get up just yet. You fainted and that nice policeman from point duty carried you in here.' The voice dropped to a whisper. 'There's been an Incident, I'm afraid.' The tongue clicked and the head shook.

Margaret shook off the restraining hand. 'I *know* there's been an incident,' she said. 'I found it, spread all over his desk.' She decided at that instant that she was going to be as clinical as possible. It wasn't Norman, bumbling, Rome-obsessed Norman, in that room. It was a murder victim, probably like dozens more the capital had seen in just the last few weeks. She looked around. 'Where am I?' And instantly hated herself for the cliché.

The voice's owner stepped around so she was standing in front of Margaret as she sat on the edge of the narrow cot on which she had been lying. 'The San,' the woman said. She also sounded rather tarter now her patient was Up and About. The matron of University College both spoke and thought in capital letters – a tartar indeed. In this regard, she and Ethelfleda Charlton spoke with one voice. She was wearing a nurse's uniform, stiff with starch, cuffs blindingly white and a goffered cap you could cut bread with. 'You fainted.'

'I know I did. You said.' Margaret stood up, pushing the nurse aside. 'I need to—'

'The Police have been called,' the matron said, patronizingly. 'I think you should stay here until you are properly rested. Who knows what Damage the Sight has done to your Brain?'

Margaret looked her up and down and bit back a remark something along the lines of at least *she* had a brain to damage, but forbore. The woman was almost certainly of the Nightingale persuasion, but Florence Nightingale had been around for *far* too long. This woman probably meant well, but judging by the extreme neatness and cleanliness of the room, her services were not in huge demand. A lecturer delivered in a fainting condition was probably the most excitement she had had all year.

'All right,' she said, with a sigh. 'Take my pulse or temperature or whatever you need to do. Then I really must get on. There is someone I need to speak to, urgently.' She looked around. 'Do you have a telephone in here?'

The matron grabbed her wrist and shoved a thermometer in her mouth. 'Of course I do,' she said. 'It is the Sanatorium, when all is said and done. Now, hush, while I count . . .' She turned the little watch hanging upside down on her bosom round so she could see the second hand and her lips moved silently. After a minute, she dropped the lecturer's wrist and yanked the thermometer from her mouth. 'Yes, well, sixty-five and a temperature of . . .' – she shook the thermometer and squinted at it – 'I'm not sure why they make these numbers so small.' She looked at it again. 'But it looks to be normal, as far as I can tell.' She stepped aside. 'All right, Dr Murray. You can go. The telephone apparatus is over there, on the wall. You might have to jiggle the thingie a bit; it's rather temperamental.' And she grabbed the bedclothes where Margaret had been lying and threw them into a wicker basket in the corner. The conversation appeared to be over so Margaret crossed to the corner where the telephone squatted on the wall like some obscene black beetle. She jiggled the thingie as instructed and finally the disembodied voice of the telephonist sounded in her ear.

'Operator,' she warbled. 'What number please?'

'I'd like to be put through to the Tambour House Hotel, please,' Margaret announced carefully. 'It's in—'

'Putting you through, caller,' carolled the telephonist, and after a number of clicks and whirrs and one ear-splitting whistle, another voice was heard.

'Tambour House Hotel,' a plummy gent intoned. 'How may I help you?'

'I'd like to speak to Mr Reid, please,' she said. 'I believe he's in room—'

'Putting you through.'

Margaret sighed. It was wrong to complain about efficiency, but really, this telephone business was making everyone forget the niceties of polite conversation.

'Reid.'

'Oh, thank goodness,' Margaret sighed. 'Hello, Inspector Reid, it's—'

'Dr Murray! How lovely to hear from you.'

Margaret narrowed her eyes but this was no time to get testy. 'I'm speaking from University College, Inspector. There's been a murder and I think the police will be here shortly. I don't trust them . . .'

'. . . further than you could throw a sarcophagus,' Reid said. 'I don't blame you. I'm on my way.'

The line went dead and Margaret jiggled the thingie.

'Hello, caller. How may I—'

'Oh, for heaven's sake,' Margaret muttered, and stomped off to find Flinders Petrie. If she didn't have a proper conversation soon, she would burst.

Athelgar Blunt crossed the room in three strides. He had already lit his pipe on the stairs and now he blew smoke over the corpse of Professor Norman Minton. Crawford stood by the door, with strict instructions to let no one past him.

There was blood everywhere. It ran from the victim's head on to his blotting pad and had sprayed in a wide arc across the glass-fronted bookcases to his right. There were spots on the floor, on the legs of the chair the dead man was still sitting in, a red mist on the wall. Lying on the desk near the victim's head was a statue of Mercury, its wings crimson and sticky. Blunt reached for it.

'I wouldn't do that, Ethel,' a voice called from the doorway.

The inspector's head snapped upwards. 'I said nobody was to come past you, Crawford,' he said.

'Technically, Eth,' the arrival said, 'I haven't actually passed the constable yet.' He looked up at the man under the helmet. 'It *is* Mr Crawford, isn't it?'

Crawford almost stood to attention. Then, realizing who the visitor was, he *did* stand to attention. 'Inspector Reid,' he half whispered.

'Do you know me, boy?' Reid asked him.

'Yes, sir. I'd only just started before you retired, but . . .'

'And that's the magic word, isn't it?' Blunt had joined them in the doorway. '*Retired.* You're a civilian now, Reid. A nobody. And you're contaminating a crime scene.'

'Not half as much as you are,' Reid said. 'And that's *Mr* Reid to you. Cliché though it is, Ethel, I pay your wages. That' – he pointed to the Mercury statuette – 'may well be the murder weapon and you were about to put your greasy little dabs all over it.'

'Oh, don't give me that fingerprints bollocks,' Blunt snarled, spinning back into the room. 'It's been years since you were on the job.'

'Directly, yes,' Reid agreed. 'Indirectly, no. I'd give you my card as a private detective but I'm not sure you can read it.'

'I haven't got to arrest you, have I?' Blunt drew himself up to his full height, slightly edging over Reid as he did so; it was only by an inch or two, but in the Met, size was everything.

'Ooh,' Reid frowned. 'Wrongful arrest is *so* messy, isn't it? So damaging to a man's career. Talking of which, remember Lady Cadwallader?'

Crawford had never seen the blood drain from a man's face so quickly. 'You wouldn't . . .' Blunt began.

'Is old Jephson still writing for Harmsworth's rag?' Reid asked him. 'I always promised him the full Cadwallader story one day. Perhaps while I'm up in town . . .' Reid pulled a small notebook and pencil from his pocket and made himself a note, with a very ostentatious full stop. He looked up with a smile and turned to go.

'Just a minute,' Blunt called out to the ex-inspector's retreating figure. 'All right,' he sighed. 'What do you want?'

'Justice for this man.' Reid pointed to the corpse. 'Constable,' he said, edging past Crawford. 'There is an increasing crowd downstairs clamouring for answers. Get down and send them away. And' – he held the man's sleeve – 'in common with the

senior investigating officer in this case, you know nothing
– understand?'

'Yes, sir.' Crawford smiled.

Reid focused on the room. 'Do you want to take notes,
Ethel? Or shall I ask Dr Murray in?'

'Who?'

'This man's colleague. She found the body – not that you've
ascertained that yet, have you? You've met her, though. She
came to see you in connection with the Helen Richardson
case.'

'Who?'

'Oh, dear,' Reid tutted, bending down to examine the corpse.
'It's not really your day, is it? Tell you what – you go downstairs and disperse the crowd. Send young Crawford up – I
can't help thinking he'd be more use.'

'You've got a bloody nerve, Reid!' Blunt snapped.

'Yes, I know,' Reid laughed, 'but I also have a really interesting story about Lady Cadwallader and a certain detective
. . . and that's still *Mr* Reid, by the way. Dr Murray came to
see you about a student of hers, known to you as Alice Groves,
a whore.'

'Oh, yes, her,' Blunt finally remembered. 'Suicide.'

'There you go again.' Reid shook his head. 'Jumping to
conclusions. This is suicide, too, I suppose.'

'Come off it . . . Mr Reid.'

'All right.' Reid was suddenly serious. 'I've had my bit of
fun. Now, let's get to work. Crawford called you in?'

'That's right. Somebody in the building had found a body.'

'Margaret Murray.' Reid nodded. 'You'll be talking to her
in the fullness of time.' It was a statement, not a question. 'I
don't know what you've touched before I got here, but Margaret
won't have touched anything.'

Reid whipped out a handkerchief from his pocket and tilted
the dead man's head. 'Stiff as a board,' he said, 'which means
he died sometime last evening. I don't suppose you know what
sort of security they've got here. Nightwatchman? That sort
of thing?'

'Er . . . no. Not yet.' Blunt suddenly remembered regulations. 'Scene of crime first, Mr Reid – you know that.'

'Indeed I do.' Reid was already tracing the blood spatters. 'He was leaning over the desk and whoever hit him struck from behind.' He swung his right arm through the air. 'Right-handed, but the first blow didn't finish him, so he did it again. And probably again.' He straightened up. 'It's a man, Ethel and he's a beginner.'

'A beginner?'

'He hasn't killed before – at least not in this way. The place has clearly been turned over. Papers all over the shop, drawers ajar. So our boy was looking for something, either before or after he struck. After, probably.' Reid was thinking aloud. 'If the professor here caught a burglar in the act, he would hardly calmly sit at his desk, would he?' Using the handkerchief again, he lifted Minton's battered head. The eyes were open, wide and staring, dried blood covering his face like a ghastly mask. 'There's something missing here,' he said. 'Look, the pattern on the blotter and here, look, on the surface of the desk. Some are neat and some are smeared – pages have been removed. They'll be covered in blood, but they may have been what our friend was looking for. That can't have been all, though. He wanted something else, hence the drawers ransacked.'

Reid looked at Blunt. 'Do you actually *have* a fingerprint department at the Yard yet?' he asked.

'Don't talk rot,' Blunt snapped. 'All that's fairy story stuff.'

'I sat on the Belper Committee last summer,' Reid told him, 'right here in London, that decided it wasn't. You're about to get a new Assistant Commissioner, aren't you? Edward Henry?'

'That's right,' Blunt said, suspicious as ever when it came to outsiders. 'Some bloody amateur from India or somesuch place. What he's likely to know about police work can be etched on a bloody tealeaf, I shouldn't wonder.'

Reid turned to go. 'From what I've read of him,' he said, 'he at least knows his loops from his whorls. By the way . . .'

Blunt looked up, glad to see – almost – the back of the man.

'That lad . . . Crawford.'

'What about him?'

'CID material, would you say?'

'CID?' Blunt guffawed. 'Never in a month of Sundays. I've rostered him on traffic until 1926 at the earliest.'

Reid turned to face him. 'Arrange a transfer, Blunt. And do it today. I know a natural when I see one.'

'You can't just dictate . . .'

'I wonder how old Jephson's dictation speed is these days? I remember now, he *is* still at the *Mail*. He's probably got some perky little secretary to do the scribbling now – he's quite senior, I believe. Gets all his stories printed, no questions asked. I expect the type writers' pool will love to hear about Lady Cadwallader, don't you? Some of it was quite . . .'

Blunt clenched his fist, but his heart wasn't in it.

'. . . unusual, as I recall.' Reid smiled innocently.

'All right!' Blunt shouted. And he was still shouting it down the stairs as Reid clattered down them. 'All right, you've made your point. Crawford!'

At the bottom, Reid turned and looked up at the man.

'*Detective* Constable Crawford,' Blunt said.

Mrs Plinlimmon looked down from her perch. Below her, Margaret Murray sat surrounded by papers. She had loosened her stays and unpinned her hair – the correct attire, she believed, for serious thinking.

'Whoever killed poor old Norman,' the lecturer said to the owl, 'was looking for something. Drawers had been ransacked, papers overturned, books strewn around.' Margaret looked up at those penetrating glass eyes and laughed. 'Yes, I know,' she said. 'Not unlike my own dear study as we speak. But Norman was neater than I am though that's not saying much; he tried to keep everything just so. Whoever smashed his head . . .' – and she shuddered at the memory – 'wanted something from his room. What was he working on?' She tapped her fingers on the desk rim, then moved the oil lamp that was shining in her face. 'Poor old Norman,' she said again, as if the man had, in death, acquired two more Christian names. 'He hadn't worked on anything new for years. Oh, his Latin was impeccable, his knowledge of Rome's catacombs second to none. But field work?' She sighed. 'That was so *then*.'

She got up, stretched, felt her back click and ferreted out the decanter of port she had stashed away for critical thinking. 'Don't look at me like that, Mrs Plinlimmon,' she said, without glancing at the owl. 'The sun is definitely over the yardarm, whatever that is. And I need to focus.' She took a sip and sat down again. 'I can't help thinking,' she said, 'that all this has something to do with that veiled Latin I showed him.' She suddenly sat bold upright. 'Oh, God,' she said. 'I have inadvertently contributed to the poor man's death, Mrs Plinlimmon!' And she downed the rest of her glass in one. She held up her hand. 'No, no, nothing you can say will placate me. I *am* involved.' She took a deep breath. 'And so, it's up to me to sort this whole wretched business out. Now,' she moved her papers around, as though a magical answer would be lying there under the pile of undergraduate piffle. 'What was that phrase that Norman read out? It seemed to stop him in his tracks. "*Turbator Josephus*" – the troublemaker Josephus.' She got up again and walked around the room. The owl watched her go. 'Josephus. Josephus . . .' She clicked her fingers. 'The other reference was to the II Augusta Legion, wasn't it? And Vespasian. That's it!' She began humming to herself as her fingers trailed along the spines of her books. It was here somewhere, she knew. Oh, damn the tune, she thought – it was 'Goodbye, Dolly Grey' again.

'Aha!' She winkled a leather-bound tome out from the shelf just above her head and flicked through its pages. 'Here he is – Titus Flavius Josephus, 37–100. Historian, of noble family, son of Matthias. Spent three years in the wilderness with Bannus the hermit. Sent to Rome from Judea in 64 and . . . oh, got on rather well with Poppaea . . .' Margaret glanced up at the owl. 'No better than she should be, Mrs Plinlimmon, wife of the emperor Nero – and it's probably best you don't know any more. Led the rebellion in Galilee in 66. Captured by the Romans and prophesied that Vespasian would become emperor, which, of course, he did. Well, that's fascinating . . .' Margaret's smile faded. 'And wrong. Not this entry.' She glanced at the spine of the book to check the author and nodded approvingly. 'This entry is no doubt accurate. But look at the dates, Mrs Plinlimmon. Born in 37. Emma's notes imply she is talking about 42 or 43 – Norman didn't argue with any of that, so we must assume she was right. Josephus may have been an annoying five- or six-year-old, but why would he be called a troublemaker by officials in Britain, best part of two and a half thousand miles away from where he lived?'

Margaret put the book down and sighed. 'Nobody said, Mrs Plinlimmon, that archaeology was easy.'

'Rudyard Kipling!' The little woman stood on the path of the house at Rottingdean with open arms.

'Margaret Murray!' The man followed suit and they squeezed each other, laughing like maniacs.

'Margaret Murray!' an American voice rang out from behind the great man.

'Caroline!' Margaret hugged her too. 'I am *so* sorry to call unannounced,' she said, 'but I needed to pick your husband's brains.'

'Come in, come in.' Kipling ushered her over the threshold. 'Carrie; tea, cakes, the contents of your larder! It isn't every day we are honoured by a visit from the world's foremost archaeologist.'

Carrie Kipling laughed and went off to organize the maids.

'You're looking well, Ruddy,' Margaret said. 'The tan is from the Veldt, I assume?'

'Ah, you know about that?'

'My dear Ruddy, the whole world knows about it.' She accepted his offer of the sofa. 'I've followed your exploits in *The Times*. Was it all as wretched as they say, our brave boys in the hospitals, I mean?'

'Worse,' Kipling scowled. 'You know how the British press clean things up for the public. But that's enough about the world and its woes; tell me, has that old deviant Flinders Petrie taken you to Egypt yet?'

'He assures me he is going to on his next dig,' she said, 'though I'll believe it when it happens.'

'Ah, a woman's touch.' Kipling smiled. 'I have to admit, I'd be lost without Carrie. She handles all my paperwork, bullies publishers and even fires the cannon for me when we have any local troops coming home.'

'Yes,' Margaret said. 'I heard about that, too. I'm sure the locals love you, Ruddy.' There was a pained expression on her face and Kipling burst out laughing. The eyes were bright under the bushy eyebrows and the jaw strong. He and Margaret were of an age, both of them brought up – she more so than him – in India. He was a household name in literary circles, a champion of the empire. But she knew that the firm jaw and bright eyes hid an unhappy child who had grown into a man oddly unsure of himself. And what Margaret knew, and what the papers had not said, was that Ruddy and Carrie had just lost their darling little girl, Josephine, and the archaeologist could not know how that felt. She would not raise it unless he did. And he would not raise it because the pain was still too raw.

Instead, 'I have a problem,' she said. 'It's to do with poetry. And, I'm ashamed to admit, you're the only poet I know.'

'Well, any port in a storm.' He shrugged.

She passed him a copy of the page she'd found in Emmeline Barker's box, the one that Norman Minton had so spectacularly – and mystifyingly – failed to translate.

Kipling fixed his thick-lensed glasses to his nose and peered at it. 'It's in Latin, Em-em,' he told her solemnly.

She leaned back in mock astonishment. 'And some people say you'll never be Poet Laureate,' she said.

He swiped at her with the paper, then tried to pick out individual words. '"*Essedum*",' he said. 'What's that?'

'Chariot,' she translated.

'Is this something military, then?' he asked her. 'Did I send you a copy of Song to Mithras, by the way? I know I meant to.'

'You did,' she said, 'and very good it is, too.' She almost told him how the final line, 'Mithras, also a soldier, teach us to die aright!' had reduced her to tears, but perhaps now was not the moment. Some other time. 'Is it published yet? You got the Romans on the Wall just right.'

'Hmmm . . . I'm gathering some things together, some jottings, you know, some ideas. I have in mind something a bit . . . otherworldly.' His eyes misted. 'Something for the children . . .' He coughed. 'I'm glad you liked it, I really am.

But Latin, Em-em. You know I never actually went to university.'

She rolled her eyes. 'You don't know how lucky you are,' she said. 'I was hoping you'd get some sort of . . . I don't know . . . rhythm. Or resonance, or . . . I'm completely out of my depth.'

'What's the importance of this?' Kipling asked.

'I don't even know that,' she told him. 'Oh, look, Ruddy, I'm sorry. I turn up, out of the blue, interrupting like this and talking gibberish.'

'What's new?' He winked at her.

'I found that page in a box belonging to a dead girl.' She could have bitten her tongue. A shiver of pain crossed Kipling's face, but Margaret carried on hurriedly. 'A girl who was murdered.'

'Murdered?' the poet frowned. 'Good Lord!'

'Her body was found on a beach in Herne Bay, Kent. That page was in a box belonging to her at her college, King's in London.'

'But . . . you're University College, aren't you? Sworn enemies, and all that?'

'Emmeline was an archaeologist,' Margaret said. 'So we're sisters under the skin.'

There was a sudden 'whoop' from the hallway and a little boy with a chubby face and brown hair barged into the room, his mother in tow.

'My boy, Jack,' Kipling beamed. 'Stop rampaging about now, Jack, and say hello to Em-em.'

The lad stood in front of her, frowning. Then he said, 'Hello, Em-em,' and held out his hand for her to shake.

'Elsie will be down momentarily,' Carrie said, moving Jack aside so that the maid could lay out the tea tray. 'She's going through a shy stage at the moment.'

'Sit on Em-em's lap, Jack,' Kipling said, 'and make sure she doesn't eat all the scones.'

The boy jumped up and Margaret held him, smiling at his dimpled cheeks and bright eyes. He turned to her. 'Don't eat all the scones, Em-em,' he said, and everyone laughed.

'Carrie.' Kipling passed the dead girl's paper to his wife. 'Does any of this make sense to you?'

Carrie looked at it as the maid passed the tea and Jack didn't take his eyes off Em-em. 'My Latin isn't what it was,' she smiled. 'Oh, wait a minute . . . "*Nubes*" – that's clouds, isn't it? "*Essedum*" – chariot. "*Agnus dei*" – Lamb of God, of course. Yes, this is William Blake.' She mock-frowned at her husband. 'And you, Rudyard Kipling, should be ashamed of yourself for not recognizing it.'

An odd silence filled the room. Then Margaret picked up a scone. 'Can I have just this one, Jack?' she asked.

He looked dubiously at her. 'All right,' he said. 'Just that one.'

Walnut Mews was more familiar to Edmund Reid in the dark rather than the light. The day was gloomy, but at least he could see if anyone untoward was dodging behind a bin or hiding in an area as he turned into the narrow street. Mews were up and coming all over London, but Walnut seemed to have rebuffed any attempt at gentrification. Even so, some of the tiny houses had tried their best, with window-boxes full of winter pansies brightening up the dull red brick and neglected green-painted windows. He referred to the scrap of paper on which he had jotted down the details and made his way across the cracked and greasy cobbles to number fifteen. It was one of the pansy houses, so he felt hopeful; their brave faces nodding under their purple hoods lifted the spirits at this gloomy time of year.

He had thought long and hard about the best time to call. He assumed that the woman he was visiting would be a student but it had occurred to him as he made his way there from his hotel that this need not be the case. If she worked, he would have to come back later. If she was a student, it would be anyone's guess. As he approached the door, painted a bright blue and garnished with a brass knocker in the shape of the Lincoln Imp, he was accompanied by a cat, well-fed and glossy, who wound herself around his ankles as he waited for a reply to his smart rapping. He had never been much of a cat man himself, but his wife had had several and it cheered him to hear the soft purr around his feet. What cheered him even more was the sound of heels tapping along the hallway.

The door was flung open and a smiling girl stood inside, a smear of paint down one cheek and a paintbrush stuck in her piled-up hair.

'Oh.' Her smile didn't fade but he clearly wasn't who she was expecting. 'I'm sorry,' she said. 'I thought you were the pigment man.' She put her hand to her cheek and scrubbed at it half-heartedly. 'He's used to seeing people covered in paint, I would imagine. But you are . . .?'

Reid touched the brim of his hat politely. 'I am Edmund Reid, madam,' he said. 'Late of Scotland Yard . . .'

'Inspector *Dier*! I love those books.' Her face lit up, then fell. 'But . . . why are you here? Is . . . is it about Emma?'

'Why would you assume that?' Reid asked. 'Umm . . . may I come in?' The cat had shot in through the door as soon as it had opened. 'And . . . did you notice the cat? It is yours, I assume.'

'Actually, it's Emma's. She adored the creature; I can take or leave it, to be frank. That's why I didn't believe the letter. For a start, it was typed.' The woman ushered Reid in and shut the door behind him. They were left in the semi-dark of a short hallway leading to a flight of stairs. 'Do go up,' she said, extending an arm. 'The studio is warmer than the sitting room and lighter as well. In fact, since Emma left, I've hardly been in there at all. There doesn't seem to be much point.'

At the top of the stairs, the big room was flooded with light. Reid wouldn't have believed that a grey London sky could provide such illumination, but added to a few lamps and a crackling wood fire, it was magical. A couch at one end was strewn with jewel-coloured cushions and a tasselled throw. At the other end, an enormous canvas depicting some of a nude dominated the space. Reid walked up to it and looked at it closely.

'I see you are not offended by nudity, Inspector Reid,' the woman said.

'Not at all,' he chuckled. 'You have depicted the . . . the . . .' – he waved a hand in the general direction of the bits in question – 'with particular skill, I think.'

'Shall we sit down?' the artist said. 'I'm Marjorie Simmons, by the way, but everyone calls me Marjy. I hope you'll do the same.' She patted the other end of the couch and Reid joined her, still casting glances at the canvas.

'I understand that you and Emma had shared this mews for a while,' he began.

'Since she came to London,' Marjy told him. 'I had moved in and to be honest was finding the rent tricky. Emma didn't have much money, but every little helped back then.' She smiled and looked down, not modestly but like someone who still couldn't quite believe the turn her luck had taken. 'My canvases sell now, though, so I don't need a lodger. But . . . well, Emma and I had hit it off, so she stayed. She would just pay for a special meal now and then, but apart from that, she was my guest. A very loved guest, Inspector, I must say.'

'Did you ever visit her in her house in Hampton?' he asked.

'Her *house*? She would laugh to hear it called that. It was a shack, nothing more. But she loved her digging and delving and all she wanted was somewhere to lay her head.'

'So you did visit?'

'Once or twice.' Marjy Simmons had become used to her comforts, that was clear. 'But honestly, Inspector, roughing it on a mattress on the floor isn't my style. It never was, but it certainly isn't now.'

'Did she have other guests?'

Marjy smiled and put a painty hand on his knee. 'You're very sweet, Inspector. I assume you mean men.'

'I didn't say so.' Reid was used to being circumspect.

'Not as such, no, that's true, you didn't. Emma didn't care much for men, Inspector, in the normal run of things.' Her blush made the streak of paint show up more. 'In fact, I rather think she loved me. Does that shock you?'

'Miss Simmons . . . Marjy . . . I don't believe anything could shock me. Not even . . .' – he tipped his head towards the canvas – 'that. But the college did receive a letter, saying she had decided to marry.'

'So did I,' Marjy said, 'which is why I took no notice of it. A typed letter from one's lover to say she is getting married doesn't really cut the mustard, does it?'

'Why didn't you report her missing, then?' Reid knew the answer but needed it from this horse's mouth.

'Can you imagine it, Inspector Reid? "Hello, policeman. I have come to report my lover missing." "Oh, really, madam."' She dropped her voice an octave. '"Could you describe the gentleman?" "Well, she's about five foot five . . ."' I rather fancy the conversation would go downhill from there.'

Reid smiled. 'Yes, I do understand. But . . . what do you think happened?'

The artist straightened her back and lifted her chin, as someone waiting for a shock. 'I assumed she had tired of me, Inspector. But I expect you're here to tell me she's dead.' She saw the look on his face. 'Don't worry, I won't cry. It will be a relief. As long as she didn't choose to go, that's all that matters. I've shed my tears.'

Reid had seen some brave women in his time, but this one was up there with the bravest. 'I'm sorry, Marjy. She is dead, yes. Down in Hampton. I . . . I found her, actually.'

Marjy dropped her head and she was wrong about having shed her tears. One dropped on to her hand with a splash. 'And was she . . .?'

Reid chose his words. 'She had been murdered, Marjy, but not . . . interfered with, as far as we could tell. We don't know why anyone would want to kill her – unless you do?'

'When?' The word was hardly audible.

'In August sometime, we think.'

The face that lifted to him bore a ghost of a smile. 'She never left me, then,' she whispered. 'I waved her off on that stupid Summer Saturday train and never saw her again. But if she died . . . well' – she rummaged in a sleeve and brought out a handkerchief stained with burnt umber – 'she hadn't left me, not even for a while. That makes it better, Inspector.' She blew her nose. 'Sorry about that. Better now.'

Reid waited for her to regain her composure. Emmeline Barker had been loved, more loved than many people ever are in much longer lives. He hoped she had known it, before she died. 'Can you tell me a bit about her? Her parents were . . . unhelpful.'

'Parents! They don't deserve the name. Her father is a pig,

her mother worse for letting him *be* a pig. When we met, she was sitting in a coffee shop in Surrey Street, trying to keep warm and making a cup of tea last all day if she could. She was homeless, essentially; she had stayed with an aunt for a week or so, but it wasn't a success, so she was trying to keep out of the house as much as possible. How any father could do that to a girl who just wanted to better herself, I fail to see. Anyway, long story short, she had a little money and when she didn't have to worry about making it last to keep a roof over her head and food in her belly for three years, she was happy to help me with the rent.' She wiped her eye again, but was smiling. 'She knew I would be famous one day, she said. I'm not famous, but I do well. I fell in love with her there and then.'

'And what about her? Did she fall in love with you?'

Marjy laughed. 'Eventually. She had had a man at home who was interested in marrying her, apparently, but she didn't want to marry. Another reason for her letter to make no sense. I think she had friends who were men – how could she not, when almost all the students she mixed with were men? She mentioned one – not his name, though – who she had become fond of, but not in what people call "that way". He understood, she said. He had other outlets, if you understand me.'

Reid understood only too well. 'Apart from all this, did you find out anything about her work?'

'Oh, goodness, it wasn't for lack of trying, but it was gibberish to me. I know she was very excited about something, but she wouldn't tell me what. Not until she was sure, she said. She had notes and everything, back at King's, I suppose. There was certainly no paperwork here, just her clothes and things. She liked to keep her two lives separate.'

'We have her paperwork,' Reid said. 'If you would like it after we're done . . .?'

Marjy batted the idea away with a grubby hand. 'No, no, keep it. I can't imagine I would be able to make sense of it. Can you? I only ask because she had the most peculiar way of remembering things. I can't do it, but I can explain it, though best of luck with understanding how it works.'

Reid was intrigued. 'Go on.'

'Well, say you want to remember to buy bread, milk and eggs on your way home. What do you do?'

Reid didn't hesitate. 'I write it down.'

'Of course. But what do you write?'

'Umm . . . milk, bread, eggs. I might add what sort of bread, brown or whathaveyou, but that's about it. I might put "buy" or "shops" or something.'

Marjy clapped her hands. 'Right. That's what I and most people would do. Not Emma. She would do a little stick drawing of a tree, with a bird sitting in it.'

'In order to . . .'

'Well, she would have constructed a story for herself. She would have imagined herself going for a walk in the country, and seeing a farmer sitting on a gate, eating a sandwich. That would be the bread. She would chat with him and he would say he was waiting there until it was time to move the cows.'

'The milk?'

'Correct. Have you done this before?' Marjy had never met anyone who got the point before.

'No. Do go on.'

'Then, she would ask him how to get to the shops from there. And he would say, go up to the top of this hill and there will be a tree. And from there, she will see the shop.'

'So she added a bird, for eggs, and then just reminded herself with the drawing. It's complex, but I could see how it would work for some people.'

'I'm so glad. She thought of it herself and she could remember whole lists of words for months, just by telling herself the story again. It was a bit of a party piece.'

'So, just to make sure I have this right' – Reid knew Margaret Murray would ask whether he had double checked – 'anything that Emma wrote was not likely to be what she meant, more a part of a story to remind herself of what she meant.' Reid paused. It sounded convoluted, even as it left his mouth.

'That's it,' Marjy agreed. 'Everything is just a reminder of something else. She used different languages sometimes. She even played about with them. She spoke French, of course, with a smattering of German. She had taught herself Latin. She . . .' She leaned forward. 'Oh, Inspector Dier, I do miss her so!'

Edmund Reid had seen a lot of sad things in his time. He had been sad himself, sadder than he had thought possible in the past year or two. So he gathered the girl to him and let her cry all over his tweed. Finally, she stopped crying, but stayed there, safe in his arms. It did them both the world of good.

'Tell me, Marjy,' Reid said as she sat up and tucked her handkerchief away. 'That painting . . .'

'Are you *sure* you're not offended?' she checked.

'Not at all. I mean, we all have one, don't we? Well, not *all*, of course . . .' He could feel himself getting a bit bogged down, so changed the subject slightly. 'It's what the picture represents. Who is it for?'

'It's a retirement present,' she said, 'from the staff at the telegraph office, in St Martin le Grand. Apparently, their manager is leaving and they wanted a painting for him as he is a keen amateur.' She saw his raised eyebrows. 'I *know*,' she said. 'I did check that they wanted a nude. But they were adamant.'

'And it portrays?'

'They didn't specify, but I think I have been rather clever. It's Mercury, the winged messenger.'

NINE

The Senior Common Room had long ago been appropriated by the teaching staff. Originally, it had been built as a bolt-hole for graduates, but few of them ever turned up so the lecturers moved in, lured by the soft leather furniture, the ginger biscuits and the port. All in all, it had the hallmarks of a gentlemen's club without the exorbitant membership fees and it was the *gentlemen's* angle that annoyed Margaret Murray the most. She was usually too busy to go there, but whenever she could, she would make an appearance just because she wore a dress. She would listen to the tuts and sighs from the older dons and wink at the younger ones, most of whom had no problem with her presence at all.

Today, however, she was on a mission and the two birds she would bring down with a single stone sat opposite each other, hogging the fireplace, looking like Tweedledum and Tweedledee – without Mr Tenniel's caps and tight jackets, of course.

'Good morning, doctors,' she trilled, causing both of them to rattle their papers.

Reluctantly, they clambered to their feet. 'Dr Murray,' one of them said. He was arguably the more approachable of the two. Henry Sacheverill was an Oxford man, wondering most days how he had ended up so far down the academic pecking order as to be teaching at University College, London.

'Dear lady,' smiled the other one. He was Alistair Wishart, a Cambridge alumnus who had long ago learned to lose his native Arbroath accent in favour of the plummier tones of the queen's English.

'I hate to bother you,' Margaret said, plonking herself squarely between them as though she were there for the duration, 'but I'd like to pick your brains on William Blake.'

The men looked at each other. 'Why us, pray?' Wishart asked.

Margaret could gush with the best of them. 'Because you, gentlemen, represent the finest brains in the English faculty. Where else would I turn?'

Their egos suitably tweaked, the lecturers made burbling noises and Sacheverill rang a little silver bell by his chair. 'Will you take tea, Dr Murray?' he asked. 'Personally, I find Blake too dry for my tastes.'

'Wasn't he a great poet?' Margaret asked. She had been around undergraduates for long enough to know how to play the ingénue.

Sacheverill snorted. 'He was mad, Margaret,' he said as a waiter hovered. 'Teas all round, Weston, and a pile of your best gingers.'

'Mad is in the eye of the beholder, Sacheverill,' Wishart said. 'I see him as a visionary, a pioneer, if you will.'

'I won't,' Sacheverill scowled. 'Why the interest in Blake, Margaret?'

'Oh, it's some random jottings that a student recently made. I'm trying to make sense of them.'

'Couldn't you ask him?' Wishart was ever the champion of the all-too-obvious.

'I'd love to,' Margaret said. 'Sadly, she is dead.'

'Ah.'

'I was particularly interested in "Jerusalem".'

The tea arrived at that moment and there was a great deal of clattering of crockery.

'Yes.' Wishart waited until Margaret did what was expected of her and poured for them all. 'Blake was working on that between 1804 and 1820 – the illustrations, I mean.'

'Margaret,' Sacheverill cut in, 'I really wouldn't waste your time on this, particularly as the wretched girl is apparently no more. When I said a moment ago that Blake was mad, I meant it. He had delusions from the age of eight. Angels talked to him in Westminster Abbey.'

'His inspiration,' Wishart came straight back. 'His muse, if you will.'

'He should have been in a straitjacket.' Sacheverill would not be moved. 'Do you know he once beat up a Westminster schoolboy for looking at him funny? That's a Bedlam case, right there.'

'He was provoked,' Wishart insisted. 'The boys were laughing at him.'

'As well they might.'

'The man,' Wishart explained, 'was profoundly influenced by the Bible; Bunyan; Milton . . .'

'Uncle Tom Cobleigh and all,' Sacheverill sneered. 'The man was a dissident. Supported the American Revolution, the French. That ghastly woman – oh, no offence, Margaret – Mary Wollstonecraft.'

'That was in his salad days,' Wishart countered. 'He mellowed later.'

'Gentlemen.' Margaret held up both her hands. 'Fascinating though academic differences are, I am trying to understand what Blake meant by his lines in "Jerusalem".'

The two English lecturers looked at each other.

'Well, that's easy,' a voice called from across the room.

'He's wondering aloud whether Joseph of Arimathea ever came to England. And whether he brought his nephew Jesus with him.'

The two English lecturers looked at him.

'Thank you, Lionel,' Wishart scowled, glaring daggers at the man. 'Helpful as always.'

'But I have to say, Lionel,' Sacheverill added, 'as a professor of art history, what the hell do you know about it?'

'Did that oaf pester you fellows?' Piers Gibbs was still seething after the week's events.

'Who?' Ben Crouch had long ago ceased to be embarrassed by talking with his mouth full. It was only toast to most people, but to gourmets like Crouch, it was the staff of life.

'That Scotland Yard chappie.' Gibbs was lighting his cigarette. 'Blunt.'

'Yes.' Rose answered on Crouch's behalf. 'Caught me in the library. Didn't seem to know the meaning of "silence". I took him outside into the corridor before the librarian had some kind of seizure. All that shushing can't be good for a person.'

'What did he ask you?' Gibbs wanted to know.

'Pass me a ciggie, there's a good chap.' Rose stretched out a languid hand. 'Wanted to know how well I knew Norman Minton.'

'Me too,' Gibbs said.

'And me.' Crouch was in mid-swallow but he carried on regardless. 'I think his needle must have been stuck in the groove.'

'But how well do any of us know anybody?' Rose asked, his face blurring momentarily in a cloud of smoke. 'What if I'd said "Old Norman was the most boring lecturer on the face of the earth and the entire faculty, led by old Petrie, queued up around the building to smash his head in"?'

'Was that what happened to him?' Gibbs had clearly not caught the essentials. 'I heard he was strangled.'

'Stabbed, I heard,' Crouch offered.

'Bludgeoned, that seems to be the word on Gower Street.' Rose shrugged.

Crouch was set on his version of events. 'From what I heard, he had been disembowelled, more or less. Mind you, I heard that from a Smithfield meat porter, so he may have got a bit confused.'

Gibbs blinked. 'How did you come to be chatting to a Smithfield meat porter?' he asked.

'All night breakfast.' As if there could have been another reason. 'They work odd shifts. Find a meat market – or fish, or flowers, come to that – and you'll find an all night breakfast not far away.'

Gibbs got back to the matter in hand. '*And* Blunt wanted to know where I was on . . . what's that appalling cliché they use? "The night in question".'

There were rumblings all round, mostly from Crouch.

'And where *were* you?' Rose asked.

It may have been a trick of the lamplight, but Piers Gibbs seemed to be blushing from ear to ear. 'Er . . . I'm not quite sure.'

'That must have gone down well with the boys in blue,' Crouch chuckled. 'They'll have you in the frame before your boots touch the trapdoors, old son.'

'I was with a lady, if you must know.'

'Aye, aye,' Crouch chuckled, winking at Rose. 'Anybody we know?'

'No.' Gibbs remained the quintessence of the public schoolboy. 'She's not from the university.'

'Excellent choice,' Rose said. 'Nothing but trouble, these women students. Did Blunt accept that?'

'Well, I had to mention the lady in question's name, of course. I hated doing that, but you can't be too careful.'

Crouch was licking his plate to catch every crumb. 'Night in question. Lady in question. It's all bloody questions, isn't it?'

'And not enough answers,' Rose said. 'Where were you, Benjamin?'

'Tuesday, was it?' Crouch had to think. 'Now you've asked me.'

'Yes, I have,' Rose agreed. 'And so did the police. What did you tell them?'

'Well, it was either the Cornucopia or the Jack o' Lantern. It may even have been both.'

'You weren't at the Jack,' Rose said, 'or I'd have seen you there.'

'There you are, then,' Crouch said, holding his hand out for one of Gibbs's cigarettes. 'The Cornucopia it was.'

'They can't seriously think that one of us killed old Minton, surely?' Gibbs said. Down to his last three cigarettes, he put the packet away.

'Don't build up your part, Gibbsy, my boy,' Rose said. 'They were asking everybody, and not just from our faculty either. Only the men, notice; not the women.'

'Not a woman thing, though, is it, disembowelling?' Crouch was lolling on the sofa.

'Strangling,' Gibbs corrected him.

'Or even bludgeoning.' Rose always had to be right.

Crouch ignored them and went on. 'Poison, that kind of stuff. Look at Helen Richardson.'

'You think a woman killed her?' Rose asked.

Crouch sat up. 'As a matter of fact, I do,' he said.

'Well,' Rose said, lapsing into a perfect Flinders Petrie, 'I shall have to ask you to justify that speculation, Mr Crouch.'

'With pleasure, Professor,' Crouch laughed. 'Angela Friend told me all the juicy details that she'd picked up from her latest squeeze, that Crawford chap.'

'He was there, with Blunt, when he was asking his questions,' Gibbs chimed in. 'He was in civvies, though. Must have forgotten his uniform.'

Crouch dismissed it. 'Apparently, Helen was found stark naked, legs apart on the bed.'

Gibbs was blushing again.

'But all that was staged. Her killer put her like that to make the police think that she had been ravaged.'

'But she hadn't?' Rose checked.

'No more than you are doing the routine of the day job when you're in her line of work,' Crouch said. 'What actually killed her was poison – a woman's weapon.'

Gibbs butted in. 'Did Angela tell you all that? She doesn't seem that kind of girl. You know, gossipy.'

Crouch waved his objection aside. 'She might not have said it in so many words,' he admitted. 'But the inference was very clear, I thought. Of course,' he went on, 'Norman is totally different.'

'Yes,' Rose agreed. 'A man. And not on the game.'

'Steady on!' Gibbs didn't care for the way this conversation was going.

'That doesn't preclude women, though, Ben.' Rose was thinking aloud. 'All right, from what we know, Norman's death was altogether messier.'

'Strangling isn't messy, particularly, is it?' Gibbs was sticking to what he had heard.

'Disembowelling is, though,' Crouch muttered.

'Bludgeoning,' Rose corrected them both. 'But a woman *could* have done it. Had a look at Anthea Crossley's biceps lately?' Rose raised a knowing eyebrow.

'I bow to your greater knowledge, Andrew,' Crouch chuckled.

Gibbs was crimson once again.

'Then there's that girl who always sits in the front row in lectures,' Rose remembered. 'Convent girl, I reckon. Built like a dray horse. She could crack a skull or two, I shouldn't wonder.'

They all looked into the fire. It wasn't pretty, pinning the blame on a woman, any woman, really. But they wanted parity with men, so they could have it, as far as that went. Murder took a lot of thought and effort and there wasn't much of either on display around Piers Gibbs's fireside that Saturday afternoon. Crouch yawned and they all followed suit.

'Oops, sorry,' Andrew Rose said, covering his mouth. 'So, we're agreed then. It *is* a woman.'

'And for my money' – Crouch leaned over and picked up the toasting fork from where he had dropped it earlier – 'it's Margaret Murray, spinster of this parish.' He brandished the fork. 'Got any more bread, Gibbsy?'

Janet Bairnsfather had had a difficult week. If she were to be absolutely honest, she had had a difficult term. Make that year. The news that she had been accepted into University College had made her mother cry and her father give one of his very

Presbyterian harumphs, which meant he was proud and also counting his money at the same time. No one in their family had ever gone into academe before, certainly not a woman. Janet's auntie Morag was known to be very clever, but also rather odd; she spent her days on a hilltop farm in the Trossachs, working every hour God sent in her mission to breed the first pure white Aberdeen Angus. No doubt when she had begun, it had seemed a worthwhile cause. Now, she was the owner of a feral herd of cows so insanely inbred that they were the scourge of the neighbourhood. No one mentioned Auntie Morag and now, Janet wondered whether she was going to go the same way. She had never even known anyone to die before she came to London, if you didn't count Uncle Fergus dropping dead of a surfeit of haggis the Hogmanay before last. And now, in a blink of an eye, there had been two murders, of people she actually knew. She blinked the tears from her eyes and tried to concentrate on her darning.

Anthea Crossley was lounging in an armchair, hogging the fire. One leg was thrown carelessly across one arm of the chair and Janet kept her eyes averted from the display of stockinged nether limb. The girl had a book in her lap, but her head was lolled back and if she was looking at anything, it was the ceiling.

Janet was in awe of Anthea. She was in awe of all of the girls she shared a house with, but Anthea most of all. Angela was nice but not in all that much. If she wasn't with her policeman, she was working in the library – and Janet wondered about that; how did she know what to study? Janet's head was a whirl of facts and the books just overwhelmed her. How did everyone seem to know which book to choose to find out more? And what *was* more, anyway? Veronica seemed a pleasant person, but was also a bit of a swot. As for the men; Janet blushed just thinking the word in her head. She sniffed.

'Must you?'

Janet looked up in mid-stitch and pricked her finger. 'Ow. Pardon?'

'Pardon?' Anthea rolled her eyes. *Who* on earth asked this strange little thing to live with them? Angela, in all probability.

If she had been reminded that it was after all Angela's house, Anthea would have rolled her eyes some more.

'I'm sorry,' Janet said. 'I didn't hear what you said. That's what I meant.'

'I imagine you couldn't hear me for the sniffing,' Anthea said. At heart, she wasn't a cruel person, but she was bored and needed some sport. 'And what are you doing there, exactly?' She raised her head for a better look. 'Are you *mending* that stocking?' Mending was not something that Anthea Crossley had ever had to worry about.

'It has a hole in it.' Janet had stockings with more mend than stocking, but there was no need to share that nugget with Anthea. Her father took frugality to levels unheard of by Anthea and her ilk. Every day in London brought something new for Janet to be horrified by. Meals left virtually untouched, simply scraped into the bin. Clothes discarded or, if the girl had a modicum of charity, given to the Salvation Army, simply because a seam had come loose or a hemline was an inch too high or too low for the fashion this week. At home with the Bairnsfathers, nothing was ever wasted. She had heard Cook say that the master would have her use every part of the pig, up to and including the squeak. It was years before Janet had realized that bubble and squeak was just potato and cabbage.

'How quaint,' Anthea murmured, and let her head fall back again. But only for a minute. 'May I ask you a possibly rather personal question?'

'By all means.' Janet had been brought up to be polite.

'Why are you here? I don't mean it in the philosophical sense, as in why are any of us here? I mean it more literally. Why are *you* actually *here*?'

Janet looked up at her, disconcerted. It wasn't as if she hadn't asked herself the same thing many times. 'My . . . my teachers at the school I went to told my parents I should . . . well, that I should go to university. I had a place at Edinburgh, to . . . to study medicine. But my father . . .' – Janet dashed away her tears now, quite openly – 'my father had a rather unpleasant run-in with Sophia Jex-Blake when he was there studying divinity . . .'

Anthea sat up suddenly, her book sliding to the floor, forgotten. 'Really? Whatever was it? Did he try to . . .?'

'Anthea!' Janet was horrified. 'I did say he was studying divinity!'

Anthea spread her arms. 'That has nothing to do with it,' she observed. 'I've had some of my best evenings spent with the divinity lot. *Very* best evenings, I might almost say.' She smiled and Janet blushed. 'Not to mention the God Squad from King's.'

'Anyway,' Janet said, wriggling back into position and picking up her mending, 'I came here because . . . well, they were the only other place that offered. So that's why. My father doesn't know it's called the Godless Institution. I expect I shall be called home when he finds out.'

Anthea shrugged. That had turned out to be more amusing than she had expected, though she had no idea who Sophia Jex-Blake might be.

'And anyway,' Janet suddenly howled, throwing her stocking aside. 'I hate it here. No one likes me. I don't like the food. I don't like the course. I don't know what's going on and . . .' – the sniff this time could have stripped paint – 'people keep getting *murdered*!'

Her Scots accent gave Anthea pause for a moment, then she worked it out. 'Murdered?' she said, unhooking her leg and going over to sit next to Janet. 'People don't *keep* getting murdered, though, do they? Hmm?' She put her arm round the girl's shoulders and pulled her to her. She would kill anyone who said it, but she would make a lovely mother one day.

'They *do!*' Tears were making Janet shrill. 'There's that girl, that girl who used to come to the lectures. And . . . there's another one, I don't know who, but people talk so. And now Professor Minton. I really liked him.'

'You did?' Anthea was amazed. Norman Minton had the students' vote for the most boring man alive year after year.

'He was . . . well, he went nice and slowly,' Janet sniffed. 'He wrote things on the blackboard.' Janet was comfortable with blackboards, not so much with the kind of lecturer who stood looking out of the window muttering something.

Anthea patted Janet soothingly. 'But this has all happened to *other people*, Janet,' she said. 'It's nothing to do with us.'

Janet pulled away and looked at Anthea. The lovely face was as smooth and unlined as a baby's. And it had about as much empathy with the human race as a snail has. 'But . . .' She was stuck for how to begin. 'But they were *people*, Anthea,' she said. 'Someone loved them, surely.'

Anthea shrugged. 'Well, possibly. But if so, we don't know them either, do we?' She looked up at the clock, ticking sonorously on the wall. 'Oh, my Lord! Is that the time? I must go and get ready. I'm dining with . . .' She narrowed her eyes. It was only Janet, but still, one had to be discreet. Some married men were very hot on that point. 'Dining. So I must go.' She dropped a kiss a foot or so above Janet's head. 'Don't worry so much, Janet. It will all work out in the end.' And, on a gust of Heliotrope, she was gone.

'Professor Inkester?'

'Ah – leave it outside, will you?'

'What?'

'The wildebeest. In the case. Leave it outside. I'll get to it later.'

'What are you talking about, sir?'

Walter Inkester adjusted his pince-nez. On reflection, he had to admit that his visitor didn't look much like a delivery man, still less a purveyor of carcases packed in ice. 'Aren't you the wildebeest man?' he asked. 'From Messrs Rowland Ward?'

'No, sir; I am Inspector Blunt of Scotland Yard.' He duly produced his leather-bound warrant card. 'I'd like a word with you.'

'Really?' Inkester peered at the taller man at Blunt's elbow. 'I don't suppose . . .'

'No, sir,' the taller man said. 'I am not the wildebeest man either. Detective Constable Crawford.' Crawford had not been on a detective's payscale for long enough to afford a leather wallet yet. He had to make do with a piece of paper.

'Well, gentlemen.' Inkester ushered them both to chairs. 'What can I do for you?'

'The late Dr Norman Minton,' Blunt said, watching the zoologist closely.

'Ah, Norman.' Inkester took off his pince-nez and polished the lenses furiously. 'Tragic. And shocking.'

'Mrs Inkester must be distraught.'

'Dear Elspeth. Any man's death diminishes her, of course, but why Norman's in particular?' The professor frowned.

Blunt smiled and looked knowingly at Crawford. 'A little bird, Professor,' he said. 'I'm sure that, as a zoologist, you are familiar with their habits?'

'Er . . . what?'

'Some of them talk, don't they?' Blunt leaned back in his chair. 'And fascinating tales some of them have to tell, indeed.'

'Inspector, I . . .'

'One of those tales is that the late Dr Minton was . . . shall we say . . . close to your wife.'

'What rot!' Inkester snapped. 'That is a slanderous concept totally without foundation.'

'Yes,' growled Blunt, 'and I'm a Boer's left bollock . . . oh, begging your pardon, Professor . . . testicle. Where were you on Tuesday night?'

'Um . . . Tuesday? Tuesday? Let me see. Nightjars.'

Crawford stopped in mid-notetake. 'Nightjars?' he repeated.

'Yes. That's all one word, if you were wondering. *Caprimulgus europaeus*, if you would prefer the Latin. I'm carrying out a survey at the moment. There's quite a little colony in Hyde Park but increasing habitations in several London squares. Normally, they've migrated by August, but there are signs of a change. Must be the climate.'

Blunt blinked. 'Are you telling me you were wandering about London looking for birds in the dark?' he asked.

'Well,' Inkester chuckled. 'Put like that, it does seem rather silly, doesn't it? But yes, in a nutshell, that's exactly what I was doing.'

'Can anybody vouch for that, sir?' Blunt asked. 'In the avian community, perhaps?'

'No,' Inkester said. 'No. I invariably carry out my research alone.'

'Tell me, sir, do the little birdies you were hunting inhabit, say, Bloomsbury Square?'

'Indeed they do. Very distinctive song, you see.' And he proceeded to give the officers of the law a demonstration of the whirring chirrup of a nightjar.

'So, you were around the corner from this very building on the night in question.'

'Yes, I suppose I was.'

'Did you actually enter the building, sir? On your nightly prowling, I mean?'

'No, I . . . Wait a minute. Yes, yes, I did. It had turned quite chilly, so I nipped in for my hip flask.' He rummaged in a drawer of his office desk and produced it. 'Keeps out the cold.'

Blunt folded his arms with the air of a man who was about to close a case. 'What time was this, Professor?' he asked. 'Approximately.'

'Oh, I don't know. One . . . two o'clock? I really can't remember. You'd have to ask old Jenkins.'

'Nightwatchman?' Crawford checked.

'That's right. Man was asleep when I arrived, of course, but he muttered something to me as I left.'

'Constable,' Blunt turned to Crawford. 'You know this building tolerably well.'

'Tolerably, sir.'

'How far would you say it is from the department of Zoology to the department of Archaeology?'

'As the nightjar flies, sir, two minutes.'

Blunt smiled and stood up. 'I'd like you to come with us, please, Professor.'

'What? Where to? I'm expecting a wildebeest . . .'

'Scotland Yard, sir. We can continue our conversation there.'

'But I've got a lecture in half an hour.'

'You did have,' Blunt said, and waited while the professor got his coat.

Margaret Murray hung her coat up on the antlers screwed at a rather rakish angle to the wall and turned to the girl intent on a book at the far side of the table.

'Did I just see your young man escorting Walter Stinkster out of the building?'

Angela nodded. She had stopped telling people that Adam Crawford was not her young man. The truth was self-evident whenever they were within sight of each other. 'Yes,' she said, closing her book but keeping her finger in the page. 'Apparently, Blunt has it in mind that he killed Norman.'

'The Stinkster? Why?'

'It is a well-attested fact, according to Blunt, that Norman and Mrs Inkester were more than just good friends.'

'Well, yes, everyone knows that. It's been going on for years.'

Angela's eyes nearly fell out of her head. '*Norman?*' she said. 'Why Norman?'

'You've seen Mrs Inkester, I assume? At functions.'

Angela shook her head.

Margaret held her hand some way above her own head, puffed out her cheeks and mimed a bust like a rolltop desk. 'She's quite an intimidating lady,' she said, letting out her held breath with relief. 'Rumour has it that Walter was looking for a silverback gorilla for his stuffed animal collection and settled for Elspeth when one wasn't available.'

Angela cast her mind back and nodded. 'I *do* know her. I see what you mean, but I think what I meant was, why Norman? Rather than why did Norman choose Mrs Inkester.'

'Any old professor in a storm, I suppose,' Margaret said, sitting down and arranging her notes for the forthcoming tutorial. 'If you had a choice between being bored to death, no pun intended, by Norman or sharing a bed with someone who spends much of his day up to his elbows in exotic animal innards, who would it be?'

Angela shrugged. 'Not easy,' she said. 'Apparently, he's waiting for a wildebeest.'

Margaret gestured over her shoulder. 'No, it's here. He met it on the stairs. He got quite aerated about it, apparently, but Blunt wouldn't take "Wait, that's my wildebeest" for an answer.'

'I dare say someone in the department will . . .' Angela didn't know what one did with chilled wildebeest. 'Will . . .'

'Yes, dear. I dare say they will. Meanwhile, how would you and the detective constable like to come to tea today?'

'Not today, I'm afraid,' Angela said. 'Not that there's an agenda in your invitation, I'm sure. Tomorrow, though. I'll make sure that Adam . . . Constable Crawford . . . is off duty. Would supper be all right if we can't make it at teatime?'

'Even better,' Margaret said. 'Mrs Plinlimmon likes company in the evening.'

Walter Inkester had never really noticed the headquarters of the Metropolitan Police before. It stood alongside the Embankment, watching the river with one eye and the Houses of Parliament with the other. Athelgar Blunt had let the zoologist sit all day, filling in the paperwork which was the lot of a detective at the dawn of a new century. He barely had time to nip down to the Clarence to wet his whistle before he nipped back to pursue his enquiries.

It irked him that Crawford was his number two on this one. It irked him even more that he was only there because that interfering busybody Reid had thrown his weight around. It didn't help that, all around him, the cult of St Edmund was still very much in evidence. They'd be putting up a blue plaque next.

'Right.' Blunt had lit his pipe. Now he blew smoke into the suspect's face. 'Let's talk about Mrs Inkester, shall we? How long had she and Norman been at it like weasels?'

'What?' Inkester had been kept waiting for hours. He was not in the best of moods.

'Oh, I thought you would appreciate the analogy,' Blunt smirked, 'you being of the zoological persuasion and all.'

'I find you offensive, Inspector,' Inkester snapped. 'That you have the barefaced audacity to infer . . .'

'I'm not inferring, sunshine,' Blunt said. 'I'm saying it straight out. It's common knowledge at the college that the late Dr Minton, otherwise boring old fart that he was, was slipping your wife one.'

Inkester was on his feet, fuming.

'Sit down, Professor,' Crawford said. He didn't like Blunt and he didn't like his methods, but he did take the queen's shilling and he had a job to do.

Inkester sulked back into the chair.

'You see,' Blunt said. 'My thinking goes something like this. The late lamented and your good lady are enjoying a bit of how's your father. You found out and . . . what? Confronted her? We have yet to find out. But you certainly confronted him – on the night in question, while pretending to be bird-watching or whatever – and things got ugly.'

'No, I . . .'

'You argued. Maybe he swung a punch, or tried to. You saw the statuette on his desk through the red mist and wallop! One less philandering bastard in the world. Happens all the time, even in the best academic circles. Now, are you going to come clean, or what?'

TEN

There was no doubt about it; Thomas was about to excel himself. From the wine to the doilies via the canapés, he had forgotten nothing, skimped on nothing. This evening's soirée did not come out of University College's hospitality budget, so it all devolved on Margaret Murray. But she had chosen her guests well and tonight she hoped for some answers.

She had hired the Senior Common Room, the fire was crackling in the grate and the college servants had been given the night off. Thomas was literally head cook and bottle washer, but he liked it that way, a jack of all trades and master of them all.

'Thomas.' Margaret was folding napkins. It gave her some-thing to do before the guests arrived, even if it was encroaching on Thomas's domain.

'Yes, Prof?' Thomas was holding up a wine glass to the light, twisting it critically this way and that.

'Can I put a hypothetical case to you?'

'Hype away,' Thomas said, huffing on the glass and polishing away a recalcitrant speck with his cloth.

'Imagine someone came across a box, a box that did not belong to them but a box that was locked and looked intriguing. As a man of the world, which I know you to be, what might be inside, do you suppose?'

Tom laid out the glasses just so, lining them up by eye. 'Would that be the box you showed me the other day?' he asked her. 'At the Bentham?'

'It might be,' she said, pulling out the centre of a waterlily with practised fingers. 'It might be.'

'Nice.' He pointed to her handiwork and she nodded, pleased. She had always been clever with her hands and it always paid to have something up one's sleeve, should archaeology ever fail to please her. 'Hmm.' He closed his eyes, the better to remember the dimensions of the box. 'Six by ten,' he said, 'give or take.' He looked at her. 'Street value's difficult,' he said, 'and the fence's role is vital. If the contents are lifted, selling on the open market's risky. And of course, if the contents are well known, even if just to experts such as yourself, then the riskier it becomes.'

Instinctively, Margaret's mind was focusing on hoards. 'Gold,' she said. 'Coins. Probably first century.'

'Top of the market,' Tom nodded. 'But coins are specific, aren't they? Got kings' heads or whatever on 'em. For that, or silver, come to that, you'd need – and you didn't hear this from me – Lemmy Izlebit of Old Jewry. Failing him – and some people have – Isaac Farben, off of Bevis Marks. The Chosen People have got the precious metals market pretty well sewn up.'

'What about diamonds?'

The archaeologist was out of her depth already, but gems were not called the killing stones for nothing and it seemed that at least two people, perhaps three, were dead as a result.

'I reckon that'll be Gregorius Hendrick, New Bond Street. Or, at a pinch, Wyndham's.'

Margaret was horrified. 'Wyndham's?' she repeated. 'But they're a reputable auction house.'

Tom tapped the side of his nose. 'And I'm Joan of Arc,' he said. 'Trust me, Prof. You show me an honest auctioneer and I'll show you a good time – oh, begging your pardon, of course.'

'We might be thinking too literally here, Thomas,' Margaret said. 'What if the box contained something of other value? Not intrinsic. It could be parchment, wood, paper, even. But it could be priceless.'

'Well, that's where I'd have to bow out, Prof,' Thomas said, counting the forks and allowing for extras. 'How do you mean?'

'Well, the Rosetta Stone wouldn't fit into the box I have in mind, but it opened the ancient world to us in a way that makes it absolutely unique.'

'Is that a diamond?' Thomas asked. 'A sort of Koh-i-Noor of Koh-i-Noors?'

Margaret smiled. 'No, it's a block of marble, but it carries vital translations, from Latin back to Greek and to Egyptian hieroglyphs. That's how we can read the tomb art of the various dynasties.'

'It might be how you can!' Thomas laughed.

'The stone was found at Rosetta by archaeologists working under Champollion.'

'Get away!'

'And he in turn was working for General Bonaparte.'

'Ah.' Thomas clicked his fingers. 'Now him, I have heard of – the man who gave the world Chicken Marengo!'

They both laughed this time.

'But if I'm right about the content of the box' – Margaret was thinking aloud – 'what could it possibly be?'

Thomas swept away in search of menu card holders. 'Well, it could be the Holy Grail,' he said. 'What's that Old Testament thing? The Ark of the Covenenant.'

'Am I right,' Margaret asked, 'in believing there are collectors out there? Men – and women, I hasten to add – who would pay a small fortune for the right article?'

'Oh, yes,' Tom nodded. 'It's just a matter of finding 'em. A lot of your millionaires have private collections they've paid through the nose for; the Rothschilds, the Carnegies, Rockefellers, all that crowd. I happen to know that old man Dietrichson has the finest collection of erotica outside the Vatican. And you can't get that stuff at the Army & Navy's – I know, I've tried.'

There was a knock at the door and Margaret answered it.

'Inspector.' She smiled as a squat, bearded man swept off his hat.

'I'm not late, I hope,' he said.

'Dear me, no; in fact, you're the first. Will you have a sherry?'

Edmund Reid's smile froze when he saw the waiter, but not as quickly as the waiter's froze when he saw the inspector.

'Hello, Tom,' Reid said through clenched teeth. 'Nice to see you out.'

'Mr Reid,' Tom said, a rictus grin on his face. 'It's been a while.'

'It has,' Reid nodded. 'Lord and Lady Adderley's, ninety-three.'

'That was ninety-four,' Thomas corrected him. 'And if you remember, nothing proved. You're thinking of that bracelet lay in ninety-three.'

Reid clicked his fingers. 'Of course I am,' he agreed. 'But what I remember in the Adderley case is that the magistrate on that occasion was older than God and didn't really understand the question. You got off lightly.'

'Well, bygones, eh?' Tom's laugh was brittle, largely because Reid's memory was long.

'I assume, Dr Murray,' the inspector said, 'from the fact that he's standing here, that you know this reprobate.'

Margaret tutted. 'Reprobation is in the eye of the beholder, Inspector,' she said. 'I take it that you gentlemen have something of a history?'

'You could say that,' Reid nodded, and took the glass gingerly from Tom.

'It's not poison, Mr Reid,' Margaret said. 'Thomas, take the inspector's hat.'

'And make sure I get it back,' Reid growled.

'You will,' Tom muttered. 'It wouldn't be worth the shoe leather taking it down to uncle.'

'Boys! Boys!' Margaret chuckled and settled down by the fire with Reid.

'This is very pleasant.' The inspector raised his glass. 'To crime,' he said.

'God rot Arthur Evans,' she riposted. 'But, funnily enough, crime is why I invited you.'

'And I thought it was for my charm and after-dinner chat.'

'Inspector Dier,' Margaret gushed, 'you are one of the most charming men I've ever met. And you can talk about what you like *after* dinner. Pre-prandially, however, can we focus on the late Helen Richardson and the late Emma Barker?'

Reid nodded. 'Back in the day,' he said, 'I'd be looking at a baize wall at the Yard. It would be covered in little pieces of paper which a minion would move about on my command. There'd be lots of tea and cigar smoke and I'm afraid the language could get quite colourful.'

'Well,' Margaret smiled, 'I'm afraid you'll have to do with sherry for the moment. And as for the bits of paper, they're in my head, I'm afraid, along with a great deal of irrelevant rubbish. As to the language, well, the night is young.'

She crossed the room and topped up their sherries. 'Imagine I'm a minion,' she said, 'a detective sergeant, perhaps. No, make me a constable. Make it simple for me.'

Reid laughed. 'I don't think *that's* necessary, is it, Margaret?' he said. 'But all right. I'll play along. Helen and Emma. What's the common ground, apart from the fact that they're both dead, of course?'

'Both women,' Margaret said. Clearly, she was taking her role as rookie constable very seriously.

'Both archaeology students.' Reid was sharpening the focus.

'But from different colleges,' Margaret came back at him. 'And Helen was very much part time. Only attended the Friday lectures for the general public.'

'How is that different from the regulars?' Reid wanted to know. 'What do full-timers get that part-timers don't, apart from the hours, of course?'

'Part-timers don't attend tutorials or write essays or undertake research. They also don't go on digs.'

'Whereas Emma did, hence the goings on at Hampton.'

'Precisely.'

'Would their paths have crossed?' Reid asked. 'In the general scheme of things?'

'Unlikely.' Margaret shook her head. 'It *is* possible for

students of other colleges to attend Friday lectures, but it's not usual. What about Helen's other calling? What we should rather inaccurately call her day job?'

'I've been looking into that,' Reid said. 'Or rather, one of my Yard contacts did it for me. She really was a telephonist, at the Exchange. We'd have to call soliciting her twilight job, I suppose.'

'And Emma?'

Reid shook his head. 'I met her friend, the girl she shared an apartment with. Her father had thrown her out, but her mother had given her some money and I think gave her more when she could.' Reid looked solemn. He couldn't shake off the memory of William Barker, and he had known some wrong 'uns in his life. 'Her friend is fairly successful, in the art world in a small way, so she managed. There don't seem to be any sudden bursts of unexplained income.'

'Immoral earnings?' Margaret checked. 'They're not sudden bursts, are they?'

'Such a silly phrase, isn't it, immoral earnings?' Reid said, sipping his sherry. 'But no; no hint of that.' He knew he would have to give more details soon and although he had decided that Margaret Murray was next to impossible to shock, he wasn't looking forward to it.

'What about men?' Margaret asked, 'Given that you're all beasts, of course.' She winked at him.

'Well, in the case of Emma, there *was* one to whom she had been close, but that seemed to be over. There was mention of another, more recently, but the apartment-mate didn't have his name. In any case, she was more interested in said apart-ment-mate, if you catch my drift.' He took a deep breath. It was good to get it over. Tom, over in his corner polishing cutlery, gave a little chuckle. It was well known Inspector Dier was a bit of an old woman sometimes.

'Ah, Sappho,' Margaret nodded. 'The Greek island of Lesbos.'

'If you say so,' Reid said. 'Whereas, almost by definition, there were several men in Helen Richardson's life – her land-lord, her rent collector, her neighbour and an unknown number of clients. What did you find in Emma's box, by the way?'

'Ah, yes, the box. Apart from the letter which you have, there were lots of cryptic notes, some in Latin, that led me to the poetry of William Blake.'

'Who?'

'Quite. It was all rather rambling.'

'Rambling?'

'Oblique. Off the point. Not – unforgivable in an archaeologist – calling a spade a spade.'

'But that's her,' Reid said.

'What is?'

'The way Emma's mind worked. Marjy – her friend – explained it to me. Quirk of the brain, I suppose. She used aide-memoires rather than direct notes.'

'I do that,' Tom said, moving round the table, laying places. 'To remember customers and what they order. You, for example, Prof, I always picture you with a crown on. Victoria sponge. Simple. That student of yours, Veronica of the butterfly cakes, is an imago. I only learned that word the other day.'

Reid nodded. 'That's it, more or less.'

'Hmm,' Margaret mused. 'It doesn't help us, though. One enigma wrapped up inside another one. Ah.'

There was a knock at the door and Margaret bustled across to answer it. 'Angela, Mr Crawford, lovely to see you. Thomas, sherries for our guests.'

There were introductions all round, though only Angela and Reid didn't know each other. Soon, while Tom brought in the food from the kitchen down the hall, they were all sitting at the dining table.

Tom and Margaret had decided to dine *à la française*, mainly because it wasn't going to work any other way, as Tom explained in his inimitable style. 'It ain't going to work, Prof,' he had said. 'If we do it Russian style, I'll meet my arse going back. It's all on the table at once, or nothing.'

The table did look wonderful, frog or not, as Tom pointed out. The curry puffs were golden and light as feathers. The Waldorf salad was a revelation to everyone but Thomas and the table was silent but for chewing.

Reid, who liked his food, pointed wordlessly at his plate with his fork, making querying motions with his eyebrows.

'Waldorf salad,' Thomas said, correctly interpreting the signs. 'A friend of mine in the catering trade invented it for some charity do and I confess I nicked it. Nice, innit?'

'It's lovely, Thomas,' Angela said. 'And what's this?' She held up a spear of asparagus covered with a brittle batter.

Thomas looked uncomfortable. He had expected well-brought-up young ladies to recognize common vegetables. 'Asparagus, miss,' he said.

'But it's out of season, isn't it?' she asked. 'Apart from that, though, it was these crispy bits I was really asking after.'

'Tempura batter, miss. Japanese, that is. And nothing's out of season in London, not if you know the right people.'

Reid raised his eyebrow.

'All above board, Mr Reid, all above board. My sister's youngest is a porter down the Garden.'

When the savouries had all gone and the desserts had taken their place, the conversation returned to the nights in question.

'What did the Kent Constabulary make of poor Emma's death?' Margaret asked Reid. 'Have they decided?'

'I thought I'd have to go a long way to find a force as moronic as the Met,' the ex-inspector told her. 'No offence, Constable Crawford, of course. And then, lo and behold, there they were, on the doorstep of the place I intend to make my new home, all along. All rather depressing.'

Crawford couldn't help but snort.

'What was Inspector Blunt's take on Helen Richardson's death, Detective Constable?' Reid asked him.

'Suicide, Mr Reid,' Crawford said, 'while the balance of mind, et cetera.'

'Well.' Reid smiled, like the crafty poker player he was. 'I'll see your suicide and I'll raise you a wandering lunatic.'

'What?' Angela looked up from her Charlotte Russe. Crawford, across the table from her, thought how adorable she looked with a blob of cream on her chin.

'The Kent Constabulary's verdict on the death of Emma Barker,' Reid said, looking hard and sideways at Tom, even as the man topped up his wine. 'The county's crawling with them.'

'Is that true?' Angela Friend was a little at sea in this conversation. She was a clever girl, quick and intuitive, but she had not been brought up to this and the only bodies she knew anything about had been dead for centuries.

'No,' Reid chuckled. 'Oh, London, yes. On the Ripper case, we had more wandering lunatics than Tom here has served . . . hot dinners.' He smiled at the man and Tom scowled in return. 'But that's the biggest city in the world for you. It breeds peculiarities; men who talk to themselves or invisible friends; women who wheel puppies around in perambulators; dribbling maniacs who feed from the gutters. But Kent? Not so much.'

'But it happens, though?' Angela would not let it go.

'No doubt it does,' Reid sighed. 'But it's incredibly rare. No one likes to think of their nearest and dearest being killed by daddy, mummy, kind old Uncle John, the vicar. They'd rather it was a menacing-looking stranger, with wild eyes and bloody teeth. And if he's a foreigner, so much the better. We never caught the Whitechapel murderer, but he was a local man, of the same social class as the women he killed. That's how he got away with it – knew those mean streets better than any of us.'

'So,' Margaret said, 'the Metropolitan Police – saving your presence again, Mr Crawford – have washed their hands of Helen Richardson. The Kent Constabulary, ditto Emma Barker. Which brings us to Norman.'

Reid smiled. 'I wondered when you'd get round to him,' he said.

'Oh, but that's completely different,' Angela said. 'Poor Helen was poisoned. Emma . . .' She suddenly wasn't sure.

'Strangled,' Reid explained. 'I may not trust the Kent police, but I trust the evidence of my own eyes. She was strangled.'

'Strangled,' Angela repeated, her point made, 'whereas Dr Minton . . .' She looked at Crawford.

'Heavy object,' he said. 'Probably from behind.'

'Probably a statuette of Mercury,' Reid added.

'Mercury!' Angela clicked her fingers. 'Of course. Mercury is a poison, isn't it? Helen was poisoned. It all makes sense now . . . doesn't it?'

Margaret couldn't help chuckling, despite the grim topic under discussion. 'There is such a thing as being *too* clever, Angela,' she said, but in a kindly way; she wouldn't have wanted to hurt the girl's feelings for the world.

'You've talked to the coroner, Crawford?' Reid asked.

'I have. Surprisingly little to go on. The murder weapon was there, in Minton's office.'

'So' – Reid was reasoning it out – 'not planned.'

'I wouldn't say so,' Crawford said, 'but please remember, Inspector Reid, I am sort of new to all this.'

Reid shook his head. 'Experience only counts for so much, lad,' he said. 'Being a copper is all about a nose, a sixth sense. You've either got it or you haven't. In the case of Ethel Blunt, now . . .'

Tom, leaving the room with a stack of plates, snorted. 'Ethel couldn't find his arse with both hands, excuse my French, ladies,' he said. 'I know blokes who'd plan their jobs for when they knew Ethel was on duty.'

Reid nodded and for once, Tom nodded back.

'So, if I'm right . . .' Reid continued.

'And you are,' Margaret said.

The ex-inspector laughed. 'If I'm right, our friend hadn't planned the attack on Minton. He lost his temper, panicked, whatever. Hence, no weapon brought with him. Hence, no attempt to cover things up.'

'It had to be someone who knew the college,' Crawford said. 'The Archaeology department isn't the easiest place to find.'

'But I've seen better security in a sieve,' Reid pointed out. 'What have we got? One nightwatchman?'

'Name of Jenkins,' Crawford said.

'Eyes everywhere,' Angela chimed in, 'but only in the direction of female students.'

Margaret forbore to mention that that included female staff too.

'Assuming that our murderous friend is male' – Reid was thinking aloud – 'he might have missed him entirely. You were present at the interview with Inkester?'

Crawford looked at the former policeman. 'News travels fast,' he said. His eyes swivelled to Margaret Murray.

'Don't look at me, Mr Crawford,' she said, hands up. 'I couldn't possibly divulge.'

Reid laughed. 'I used to live in this town,' he said. 'My patch. My manor. It doesn't take long to winkle things out.'

'He had no alibi for the night Minton died,' Crawford said, 'and, if rumours are true, he had the motive.'

'Oh, they're true all right,' Margaret said. 'I hate to be the one to gossip, but the Stinkster must be the only one in the college *not* to know about Elspeth's peccadilloes. He's very focused, is Walter; more concerned with armadillos than peccadilloes.'

'Unless that was a front,' Reid reasoned. 'Unless he knew all about Minton and the missus, or had recently discovered it. It must have festered, too. He surely didn't catch them in flagrante or he'd have caved the man's head in, then and there. He thought about it, worried at it. And then . . .'

'But if he didn't take a weapon with him,' Crawford pointed out, 'there's no intent.'

'His Defence could argue that, certainly,' Reid said. 'Perhaps he just went to confront him; to have it out, man to man.'

'We're all forgetting one thing,' Margaret said. 'The state of Norman's study. The killer was looking for something. And I think what he was looking for was the papers I was talking about earlier, Edmund – Emma Barker's oblique ramblings. There has to be a link with the girls.'

'Crawford?' Reid turned to the man.

The constable shrugged. 'Don't know,' he said. 'Different gender, different age. Three different settings, two inside, one out. Of course, we don't know exactly where Emma Barker was killed, do we?'

'No, we don't,' Reid admitted. 'Only where she was left.'

'Well,' Margaret sighed, finishing her wine. 'While we're all pondering that one, while Thomas is clearing away, let's retire to my inner sanctum for coffee and a rather delectable little port I have waiting. I think I can make the kettle work.'

They clattered along the corridors, past the marble busts of the great and good who had been there at University College's birth pangs. They padded up the carpets of the annexe stairs, past the scene of a man's death. They'd all been there – Angela to the occasional tutorial; Margaret to discuss all manner of arcane matters with her colleague and to get back the books he had borrowed on a weekly basis; the two policemen treading carefully to avoid that same colleague's blood and worse.

'And what of the Stinkster?' Margaret asked Crawford. 'How is Walter bearing up under all this?'

'We bailed him,' Crawford said. 'Couldn't do much else at this stage. My guv'nor, of course, still thinks he's got his man.'

Margaret's eyes rolled heavenward. 'Oh, God.' Her hand flew up involuntarily to her mouth as she opened her study door.

'What is it, Margaret?' Reid asked, looking around for what might have startled the woman.

'I've been robbed,' she said.

'What?' Crawford said. 'How do you know?'

'Well,' Margaret said, bustling into the room, 'when I say "robbed", that may be a supposition too far. But I've certainly been disturbed.'

Angela frowned, looking in all directions. She knew this office well, the scrolls of parchment, the untidy piles of books, some of them toppled, the artefacts from Ur and Nineveh and Luxor. She couldn't see anything different.

'Well,' said Reid, hands on hips. 'Somebody's certainly had a right old go at this place.'

Margaret snapped at him, despite herself. She had a soft spot for the retired inspector, it had to be said, but he was, after all, a man and she couldn't let her reputation take that sort of knock without a challenge. 'Don't be ridiculous,' she said. 'It always looks like this. Except . . .' and she pointed to a high shelf.

'Except what, Dr Murray?' Crawford asked.

'Except for Mrs Plinlimmon,' she said, wide-eyed. 'I may not know as much about stuffed owls as Walter Inkester, but I do know they don't move by themselves. She's five inches to the left and looking in the wrong direction.'

All eyes turned to the owl, who wore her usual inscrutable expression despite having been interfered with. Mrs Plinlimmon wasn't even dusted on a regular basis, so it was extraordinary that she had taken it all so well. Checking on the rest of the room wasn't so easy. The chaos was, according to its resident, deliberate and, like Sherlock Holmes, she could tell how important things were from the thickness of dust. This was quickly proved to be untrue, however.

'Dr Murray!' Angela's voice was shrill with outrage. 'What's this?' She waved a slim wodge of paper in the air.

Everyone stopped what they were doing and waited with bated breath while Margaret thumbed through it.

'Oh, goodness, Angela. Nothing to get excited about. Continue the search, everyone.'

'No, don't let's continue the search,' Angela said, rather coldly. 'It's pointless as only you will know what has been disturbed, Dr Murray. And thank you for telling me that an unmarked essay of mine from March 1898 is nothing to get excited about. It's not great research, probably, but it meant a lot to me.'

Margaret drew herself up as much as possible and looked disposed to argue.

'That is a little unreasonable,' Reid said, in placatory terms. 'I don't know if you agree, Dr Murray, but I think it would be helpful if you could go through this room with a fine-tooth comb and perhaps weed out everything that you no longer need. Starting with the piles of paper. Miss Friend is quite right, we are not helping at all. We can't possibly know what belongs here and what doesn't.'

'But I . . . but I'm terribly busy,' Margaret blustered. 'It's hard to keep up with everything . . .' No one in the room had ever seen her look deflated before, but Angela's outrage had won the day. Polite to the last, her guests said goodnight and thank you for a lovely evening, finally leaving her alone with the owl. She heard their voices dwindle down the corridor and then everything was silence. She pulled a chair over and climbed up to reposition what seemed to be her only friend.

Clambering down, she spoke as much to herself as to Mrs Plinlimmon. 'Well,' she said softly. 'Where to start? To dust or not to dust? Throw or keep?' She picked up Angela's essay from where it had been thrown down on the desk and looked at it with a sigh. 'Perhaps the living do deserve more attention than the dead, eh, Mrs P?'

Coming to a decision, she extinguished the lights. 'But that's for another day, I think.'

On their way out of the building, Reid, Crawford and Angela passed the Senior Common Room just as Tom came out of the kitchen and turned the key.

'Oh, you leaving already?' he said in some surprise. 'The Prof's parties usually go on longer than this. I've known 'em all come over to the Bentham for breakfast before now.'

'There was . . . an incident,' Reid said, diplomatically. 'Dr Murray thinks someone may have been in her room without her knowledge.'

'Blimey,' Tom said. 'How could she tell? I've seen dustheaps tidier than the Prof's room.'

Angela was rebuilding her head of steam but quiet pressure from Crawford's hand on hers pre-empted the explosion.

'We've left her tidying up, checking if anything is missing,' Reid said.

Tom glanced along the corridor. 'I suppose she needs a hand . . .' His unwillingness to get involved was palpable.

'I think she's best left to do it herself,' Crawford said. 'Like you say, it's a bit of a tangle in there.'

Tom nodded. He could read a hidden meaning as well as the next man. 'Right, then. I'll just give the table in here a final wipe and I'll be away. Goodnight, all.'

'Goodnight, Tom,' Angela said. 'What was that thing, that nut thing called again?'

'Waldorf salad,' Tom said. 'Put your head into the kitchen at the Bentham any time and I'll give you the recipe.'

'Thank you.' Angela turned up the collar of her coat and Adam linked his arm in hers. 'I'll be in soon. Goodnight.'

''Night.'

At the front door, they had a quick word with Jenkins, having woken him up, Adam keeping Angela on the lee side, away from any wandering hands. They had the problem of all parties the world over since the first hominid shared a bit of leftover mammoth with his neighbour. How to walk away from someone you have spent the evening with, without seeming rude. But eventually, the small talk petered out and, with gestures as to which way would lead them home, they turned, two to the left, one to the right, into Gower Street.

Reid took a few steps and turned to watch the other two. He would not have said he was lonely, but he missed the company of younger people and watching Angela and Crawford walking arm in arm, his fair head bent to her dark one, her face turning up to his for what he assumed was an illicit kiss, made him feel young again. He smiled; they had it all to come and he hoped that the smiles would outweigh the tears. As he turned to continue his walk back to his hotel, he heard Tom behind him, talking to Jenkins behind the closed doors of the University building. He smiled again. Tom was one of the bad 'uns he wouldn't mind meeting again. His crimes never hurt anyone, except in the pocket, and he was pleased to see that he had made good. It had been a long time coming, but he had made it in the end.

Turning his collar up and rewrapping his scarf against the cold and foggy night, he set off. The Tambour House Hotel was a step up from his temporary home in Hampton-on-Sea. Instead of the terrifying Mrs Mulvahey there was a rather snooty clerk in attendance at the front desk, the day one being rather the snootier of the two. He pulled his watch out of his waistcoat pocket after much fumbling with layers of coat and scarf and noted with approval that the night clerk would be on duty now. He had discovered that with the swift application of a florin, he could have a brandy and hot chocolate delivered to his room. He squared his shoulders and picked up his pace; if he didn't dawdle, he could be there in another twenty minutes or thereabouts.

Angela and Crawford wandered slowly and even more slowly as her front door drew nearer. The evening had been a success until the last few minutes and Angela was beginning to feel a little silly for reacting so badly to finding her essay languishing there. After all, how much did it matter, in the end? She had her degree, she had been taken on to do further research towards yet another and she would be a doctor soon, perhaps, like Margaret Murray. And yet . . . she snuggled up to the warm body next to her and clutched his arm a little tighter. Was that, when everything was said and done, what she wanted out of life? Was being a wife and mother that bad? Bringing children into the world, teaching them all she knew; that was all right, surely?

Finally, they reached the front door. However slowly you walked, Crawford thought, a destination would be reached eventually. He turned to Angela and pulled her to him. This evening, being invited as a couple, walking home alone in the cold in companionable silence, seemed to be a bit of a watershed. Something had happened, but he wasn't sure what.

'Adam, I've been thinking . . .'

Ah, perhaps he knew what now. He had heard those words, not often but often enough, before.

'What? What have you been thinking? Because I have also been thinking.' Better to take the bull by the horns.

'It's about my degree . . .'

'It's about us . . .'

'I don't want to do it any more . . .'

'Will you marry me?'

'I just want to get married, have babies . . . pardon?'

'What?'

And after that, silence.

ELEVEN

Tom didn't like old Jenkins much, but knew the importance of not annoying the bloke with the key. He had built up quite a nice little sideline in private catering and if you had to argue the toss with the doorman when setting up and clearing afterwards, it became more of a pain than a pleasure. So he passed a few pleasantries with the man, made appropriate noises relating to the neatness of Angela's face and figure and then, as soon as was politic, made his way out and stood on the step, listening to the bolts being shot behind him.

He worried a little about the Prof. She didn't often get

blindsided and although he thought that probably it was good for her sometimes, her little face in the lamplight when he had looked in to say goodnight was quite heartrending. She needed a good man in her life, not those dusty professors, many of whom had less than academic thoughts about her, he knew. She needed someone to take her out of herself. He smiled to himself; he knew he was the very man, but that it would only happen should hell choose to freeze over. He only had to cross the road and head down a bit, but even so, the night was chilly, so he turned up his collar and wrapped his scarf a bit closer and stepped down to the kerb. There was little traffic at this time of night but he looked both ways, even so. Of Angela and Crawford there was no sign. Off to his right, he could see the stocky figure of Edmund Reid, pacing smartly along Gower Street, just about to turn right into Gower Place. He watched him, almost fondly. Some coppers he wouldn't piss on if they were afire, but Reid was one of the good ones. Too many of that sort had gone now, leaving the Blunts to rule the roost. Tom shook his head; times were changing with the century and not necessarily for the better, either.

Then, just as Reid turned into the side road, Tom saw something that made him look twice. A dark shadow had detached itself from a portico opposite the turn and was crossing the road, keeping to the shadows where it could. It was hard to tell, in the fog and the dark, who it might be but Tom knew that posture. The slight bend to the back, the hat pulled down, the collar up. The shoulders hunched and the face turned away from any light. Tom stepped down on to the pavement and started up Gower Street at a half run. Reid was being followed, and by no well-wisher either, if he was any judge. Tom felt for the knife roll in his inside pocket; all present and correct. He chuckled, but quietly. Being a cook made 'going equipped' a whole new thing; who would have guessed, years ago, that he would be carrying a ten-inch blade as part of his work tools and be on the right side of the law?

He turned the corner and, for a moment, couldn't see anyone. Then he got his eye in and saw Reid, still stomping along at a goodish pace, considering his little legs. His follower was nowhere in sight and Tom began to wonder if he had imagined the whole thing and it was just some innocent householder heading home with his coat collar turned up against the damp. He skidded to a halt, glad that he hadn't hailed Reid as he caught up with him. He would have felt a proper Charlie. He turned to go, just as a man leapt out of an area and ran at Reid, knocking him to the ground.

Tom broke into a run, not a trot as before and as he got nearer could hear the thud as the man's fists landed on Reid's jaw. Reid was doing his best, but he had been taken by surprise and was winded. He was fighting for breath with whooping sounds and clawed at his assailant as best he could, between blows. What Tom couldn't hear, though, to his surprise, was any words. He had made up his mind as he had followed the men that the attacker was a disgruntled old lag who had discovered that Reid was back in the manor and wanted to get his own back. In Tom's experience, attacks of this kind usually came with streams of invective; it was no good beating a man to a pulp if he didn't know why you were doing it. And if it got you your collar felt the next day; well, that was the price you paid for putting a copper in the hospital. But the man was just punching in silence. That just wasn't right.

Tom felt as though he were running through treacle, but it was only seconds before he got there, fumbling for his knife roll as he ran. He grabbed the man on top by the back of the collar and hauled him off the fallen detective, leaving the older man rolling on the ground, catching his breath. Tom swung a mistimed haymaker at the other, who he could tell was younger and fitter than either him or Reid, but clearly inexperienced.

Despite the punches, Reid was now on his hands and knees; that many landed by anyone with half an idea of fighting would have half killed a man of Reid's age and condition. Even so, that youth and fitness was not for nothing. The man twisted out of Tom's grasp and aimed a sneaky knee which missed Tom's essentials by a whisker. It was at that point that Tom felt his patience give out altogether. For a bludger to knock a copper about was one thing. For some random rampsman to whale into an elderly gent with the probable intent to rob, that was entirely another. When that same rampsman then tried to knee him in his tackle, it was no holds barred. To add insult to injury, he was wearing a scarf tied tightly round the lower half of his face. Tom didn't hold with disguise. If you couldn't go out thieving wearing the face the good God gave you, then you shouldn't go out at all, in his opinion.

The next knee found its mark and Tom collapsed in a world of pain, his knife roll clattering to the pavement, scattering its contents as it did so. Tom grabbed for the younger man's leg and brought him down. He held on to a sleeve and reached for a knife. His hand closed round a familiar handle. Damn! It was only the parer, but it was better than nothing. Still seeing the world through dancing lights, he lashed out wildly. He knew he had found his mark, because he heard a hissed intake of breath, followed by running feet.

He rolled over on the pavement and came eye to eye with Edmund Reid, leaning back against the railings of the nearest house, fetching his breath in shuddering gasps.

'Well, Tom,' he said at last. 'Almost like the old days, eh?'

Tom nodded, about all he could manage. Then, 'I hope your hotel ain't far, Mr Reid,' he said. 'Because I don't think I'll be able to carry you if it is.'

'Carry me, Tom? I'll carry you if you like.'

Giggling like schoolgirls, from the shock and pain, using each other and the railings to clamber upright, the ex-burglar and the ex-policeman stood there, clutching each other in relief.

'Hello, hello, hello,' a voice said, almost in their ears. A bull's-eye lantern flashed its shafts of light. 'This is a respectable street, gents. Now, run along before I run you in.'

And the two men, brothers under the skin, limped off, to give the night clerk at the Tambour House Hotel the surprise of his life.

The History department and the department of Archaeology had circled each other for years, like duellists back in the good old days, before there were any rules. Each looked on the other as inferior, an interloper making a mockery of the highest intellectual discipline known to man.

But sometimes, in the search for the truth, the devil drove, and Margaret Murray knocked on the study door of Professor

Hilary Mayhew, a man as regius as they came.

'Hilary,' she said. 'I'm sorry to bother you.'

Mayhew stood up, a tall and still imposing figure despite the fact that he looked as though he should have cobwebs trailing from his obsolete Dundrearies. 'It's Mildred, isn't it?' He was putting his pen away.

'Margaret,' she corrected him. 'Margaret Murray.'

'Yes, of course. Have a seat, would you?'

She would. And did.

'How can I help?' he asked. 'Some nugget of historical perspicacity which will lighten your darkness?'

'Something like that,' she said. 'I know ancient Rome is a speciality of yours.'

'Ancient Rome,' he said, 'ancient Greece. Byzantium. Oh, and the early Church, of course. We must never forget the early Church.'

'No, indeed,' Margaret smiled. 'I've come across a reference in one of my students' researches, to a first-century troublemaker called Joseph. Can you shed any light?'

'Troublemaker?' Mayhew repeated.

'*Turbator*.' Margaret gave him the Latin original.

'What's the context?'

'Something found in an outpost of a Roman fort near Herne Bay in Kent. Specifically, the line was "*Josephus turbator ex Judea hic est*".'

'The troublemaker from Judea . . .' Mayhew was translating.

'Is here.' She ended the sentence for him.

'You're sure the Latin is correct?' he checked. In his experience, the purest language in the world, and students' evaluation of it rarely lived up to expectations.

'Absolutely,' she said.

'Well, what do you want to know?'

'Who this Josephus was,' she told him.

'And you're sure about the date?' he asked. 'First century? Later?'

'First, I am reliably informed,' she said.

'Well, Mildred, it's not likely to be Titus Flavius Josephus. He has no links with Britannia at all.'

'What about Joseph of Arimathea?' she asked him.

Mayhew laughed, his cheeks widening and his side-whiskers floating in the draught from his slightly open window. 'My good woman, this is the department of History, not the Music Hall. Joseph of Arimathea is the product of the deranged mind of William Blake, poet, artist and visionary. There's a tree in Glastonbury he's supposed to have planted – Joseph, that is, not Blake. But it's all legend, Mildred, a fairy story. Surely even an archaeologist knows that?'

Margaret stood up, clearly getting nowhere with this man.

'Yes, Hilary,' she said. 'I knew that. And my name is still Margaret, by the way.'

George Carey Foster was pacing his enormous study, arms locked behind his back as if in irons, his brow wrinkled and his jaw grim. In all his years in academe, he had never known anything like this. He'd known difficult colleagues, obstreperous students, the odd rogue chaplain, but never anything like this. One of his senior department heads, no less, had been . . . what was that ludicrous police phrase? Interviewed under caution. The next step, which was clear to everybody, was an arrest for murder.

There was a timid knock on the door and a cowed secretary ushered an even more cowed senior department head into the principal's office. Walter Inkester had lost the dash and fire he usually had; a day and a half in the cells of Scotland Yard had cured him of that. He looked old and haggard, his skin pale and crusty, rather more like a man whose head was barely bobbing above water at Execution Dock.

Foster waited until the lowly woman had gone and Inkester had slunk into a chair before he delivered his broadside. 'The youngest graduate out of Oxford in years,' he said, circling the man as he laid out his greatness and his former glory. 'The Philomena Kardashian Prize for Zoology; the discoverer of the role of ascariasis roundworm in the yak; accolades and plaudits from . . .' – and he shuddered as he said it – 'Harvard and Yale. An emeritus chair when you leave us at the very least. God, man, there was even talk of a knighthood.'

'I—' was as far as Inkester was likely to get today.

'All of it flushed down one of Mr Twyford's toilets. It can only be a matter of time, Walter, before the Yard comes knocking on your door again. And I have to say . . .' – he closed to his man, eyes burning into his – 'it doesn't look good.'

'I—'

'Yes, well, you would say that, wouldn't you? Let me play devil's advocate for the moment.'

Walter Inkester didn't know that Carey Foster could play anything else.

'Your wife is having an affair with one of your colleagues . . .'

'I—'

'Don't give me that tripe, Walter. Of course you knew. The whole wretched business is so sordid. They're having an affair and you get wind of it. Instead of sorting it out behind closed doors, via a solicitor of repute and discretion, you knock the man's brains out.'

'I—'

'And you didn't even have the chutzpah to do it in some dark alley. No – you did it here, in Norman's own room at University College. However this ends, Walter, I expect your resignation by the end of the day.'

'I—'

'Oh, it's too late for all that now.'

There was a sharp rap at the door and Carey Foster broke off his attack. 'Come in,' he growled.

A little woman stepped into the room, followed by a much larger man.

'Principal.' Flinders Petrie nodded in the man's direction. 'You sent for us.'

'Walter.' Margaret Murray laid a colleaguely hand on the man's shoulder. It was the first gentle touch that he had felt in years. He wanted to cry.

'That's enough of that, Margaret,' Carey Foster snapped. 'I was just in the process of telling Inkester here the appalling opprobrium he has brought to the college.'

'Why, pray?' Margaret raised an eyebrow.

For a moment, words failed the principal of University

College and one sleeve of his gown slipped off his shoulder. 'Why, madam?' he shouted. 'Why?' He was turning all colours of the rainbow.

'George,' Petrie said quietly. 'Think of your blood pressure.'

'I am thinking of the Press headlines!' Foster bellowed. 'Have you seen this?' He held up the first of several papers on his desk. '"Lecturer in archaeology found dead". That's headline news, above the piece about Kruger doing a runner out of South Africa.'

'That's just *The Times* . . .' Petrie dismissed it.

'What about this? The *Mail*. "Archaeologist becomes a body". Another attempt on the Tsar's life is buried on page three.'

'Alfred Harmsworth.' Petrie stood his ground. 'What can you expect?'

'The *Star*.' Foster waved it in the air. 'Front page news – "Godless goings on at the Godless Institution". And on their page three, they've got . . .' – and he shuddered anew – 'an advertisement for knickerbockers.'

'The Rational Dress League believes—' Margaret felt the need to defend the new fashion.

'Damn the Rational Dress League to hell!' Foster thundered. '*My* college – *our* college' – his demon eyes raked them all – 'on the front page of every newspaper in the country, I shouldn't wonder. God knows what'll happen when the *Illustrated Police News* gets hold of it.'

A ghastly silence fell on the principal's study. In the outer office, the three secretaries who had had their respective ears glued to the door broke away and got back to their typing. Foster did his best to compose himself and sat down for what seemed the first time that day.

'I have called you here, William, and you, Margaret, because you were colleagues of Norman Minton. I have already accepted Walter's resignation.'

'I—' Inkester began.

'Don't say another word, Walter.' Petrie gripped the man's shoulder. 'I'm going to say this, George, because Walter is too much of a gentleman, and if Margaret says it, you won't listen anyway. In this great country of ours, one of the guiding principles by which I hope we all live is that a man is innocent until proven guilty. Walter here has not even been charged.'

'It's only a matter of time,' Foster snapped. 'Scotland Yard is on to him.'

And it was only a matter of time before Margaret Murray snapped too. 'And I have lost count of the times over the last few years when Scotland Yard has got things wrong,' she said. 'When they've failed to arrest anybody or have arrested the wrong man. Let's not put too much faith in the long arm of the law, George, please.'

Another heavy silence. Carey Foster's eyes swivelled to the top drawer of his filing cabinet, the one that bulged with Margaret Murray's wrongdoings; he'd have to begin a second level after this.

'Why did you send for us, George?' Petrie asked.

'I had hoped,' the principal said, calmer now but in a barely restrained, homicidal way, 'that I could rely on you two to say nothing whatever to the press. Walter here has assured me he won't say a word.'

'I—'

'Precisely,' Foster nodded. 'But after *Miss* Murray's recent outburst, I clearly can't rely on that.'

'You should be more concerned about my outburst, George,' Petrie said. 'And if you'd like *all* our resignations, pass the relevant bit of paper, will you? I have my own pen.'

Carey Foster was speechless.

'You look as though you could do with a stiff cup of tea, Walter,' Petrie said, helping the man to his feet.

'Come on, Stinkster.' Margaret linked her arm with his. 'The Jeremy Bentham awaits.'

Twice in one week. Margaret Murray was making rather a habit of visiting King's College and she hoped that none of her own colleagues would find out. She got off the bus at the Aldwych and threaded her way across lethal thoroughfares, past Wren's grim little church of St Clement Danes, to the college's main entrance.

The History department was, if anything, even more obscure than in her own dear college and she had to ask for directions three times before she found it. She didn't know Professor Honorius Godbolt very well, but she knew enough about him to know that he was the very man to help her out of her current dilemma. She knocked on the frosted glass door and waited for the command to enter.

Honorius Godbolt was a ferret of a man, of Edmund Reid's height but half his width, and he wore the thickest glasses Margaret had ever seen. Behind them, his eyes were pinpricks, not so much irises as speedwells.

'Good of you to see me, Professor.' She held out a hand. Godbolt stood up and nearly missed it first time but compensated for the error by gripping the woman with both hands.

'The pleasure is mine, dear lady,' he said. 'To what do I owe it?'

'Well, I must confess I was talking to Professor Mayhew the other day . . .'

'Hilary?' The voice hardened. 'No avoiding it, I suppose, in that you work in the same establishment.'

'Indeed. I went to see him on a matter of scholarship, but . . .' – she timed the rest of the sentence to perfection – 'I'm afraid he let me down.'

'Tcha!' Godbolt scoffed. 'Nothing new there. What was your matter of scholarship?'

'Joseph of Arimathea,' she said.

'Ah. Can I interest you in a Peek Frean?' The professor held out a plate of ginger biscuits.

'How kind,' she said, and helped herself.

'It's funny, that.' Godbolt said as the ginger hit his nostrils and he momentarily fought for air. 'You are the third person to ask about him in as many months.'

'Really?' she said. 'Who were the others?'

'Well, the first – and this was quite a while ago now – was one of our archaeology students, appropriately enough. A . . . let me see, now . . .' He ferreted among the papers strewn over his desk. 'Here we are . . . no.' He peered closely at it. 'No, that's my college mess bill – I really *must* pay that. Now, where . . . ah.' He picked up another scrap of paper. 'Oh, no,

no, that's my laundry list. Ah!' He reached across for a book.
'The diary. Of course. Just give me . . . yes, here it is. Wednesday.
Miss . . .' The professor suddenly turned puce and his glasses
steamed up. 'No, no, that's something else entirely. Here.' He
tapped another page. 'This is the one. Emmeline Barker. She
was doing research, as I remember it, on a . . . what do you
people call it, a dig?'

Margaret nodded, smiling.

'A dig in . . . um . . .' He squinted at the page. 'Hampton-
on-Sea. She said she'd found something extraordinary but
couldn't tell me what.'

'Because she didn't know or because it was a secret?'
Margaret felt obliged to ask.

'Er . . . oh. To tell you the truth, I don't exactly know. But
she said it was first century *Anno Domini*, specifically the
forties. Whatever it was referred to a Joseph who was from
Judea. Well, of course, that could be anybody.'

'Not Titus Flavius Josephus?' Margaret needed
confirmation.

'Oh, no, no.' Godbolt shook his head. 'No, there's no
evidence for that at all.'

'And Joseph of Arimathea?' she asked.

'Well . . . what did Hilary Mayhew say?'

'He laughed at me, Professor,' she said, eyes all large and
little-girl. 'Called it a fairy story.'

'Laughed?' Crawford was appalled and passed her another
ginger biscuit passing itself off as a Peek Frean. 'Oh, that's
shocking, dear lady, shocking. But Mayhew . . . well, what
can I say?'

'And Joseph of Arimathea?'

'Oh, he's real enough. He was a wealthy Jerusalem merchant,
possibly a Pharisee, but he was an early Christian convert.
Some accounts say he was Jesus' uncle, but that's stretching
things a bit far. The story goes that he paid for Christ's funeral
and arranged the tomb, and so on.'

'The story?' Margaret repeated.

Godbolt laughed. 'You know as well as I do,' he said, 'that
there are stories and stories. Some are based on evidence,
rooted in fact. Others . . . well, of course, there are those and

have been since the days of that bounder Huxley, who say that every word of the Bible is a story; none of it's true.'

'Do *you* believe it, Professor?' she asked.

'Dr Murray,' he chuckled. 'I teach at King's College. We were founded, as you very well know, in rebuttal of your own Godless Institution. I could turn the tables and ask if *you* believe.'

Margaret smiled. 'There are more things in heaven and earth,' she said. She could have told this pleasant man of the times on digs when she could all but see the souls gathered thick above their mortal remains, but it was important to keep things on an earthly level.

'Indeed, dear lady.'

'You said there were three people,' she reminded him.

'I'm sorry?'

'Three people, including me, asking about Joseph of Arimathea.'

'Yes, that's right.'

'Emmeline Barker was one. Who was the other?'

'Ooh, now you've asked me.' He rummaged among his papers again. 'No, there's no point. I *know* I didn't write it down. He was not from King's, though. I'm certain of that.'

'But a man? And a student?'

'Man, definitely. Student – I couldn't be sure.'

'And he wanted to know about Joseph of Arimathea?'

'Yes, that's right.'

'Did he know Emmeline Barker?' Margaret asked.

'I didn't ask,' Godbolt said. 'It didn't occur to me.'

'This man.' Margaret tried a long shot. 'What did he look like?'

'Oh, average, you know.'

'Hair?'

'Yes, I'm pretty sure he had hair.'

'No, I mean, what colour was it?'

'Ooh, now, then . . .'

'Tall? Short? Thin? Fat?'

Godbolt shook his head and sighed. 'I'm sorry,' he said. 'As you know, historically, my reputation is second to none, particularly that oaf Mayhew, but I'm absolutely useless with faces.' He passed her the biscuits again. 'Mint imperial?'

'Piers?' Anthea Crossley had been voted 'the girl most likely to' when it came to getting a favour out of Piers Gibbs.

'Anthea.' Gibbs was on the alert. Although he had twinkled and smiled at Anthea for some time now, he had never had much effect. 'How can I help you?'

'Goodness, Piers,' she bridled, tapping his arm with her perfectly manicured fingers. 'Surely I can speak to you without wanting a favour?'

'Well, that's always possible, of course.' Piers Gibbs came from the sort of family that didn't bother with beating around the bush. 'But as I appear to have been invisible to you until about . . .' – he fished a gold half-hunter out of his pocket and consulted it ostentatiously – 'two minutes ago, I assume that a favour is on the cards. So, how can I help you?'

Anthea Crossley looked at him with new eyes. He wasn't as handsome as Andrew Rose. But mercifully, he could hide behind Ben Crouch and not show around the edges. He clearly was no fool, as his place at University College attested. But he couldn't hold a candle to her intellectually. On the other hand – she had run out of hands some time ago, but no one was counting – he didn't exactly curdle milk and he obviously had more money than he knew what to do with. 'I'll come straight to the point,' she said.

'I wish you would.' Like most men, Piers Gibbs found Anthea Crossley almost too attractive; her face and clothes were perfect, she clearly had a mind like a razor, but there was something about her which was a little off-putting. She certainly wasn't a girl you could take home to mother.

'You've heard about Angela and Constable Crawford, I suppose?' Anthea said, smiling as brightly as any woman can when a friend has managed to snaffle a man who looked very like Michelangelo's *David*, but more handsome.

'It depends.' Gibbs had sisters. He knew it was never wise to say he knew something when they could well be talking about something else entirely.

'About their engagement.' Anthea's smile could etch glass.

'I don't know what her family will think, of course. He is, after all, only a policeman.' Another smile, of sorts. 'But she has enough money for them both, so he'll probably stop all that nonsense and go into business in some way, I expect.'

'Why?' Gibbs was beginning to edge away. He had been right; this conversation wasn't one a mere man could win.

'Well . . . a *police*man, after all. It isn't quite . . . well, it isn't, is it?'

'We'd be pretty much in the soup without them, generally speaking,' Gibbs said mildly.

'They don't seem to be doing too well on our little murders, do they?' Anthea sneered. 'Arresting Walter Inkester; what are they thinking? According to a friend of mine who is in his department, he is as mild as milk toast.'

'Really? That's what she said, was it? Mild as milk toast.'

'He. And no, not exactly. That's just my reading of it.'

Gibbs stood looking at her. Eventually, he had to know. 'So, what's this favour, Anthea? I have a tutorial with Flinders Petrie in . . .' – again, he flourished his gold watch – 'ten minutes, and his room is eight minutes from here. So, you either walk with me and get ten minutes, or we talk here and you get two.'

'We'll walk,' Anthea said, tucking his arm in hers. 'But if we see Angela, change the subject.'

'Umm . . . all right. If I knew what the subject was, perhaps . . .'

'Yes. Right. Of course. Well, the engagement. I gather they don't intend it to be a long one . . .'

'Oh.' Despite protestations, Piers Gibbs liked gossip as much as the next man. 'That's how the wind blows, is it?'

Anthea thumped him lightly. 'No, indeed. It's just that poor dear Angela isn't getting any younger, is she, and they don't have their way to make or anything. Angela is one of *the* Friends, you know.'

'One of *the* Friends?' Gibbs had no idea what that meant.

'Friend's Scouring Paste. Surely you had some in the kitchen at home. *Have* some, perhaps, in your home in town.'

'I am happy to report that I have no idea. But now you come to mention, I have seen the advertisements, I think. In *The Times*.'

'That's the one.' Anthea waved an arm. '"If you want that rust to end, Buy Scouring Powder from your Friend". Well, she's one of those, so she is richer than God.'

'And so this favour is?' Gibbs could see Flinders Petrie's door by now, and time was short.

'In a nutshell, can we hold a little soirée for Angela and her young man at your house?'

Gibbs blinked. 'That's it?'

'Yes. I suppose it is.'

'Well, yes, of course. I'd be delighted. Just check with Crouch and Rose, pick your evening and I'll tell Cook. Canapés all right? A little champagne?'

'You have a cook?'

'Of course. Don't you?'

'We have a woman who does.' Anthea could tell she had underestimated Gibbs. She was losing her touch.

'Well,' he said with a smile, tapping on Petrie's door. 'Angela may have more money than God. But when God needs an extra bob or two to tide him over, he comes to the Gibbs family. Let me know when the party is – as long as I'm invited, of course.' And in answer to a muffled 'Come!' he disappeared through the door.

TWELVE

There was no doubt about it; carrying out a murder investigation took one to alien parts and expended a considerable amount of shoe leather. Margaret Murray *had* been to the Physics department before, but that was years ago and she'd been looking for the new library at the time.

Laboratories other than those used by archaeologists were a mystery to Margaret Murray. Body parts, hair, teeth, bones and grave furniture were her stock-in-trade, not so much wavelengths and linear coefficients. So it was comforting, if a little surprising, to see a face she recognized as she rounded a corner of the annexe in Torrington Place. A statuesque woman, looking a little flushed, was coming out of a side door.

'Elspeth.' Margaret nodded to her. 'What a small world!'
'Isn't it, though?' the woman said, colouring up a little
more. She called back to a man emerging from what appeared
to be a cupboard, 'Thank you for your donation, Arnold.' She
turned an acid smile on Margaret. 'I'm collecting for the
cavalry horses,' she said. 'Half a million of the poor things
have perished on the Veldt already.'

'I was so sorry to have heard about Walter,' Margaret said.
'Wretched business.'

'Oh, utterly,' Elspeth Inkester's smile had vanished and she
wore her concerned wife face. 'Still, these things are sent to
try us, aren't they? À bientôt, Arnold.' And she swept out.

Arnold Hinchinbrooke looked rather exhausted after giving
Elspeth his donation, but it was hardly Margaret's place to say
so. She barely knew the man except by reputation, and that
reputation had changed subtly in the last few minutes.

'Are you collecting too, Dr Murray?' he asked. Hinchinbrooke
was an unprepossessing man of indeterminate years. His white
coat might well have hidden a multitude of sins; it was not
for Margaret to judge. She had a murderer to unmask and
Arnold might just be the answer to her prayers.

'Your in-college memorandum spoke of a bag, as I recall,'
Hinchinbrooke reminded her. 'Is that the bag in question?' He
was pointing at Margaret's portmanteau, heavy as it was with
learned tomes and the thigh bones of a high status burial from
Mycenae.

'Lord, no,' Margaret said, and fished out some brown paper.
'It's not a bag per se, but a roll of paper which I suspect has
been made into a bag, or wrapping of some sort. I was
wondering if you could tell me what it once contained.'

Hinchinbrooke looked at it, out of the light, in the light,
sideways, backwards, forwards. 'In matters such as this,' he
said, 'I always bow to August Köhler.'

'Who?' It was not like Margaret Murray not to know a
name.

'Works for Zeiss.' Hinchinbrooke perched himself on his
upright stool and did his best not to laugh when Margaret tried
to do the same. He gently lifted her by the elbow and spread
the paper out on a glass tray. Taking a wooden stick with

cotton wool twisted over one end, he took a sweep across the paper, left to right, then, with another swab, right to left, placing the ends of each one on a glass slide. When he had quartered the paper with deft sweeps, he took up each glass slide and tapped the cotton over it. He then, with infinite care, holding his breath, slid the first slide under the lens of his microscope. Margaret was transfixed. If Arnold put this much care and attention into everything he did, she had a sneaky feeling that Elspeth Inkester would be back for another donation before too many days had passed.

Arnold Hinchinbrooke finally had enough brain cells left to speak as well as work. 'August Köhler invented this natty little illumination device a few years back, and what a Godsend it's been.' He tapped the paper gently with an acid-stained forefinger. 'This is standard enough, don't you think?'

Margaret murmured assent. It was nice to be included and she thought that Hinchinbrooke had a lot to teach the men in her own department.

'Nothing special. You can buy it in any hardware or stationery shop in the country. In fact, I think we have a roll in the cupboard where we keep such things.' A strange, mottled blush crept up his neck but he kept talking. 'As to contents, let's see.' He twiddled knobs and tweaked lenses. 'Silica,' he said, and, for clarification, 'sand.'

Margaret smiled. She was often knee deep in the stuff and she hadn't even been to Egypt yet.

'Would you like to look?' Hinchinbrooke leaned sideways and back at a perilous angle and turned the eyepieces round so Margaret could peer down them.

She wasn't ready for what she saw. It was a fairyland of cubes and hexagons, rainbow colours and rocks like diamonds. It seemed to her untutored eye that every one was different. The light from below gave each one a halo of its own. 'Arnold, it's beautiful,' she said. It seemed ungrateful to ask a question. 'Can you tell where it's from?'

'Ooh, place of origin can be tricky,' Hinchinbrooke said, sitting up straight and turning the binocular back in his direction. 'You'd really have to ask the geology lot. It's coastal, though.' He peered closer, catching his eyebrow ridge a nasty one on a lens rim. 'Ow. Yes, tiny bits of shell residue. If I had larger mag, probably diatoms in there as well. If I had to guess . . .'

Margaret held her breath.

'I'd say South-East England, but I wouldn't die in a ditch over it.'

But Emma Barker *had* died in a ditch, or something like it and Margaret couldn't let it go. 'Anything else?' she asked.

'Such as?' In Hinchinbrooke's experience, it helped to know what a client expected; especially if said client was paying for his expertise – which, by the way, Margaret Murray wasn't.

'I don't know,' the archaeologist said. 'I don't want to put words in your mouth, but, well . . . stone, marble, lead at a pinch.'

Hinchinbrooke went back to the microscope. 'There is a way of testing for lead,' he said, 'but that would mean the paper would be tested to destruction, which I assume you wouldn't want. Hmm . . .' he breathed carefully through his mouth as he swapped the slides over and looked them over one by one. 'Stone. Well, if it's sandstone, it would be indistinguishable, of course. Marble would need to be damaged to leave a trace and that would be a powder . . . nothing like that here.'

He picked up the final glass slide. 'Let's see what this one can tell us. Last one lucky, as we physicists say.'

'Do you?' Margaret asked. 'Why?'

Hinchinbrooke shrugged. 'I have no idea. But it can be a bit of a boring discipline, physics, if I'm honest with you, Margaret. These little witticisms make the day go by.'

She tried hard to see the wit in 'last one lucky' but failed. He suddenly jabbed her sharply in the ribs and she almost fell off her stool.

'Sorry,' he said. 'Excitement. I don't know if you were expecting this at all, were you?'

'What?' Margaret felt a little testy. She had almost died of shock when he suddenly poked her like that.

'Wood,' he said. 'Here. See for yourself.' He did his leaning back trick and she leaned over rather gingerly to peer down the microscope again. The rainbow of sand filled her vision again.

'What am I looking at?' she asked.

'Squiggly brown things.' Hinchinbrooke used the technical term. The Botany department would have been proud.

'Ah, yes.' She looked up and focused on his face with difficulty. She really didn't know how people did this day in, day out. 'Any idea what sort of wood?'

Hinchinbrooke laughed. 'The impossible, Dr Murray,' he said, 'I have just done. Miracles take a little longer.'

'That's funny,' she said, but she wasn't laughing. 'A girl who is now dead said that to someone shortly before she was murdered. Apparently, according to my police informant, she said "miracles do happen".'

He didn't know why, but Hinchinbrooke felt the hairs on the back of his neck crawling. And not just because this woman had a police informant. He, the stoic physicist. He, who did not believe in the supernatural at all. He cleared his throat and stuck to what he knew – or thought he knew.

'It's a soft wood, certainly,' he said. 'Very degraded, though. The cell walls are broken, some of it seems to have been eroded away. Probably by the sand, if they were wrapped together. But if I were to stick my neck out, going by the length of the fibres and the tiny bit of remaining pigment . . . did you notice the cells were different colours?'

She shook her head.

'Well, you'd need an expert, as I say, but at a guess, I would say olive wood. Does that help?'

'Right, gentlemen.' Inspector Athelgar Blunt called his people to order in the smoke-filled ante-room next to Lost Property. 'Time for morning prayers.' He scanned the room, looking at the careworn faces he had looked at now for the best part of six years. 'We are particularly honoured this morning to have with us Temporary Detective Constable Crawford.'

There were mutterings and murmurings all round and somebody banged the table. Crawford felt a little uncomfortable in his serge suit and, as the tallest man in the room, even sitting down, he was not likely to blend in.

'Right.' Blunt flicked open a ledger on the desk in front of him. 'Gleeson. Katharine Docks?'

'Still observing, guv,' the detective said. 'We're on to three bargees now, so the problem's growing.'

'Bluebottles helpful as usual?'

'What would we do without them, guv?' Gleeson rolled his eyes and everybody except Crawford guffawed. He'd always assumed that the River Police actually *were* helpful. He told himself quietly that he had a lot to learn.

'Winter.' Blunt swivelled his chair to talk to the man on his left. 'Immoral earnings down the Elephant?'

'It's pretty much what we thought, guv,' he said. 'Widespread south of the river. Bishop of Southwark wasn't interested, though, even when I mentioned a certain member of his flock being involved.'

'Maybe it's time to feel his backwards collar,' Blunt suggested. 'Take a cohort or two of uniform; be seen to be seen. Nothing puts pressure on the bloke at the top like an ostentatious police presence. Biddulph, any joy in the Anthropometry department?' Blunt looked pleased with himself; with the possible exception of Crawford, he was the only man in the room who could pronounce that word.

'Well.' Biddulph had a Gladstone bag in his lap, bulging with notes. 'From the various tarts' descriptions, I'm looking for a tall bloke with a gammy left leg, who at the same time has the ability to leg it over rooftops and squeeze through gratings. He's got the large ear lobes of a sex maniac, the long hooter of a fraudster and is given to solitary vices – hence his blindness.'

'Any sign of him in Anthropometry?' Blunt had to ask, just to say the word again.

'Nothing, guv.'

'Thought not,' the inspector sighed. 'Time they closed that bloody place down.'

'Oh, have a heart, guv,' Biddulph pleaded. 'Sergeant McIndoe down there's got a great line in toasted teacakes.'

More guffaws. Then things got serious.

'So, Crawford. The University College murder.'

'*Murders*, guv,' the rookie corrected him.

'Come again?'

'There are actually two linked with University College, and probably a third – from King's.'

There was a silence.

'What we *don't* do in morning prayers, Temporary Detective Constable,' Blunt said, 'is to speculate. We merely report progress. Notice that Detectives Gleeson, Winter and Biddulph didn't give us their airy-fairy thoughts on their respective cases, merely the current situation regarding them. Now, bearing in mind that no one in this room except you and me know the ins and outs of this particular case, try again.'

Crawford looked at the others. All eyes were trained on him and he could already feel the tightness of his old tunic collar and the chafing of his helmet rim as he contemplated the rest of his career back in the horse troughs. 'Dr Norman Minton was bludgeoned to death in his study at the college,' he said, 'week ago Tuesday. The murder weapon was almost certainly a statuette found lying on his desk.'

'What about the man in the frame?' Blunt asked.

'There is the possibility—' Crawford began.

'We deal in probabilities here, lad,' the inspector told him, 'which, with the weight and gravitas of years of police experience, become certainties. The probable is Professor Walter Inkester. You were present at my interview with him. What do you make of him?'

'An innocent man, in my view,' Crawford said.

Blunt sighed and pushed his chair back from the desk. 'Winter,' he said. 'Flick that curtain aside, would you?'

The detective obliged and a green baize-covered wall appeared, fluttering with notes written in Blunt's hand. He got to his feet and picked up the silver-crowned tipstaff that was his badge of rank twenty years ago and pointed at the name in the centre. 'Norman Minton,' he said. 'Lecturer in archaeology at University College. That's a glorified teacher to you and me, gents. And we've all got memories of old teachers we'd like to brain, haven't we?'

Guffaws all round.

'But, ruling out the student body, snowflakes who wouldn't have the bottle for anything bloody, who wants Minton dead, eh? As that great Roman policeman Marcus Tullius Cicero

used to say, "*Cui bono?*" "Who benefits?"' Blunt's tipstaff
flashed across the wall. 'This bloke. Walter Inkester, lecturer
in zoology at the same college. What's his motive, I hear you
ask? Tell 'em, Crawford.'

'The dead man was having an affair with Inkester's wife.'
There were 'aye ayes' and whistles in all directions.

'So, it's the oldest motive in the book,' Blunt said. 'Revenge.
It's best served cold and delivered by a rather sharp statuette
of Mercury.'

He paused for effect.

'So, all this' – Blunt waved his tipstaff across the wall – 'is
just so much rubbish.' And he tore them all down. 'Winter,
put those in the bin, will you?'

Crawford's heart sank. It had taken him hours to collate
that wall, each piece of paper carefully worked out with
relevant evidence, from Helen Richardson to Emma Barker
to Norman Minton. There were the scraps of Latin he had
gleaned from Margaret Murray, maps of Hampton-on-Sea,
lists of physical evidence like the cyanide phial from Storey's
Yard, the wooden box from the same place and the paper
wrapping that had once contained whatever really lay at the
heart of this mystery. All of it had just been consigned to
the litter bin.

'So, Temporary Detective Constable.' Blunt sat down again.
'There's a little lesson for you. How *not* to present a case at
morning prayers. Now, unless you want to accompany Winter
here to the Bishop of Southwark's palace, just to make the
ecclesiastical gentleman a little nervous, I'd get myself over
to Inkester's if I were you. If the college has any sense, they'll
have fired him by now and he'll be starting to let things slip.
If he so much as farts, I want to know about it. Do we understand each other, Temporary Detective Constable?'

Margaret Murray was usually getting ready for the public
lectures on a Friday afternoon, but somehow, for once, a cup
of tea and a slice of Victoria was more important. She slipped
into one of the rear booths at the Jeremy Bentham and sat
there, fingers to her eyes, waiting for Thomas to work his
magic. She felt rather than heard someone slip into the seat

opposite and, heaving a sigh, moved her hands, opened her eyes and had to smother a small scream.

'Inspector Reid! What . . . whatever *happened*?'

'I would love to say I walked into a door,' Reid said, 'but I know you wouldn't believe me. After your little soirée on Tuesday night, I'm afraid I was set upon by brigands. Or something like that, anyway.' He smiled and immediately regretted it as his swollen eye crinkled painfully. 'Ow. I keep forgetting.'

'It happened on Tuesday and you still look like this?' Margaret was appalled. 'How many of them were there, for heaven's sake?'

'Twelve. Tell her twelve, Inspector Reid.' Thomas was at the table, with a tray. 'It sounds better that way.'

'Thomas!' Margaret was aghast all over again. 'It wasn't *you*, was it? I would never have let you meet if I had known.'

Thomas was sporting a black eye almost as colourful as Reid's. But other than that, he seemed moderately unscathed. 'It wasn't *me*!' He was horrified. 'Let me put this tray down. I still . . .' He winced as he bent to his task. 'My damage is a bit more hidden,' he explained to a confused Margaret.

'But none the worse for that,' Reid said, patting his arm kindly. 'How are . . . they?'

'Still a bit twingey, Mr Reid, thank you for asking.'

Margaret decided not to delve. 'But . . . what happened?'

'Nothing we couldn't cope with, Prof,' Thomas came in quickly. 'Just a bit of rough and tumble. Between us, we saw him off, didn't we, Mr Reid?'

Reid nodded, with some care. 'A roughneck, Margaret, nothing more. Tom here nicked him, we think, on the arm. Lucky not to be killed – his knives were all over the road and it was touch and go who got there first.'

Thomas looked modest. 'As you say, Mr Reid. Just luck.'

Margaret looked from one battered face to another. As she got her eye in, she could see more bruises. Hidden in his facial hair, Reid was sporting a split lip and Thomas had the beginnings of a fine cauliflower ear. Both men had sundry grazes and Reid had two fingers taped together.

'Have you been to the hospital?' she asked. 'Just to be sure.'

'Nah.' Tom was dismissive. 'It was just—'

'A bit of rough and tumble. Yes, you said. But neither of you are as young as you were.' She looked from one outraged face to another. 'Well, you're not. It's silly to take risks.'

Reid leaned in and proffered his bruised eye to Margaret. 'See this,' he said, lisping slightly because of his lip. 'See the yellow? Well, it's healing, that means. Tom's is the same. So, really, Margaret, stop worrying.'

'Do you know who it was?' she wanted to know.

'He wore a scarf right up to here.' Tom put his hand just under his eyes.

'And he had no distinguishing features,' Reid chimed in. 'Average height, average weight. Aren't they always?'

'Age?'

They both shrugged.

'Average. I see.' Margaret had heard this description before, and recently. 'All right, you two. I can see that I'm not going to get anywhere with you. Let's pour this tea before it's stewed out of all recognition.' She glanced at the tray. 'I see you have already brought two cups, Thomas. Very forward-thinking.'

'Well, I seen him come in.' Thomas, always the perfect host, thought of everything. 'D'you want another slice?' He gestured to the sponge. 'Or just two plates?'

'Good heavens, Thomas,' Margaret said. 'I may be a little concerned, but not enough to share my Victoria sponge. Inspector Reid, would you like the same or something different?'

'Something that doesn't need chewing?' Reid suggested.

'Custard tart, on its way.' Thomas bustled off, as far as he could bustle just then.

'You didn't come to see me eat cake,' Margaret said to Reid.

'No, that's true.' He stirred his tea.

'Or to let me see your battle scars?'

'Also true.'

'So, why . . .?'

Reid smiled on one side of his face only. 'I just came to make sure you were all right. You were . . . upset, on Tuesday.'

'It's Friday now,' she pointed out.

'Yes. So, this is how my week has been. Tuesday night; beaten almost senseless. As you pointed out, I am not as young as I was. Wednesday; stayed in bed, having been beaten almost senseless the day before. Beef tea through a straw and little else. I think the Tambour House Hotel is still rather shocked – they don't have beaten-senseless guests as a rule. Still, they were very kind. Thursday; walking about, but only just. And that brings us to Friday.'

Margaret made a lot of counting sugar lumps into her tea. 'I'm sorry,' she said at last. 'I have been rather worrying at it. I thought perhaps . . . well, I thought perhaps you were angry.'

He patted her hand, using the one of his with all the functioning fingers. 'We've all been under a lot of strain,' he murmured.

'Some good news, though,' she said. 'Angela Friend and Constable Crawford are engaged to be married.'

Reid would have raised his eyebrows under normal circumstances, but chose not to this time. 'That *is* good news. Long engagement planned?' He knew how it worked for policemen. The pay was never that good, but keeping a wife on it in the early years was next to impossible.

'Short. Angela is a Friend.'

'Yes, I know.' Reid was puzzled. He had heard of Margaret's 'gang', but even so.

'No, I mean *a* Friend, as in the Scouring Powder.'

This time, Reid's eyebrows shot up and dang the consequences. 'Oh, I *see*. I hope he doesn't leave the police, though. Good instincts, that lad has.'

Margaret sighed. 'Angela is leaving academe, though,' she said. 'She came to see me this morning. Her mind is made up, I'm afraid. She is looking forward to being a policeman's wife and mother of a policeman's children.'

'Oh.' Reid was broadminded, but this was a facer. 'I didn't know.'

A waitress brought Reid's custard tart and placed it in front of him with a bob. He smiled his thanks and she dimpled away.

Margaret frowned. 'No, Inspector, Angela is not as friendly as all that, as far as I know. She just wants what she wants; I can't argue with that. Her companions from her house are putting on a surprise party tomorrow evening. We're invited.'

'That's very civil of them.' Reid was more pleased than he let show.

'Isn't it? It's at Piers Gibbs's house. I haven't been there, but I know where it is. Rather grand, as I understand it.' She chuckled. 'Probably a little less grand than it was, since Benjamin Crouch has been living there. But if they wipe the grease off, I am sure it will be lovely.'

'Do we have a time?' Reid asked.

'Seven for seven thirty,' she said.

'Well, how about this?' Reid said. 'You come to the Tambour House Hotel for a very early supper, we'll call in on someone I think you'd like to meet and then we can go on to this party and be fashionably late?'

'That sounds ideal, as well as somewhat intriguing.' If there was one thing Margaret Murray liked, it was intriguing. She patted his good hand. 'I'm so glad we're still friends.'

'Always,' he said. 'Always.'

Angela Friend sat at the breakfast table the next morning with a card propped up on the marmalade. 'This is odd,' she said, pointing to it with a butter-smeared knife. 'Piers Gibbs has invited me to sherry this evening.' She looked up at the six eyes all fixed on her. 'Have you had one of these as well?'

Janet Bairnsfather couldn't lie to save her life. Veronica Halifax was better, but bowed to the mistress.

'We've all had one,' Anthea said, not meeting anyone's eye. 'I understand that Piers Gibbs's mother is in town and wants to meet some of his friends. You know what mothers are like.'

The other students round the table made twittering noises to denote agreement. Angela looked around. She wouldn't call them friends, exactly, but they all rubbed together all right, taking one thing and another into consideration. Janet Bairnsfather tended to the frugal and labelled all her food in the pantry. As no one had ever heard of, let alone eaten, a clootie dumpling, the label saying 'Janet's clootie dumpling. Please do not touch' was superfluous to say the least. Veronica was almost too sweet and good for words. Unlikely ever to matriculate, but she was harmless enough. Anthea . . . well, she would have to speak to Anthea. When Angela and Constable Crawford were married, they were moving into another of the family's homes, backing on to Regent's Park and altogether better for children. So Anthea would become the senior student in this house, which Angela couldn't bring herself to throw them out of. Bringing various men home at all hours – most of them appearing to wear hobnailed boots and to have particularly piercing whispers – simply wouldn't do. Also, she would need to oil her bedsprings. Angela sighed. It was a responsibility, without a doubt.

'Well, in that case . . . are you going?' Angela looked at them all in turn.

'Ooh, yes,' Veronica said brightly. 'It sounds like fun, don't you think?'

Angela frowned at her. 'Sherry, with Gibb's mother. With Ben Crouch drooling canapé crumbs all down one's front.' That sounded like a memory of an actual event and the others raised their eyebrows. She flapped a hand. 'Don't ask. But, really . . . are we going?'

'Piers is a sweet boy,' Anthea announced.

'Goodness, Anthea,' Janet said. 'It sounds as if you've been licking him.' She chortled at her witticism but Angela merely gave Anthea an old-fashioned look.

'*Have* you been licking Piers Gibbs, Anthea?' she asked sternly.

'Not at all,' Anthea laughed. 'Though I wouldn't mind . . .'

'*Pas devant les enfants*,' Angela reminded her. She put down her buttery knife at last and dusted her fingers on her napkin. 'All right, then. I'll come as well. I will need to let Adam know, though. I was planning to see him this evening; wedding plans.' She ducked her head and smiled the way only women in love smile.

'I have an idea!' Veronica piped up. 'Why don't you bring him?'

'What a good idea!' Anthea enthused. 'The more the merrier! We're short on chaps.'

'We? *Are* you licking Piers Gibbs, Anthea?'

Anthea blushed, a rare event. 'No, no. Slip of the tongue. I meant to say that probably, Piers was short on chaps. I don't see him round with lots of friends, so . . .' Even to Anthea's own ears, it was sounding less and less convincing. 'Anyway, I happen to know Em-em is bringing Inspector Reid, so they can make a policemanly huddle in the corner if they want.'

Angela stood up. 'I'll ask him. I can't promise.'

'I'm sure that that is all Piers would expect,' Veronica said, smiling.

Angela left the room to go and have a word with the woman who did. It was fair enough, she wasn't a professional cook, but it would be nice if the kippers were shown the grill for at least a while. They had a Scot in residence now; there could be no skimping on that kind of thing. When the green baize door had flapped shut behind her, the other three let out their breaths as if they had been holding them for hours.

'Well,' Veronica, for ever the optimist, said. 'I think that went quite well, don't you?'

Anthea looked askance and Janet just looked down. She was not happy about parties in the first place. And secret ones even less so. And what was all this talk of licking? It was perhaps time she went back home to the manse and be done with it all. She was homesick for Abergeldy and London was just too confusing for words.

The Tambour House Hotel was never going to win any prizes for its cuisine, but the very early supper that they put on for Inspector Reid and his lady friend was one of their best collations. The ham was freshly carved off the bone, the accompaniments carefully chosen to avoid vinegar breath; although a gentleman of certain years, the inspector could still cut a dash and they didn't want to cramp his style. The bread was warm and crusty, the dessert just the right side of unbearably chocolatey. Margaret wiped her mouth delicately on the freshly laundered napkin and sat back, full and as happy as a woman could be who is in the throes of tracking down a habitual homicide.

'That was quite delicious,' she said to the waiter who was clearing the table. 'Quite my favourite kind of high tea. Thank you, Edmund.'

'You are very welcome, Margaret.' They had been uncertain

how to play this semi-leisure setting and had decided to try Christian names all round, see how it went. 'Coffee?'

Margaret consulted her delicate little watch, worn on her breast like a brooch. 'Do we have time?'

'The coffee is brewed, sir,' a hovering waiter told them.

'We'll have two cups, then,' Reid said.

'Am I to be told who this person is?' Margaret said. 'I do like a surprise, but I want to be prepared.'

'It's no big secret,' Reid said. 'It's Marjorie Simmons, Emma Barker's friend. Very special friend, perhaps I should say.'

'I'm glad she's missed,' Margaret said. 'Not because I wish Marjorie pain, but I can't help thinking that, without being missed, every life is a little pointless. Do you think that Marjy has anything new to tell us?'

'Not specifically.' The coffee arrived at their table and Reid added his usual two lumps. Margaret, also as usual, added an indeterminate number; she was waiting for the day when coffee was drinkable, a day that might never come. She took a sip and wrinkled her nose. 'Why do you have coffee if you don't like it?' Reid asked.

'Hope springs eternal,' she said. 'A bit like with this case, don't you think? We have three people dead, and I almost feel like adding "so far". Without Thomas's intervention, you would have been the fourth.'

'Possibly.' Reid stirred his coffee round and round. It was an annoying habit, but it helped him think. 'The attacker didn't seem to have a weapon of any kind. Perhaps he just meant to scare me off.'

Margaret chuckled. 'Is that likely?'

'Well, I suppose to the uninitiated, I look a typical easy target. None too fit.' He patted his stomach. 'A bit of a short arse.'

'Steady,' Margaret said, sitting up straight. 'Size isn't everything.'

'A certain age.'

'You don't look it,' Margaret said gallantly.

'Thank you. I feel it, though. That I can't deny.' He drank off his coffee in one. 'Shall we? Or do you want to have another go at liking coffee?'

'No. It's time we were on our way, anyway. We don't want to keep the happy couple waiting.'

'Do you think they'll even go?' Reid asked. 'These surprise parties can sometimes be a bit of a damp squib.'

'I think that Constable Crawford will have worked out what's happening,' Margaret said. 'He's a very bright young man. I wish he would do archaeology full time, but we need people like him in the police, don't we, Edmund?'

'As an antidote to Blunt?' Reid held her coat. 'As many as we can get.'

A cab was waiting outside. Neither of the destinations was far from the Tambour House Hotel, but the night was cold and Reid was a gentleman. He handed Margaret up and gave the first address to the cabbie, hunched on his box.

'It isn't very salubrious on the outside,' Reid told her, 'but they had made it very cosy in the studio. I'm sure that's where Marjy will take us. She seems to spend her life up there these days.'

The cab rattled off down Gower Street, heading for the river.

'I'm cutting down Munmuff Street, guv,' the cabbie said over his shoulder. 'There was anorse down Charing Cross when I come to getchya.'

'Whatever you say,' Reid said. He knew it wouldn't add anything to the fare; the old cabbies had not forgotten Inspector Reid, and probably never would.

'I confess,' Margaret said, 'I am in awe of your encyclopaedic knowledge of London. Sometimes I struggle one road west or east of Gower Street.'

'You just need to keep a picture in your head,' Reid said. 'A little like young Emma used to do.' He raised his voice to speak to the cabbie. 'Don't worry about turning into the Mews,' he said. 'It's a tight turn.'

'Where're you going next?' the cabbie wanted to know.

'Furnival Mansions,' Margaret told him. 'Number five.'

'Right. I'll let you down across the road for the Mews, then, guv, if that's all right. Then I'm facing the right way. Here we are; watch your step, lady.' The cabbie looped the reins around the whip and took out a tobacco pouch. It wasn't

perfect weather for being outside waiting. And he liked it when
he didn't have to go south of the river. He remembered Reid
as a good tipper; he hoped retirement hadn't changed that.

Reid took Margaret by the elbow – something she usually
detested – and steered her across the road into the grim little
Mews. He kept hold of her over the cobbles, slick with the
damp and nameless grease. Marjy was expecting them this
time and was waiting inside the door for Reid's knock.

'Come in, come in,' she said, stepping aside. 'Dr Murray,
it's such an honour to meet you. Emma talked of you often.'

'Really?' Margaret was secretly delighted. 'From a King's
woman, that is very heartening.'

'She used to say that she wanted to be like you, one day.'
Marjy's smile was brave and bright. Emma was no longer the
missing, she was among the dead, and knowing where she
was had brought the artist peace. 'Up you go. Door at the top.
Can't miss it.'

The studio was bright with candles. The scudding clouds
across the moon were luminous with its light and the odd
star seemed to be placed by an expert, artistic hand. Margaret
could hardly take her eyes off the expanse of sky.

'Goodness,' she said. 'I don't think I have ever seen the sky
above London looking so lovely.'

'It's always there,' Marjy said, piloting her to a chair. 'You
just need to look.'

'I suppose I look down too much,' Margaret said. 'That's
my problem, really. Always looking for a likely place to dig.'

'Emma was the same,' Marjy said. 'Sherry?'

Reid looked at Margaret. 'Just a small one,' he said. 'We
can't stay long. We have another engagement later.'

Margaret looked at the mantel clock. 'Actually, we have
another engagement now, but we have decided to be fashionably late.'

'The best way,' Marjy agreed. 'It saves all that awkward
foot shuffling if you're the first.' She handed them each an
exquisitely thin glass, with pale sherry shining through the
etched design. She raised her glass. 'Cheers,' she said. 'To
Emma.'

'To Emma,' Reid said.

Margaret held her glass in the air but was looking into the corner of the room, apparently transfixed.

'Dr Murray?' Marjy said. 'Are you feeling quite well?'

Margaret blinked and came back to the present. 'Umm . . . yes, I do apologize. I was just wondering . . . why have you got a picture of Helen Richardson over there, leaning against the wall?'

THIRTEEN

Piers Gibbs was feeling quite pleased with himself. The house he lived in with Crouch and Rose was rather splendid, he didn't need reminding of that. But with fresh flowers in the hall, sent up from his parents' place in the country, candles in every available holder and the brass and copper gleaming, it looked like a fairy tale. Cook had excelled herself. He had worried about asking her, but she was so overjoyed to be cooking what she called 'real food' that she had sung about her work for days and had brought in every relative and friend's relative she could lay hands on, to do the Young Master proud. The smell of hothouse lilies vied with melting beeswax and caviar puffs. Piers Gibbs stood in his lighted hallway and awaited his guests.

Soon, they began arriving. The gang had been here for what seemed like hours, Ben Crouch manfully leaving the food alone. Crouch and Andrew Rose had risen to the occasion and gone to fetch the others in a barouche, which the Gibbs family kept under a tarpaulin in the mews at the back. Crouch and Rose had no idea it even existed and from the light in Rose's eye, it looked as if it would not be back under its tarpaulin for long. The girls had twittered and cooed and Piers Gibbs had seen a light in Anthea Crossley's eye he hoped never to see again. It was, he imagined, very like the last thing an antelope at the watering hole sees when the crocodile breaks the surface of the previously innocent pool.

Janet Bairnsfather anxiously watched the door. She was a

worrier to her fingertips and had felt sure, ever since this plan had been hatched, that Angela and Crawford wouldn't come. She was weighing up in her troubled mind which would be worse; that *neither* turned up; that *Angela* turned up on her own; or – heaven forbid – she or Crawford turned up with someone else. But even Janet, the Job of University College, had to admit that was unlikely. Every person who arrived who wasn't Angela or Crawford sent her further into her morass of pessimism.

Veronica Halifax was beyond excited. She was almost bouncing, although to Ben Crouch's eternal disappointment, she didn't quite follow that through. After all the horrors of recent weeks, she was ready for some fun and just being in this lovely house, waiting for her friend to arrive and be the belle of the ball with her handsome prince – well, handsome temporary detective police constable, at least. She recognized some of the arrivals, but for her, no one had arrived as yet.

Anthea Crossley had been in every room and had made a rough inventory, arriving at a total that made her eyes pop. She leaned provocatively in a doorway, watching Piers Gibbs standing near the door, spangled in candlelight, wreathed in the perfume of exotic flowers, and she began to make plans. She didn't know that he was on to her, and, after all, the hunt was more than half the fun.

Ben Crouch's self-control was hanging by a thread. If the golden couple didn't arrive soon, he was going to have to extract a plate of curry puffs and hide in the study and scoff the lot. He hadn't gone this long between snacks while awake since he was about twelve and it was taking its toll. Angela and her beau couldn't arrive soon enough for his liking.

Andrew Rose was not a party animal. It would be true to say that he liked people, particularly women, but for preference in numbers small enough to count on the fingers of one hand. This crowd was not to his liking at all; although he thought Anthea Crossley was looking particularly delicious this evening. Something about the gleam in her eye, perhaps. He and Anthea had had the occasional Moment in the past weeks, but more in an any old port in a storm way. Perhaps it was time to make it more official. He started making his way, in small increments, over to her doorway.

But still, no Angela and Adam.

Reid and Marjorie looked at Margaret and then in the direction of her pointing finger. A small painting, canvas with no frame, was leaning against a pile of others in a corner to one side of the enormous nude Mercury, now almost complete. Gazing out from a dark background was the face of a girl, peaceful and contented as she held a posy of primroses under her chin. Compared to the rest of Marjy's work around the room it was rather chocolate boxy, but pretty enough and commercial; after all, even artists need to eat.

Marjy bounced up from her chair and went to fetch it. 'I'd forgotten her name,' she said. 'She came up to me one day at a small exhibition I was putting on in a gallery in Soho. She asked if I needed models, that she didn't mind taking her clothes off, the usual thing. But there was something about her, an intelligence in her eyes it isn't normal to see in . . .' – she paused, not wanting to offend – 'sort. How do you know her?'

Reid spoke up quickly, before Margaret could get a word in. 'Her sort turns out to be not so easy to identify,' he said. 'She was a telephonist by day, a lady of the night by . . . er, by night, and a part-time student at University College on a Friday. So, a busy lady with more than one iron in the fire. And as for how we know her – well, she's dead.'

'Dead?' Marjy was horrified. 'Not . . . not suicide, was it? She seemed to need the money, though with two jobs, I don't know why.'

'Murder,' Reid said shortly. He didn't go on to say that Helen and Emma shared more than Marjy; that they also shared a killer.

'That's terrible.' Marjy's eyes darkened with memory. 'I thought when I met her that she was more than met the eye. But when she approached me, she was definitely not dressed like a telephonist. Or a student, come to that. It was all tatty lace and a dress just a thought too tight and too short. Her hair was piled up in the fashion, but not very well done. She was a copyist, if I were to describe her in one word. I would imagine that she would be whatever you wanted her to be. A chameleon. I mean, look at that picture. Could anyone look more innocent?'

Margaret tilted the picture to the light and what the artist said was true. The picture, though a little sugary for many tastes, showed a face which had never known pain, want or need. The lips were parted as if about to smile. The lids were lowered over smoky blue eyes. 'Artist's licence?' she suggested.

'No.' Marjy shook her head. 'I painted what was there in front of me. The picture of innocence. Actually, it has been a bit of a dud. I was hoping that I could sell it as an advertisement piece – Pears, you know, something like that. But those days are gone. I think Leighton and Millais rather queered that pitch for us. Advertisers now use black and white pen and ink scrawls in newspapers and on hoardings. It's a shame.' She reached down behind her chair. 'I've got a frame here that would fit it. Would you like it?'

'Goodness me, no,' Margaret said. 'I'm afraid my salary doesn't run to art.'

'A gift. Now I know she was murdered . . . well, I wouldn't like to sell it to anyone, knowing that. It's somehow . . . well, it's not right. It will just take me a minute to put it in the frame. I've got some paper here as well.'

Reid nudged Margaret. 'Take it,' he said. 'You might not want it now, but when this is all over, you might be grateful to have a memento. Make a change from bones and owls.'

Marjy didn't understand where owls came into it, but sat there waiting.

'Oh, all right, then.' Margaret allowed her arm to be twisted. 'I can't take it now, though. Can you get it delivered to me at University College? It's in—'

'Gower Street. Of course, no problem. I'm sorry; this has taken us off the subject, hasn't it? You wanted to know about Emma.'

Margaret and Reid looked at each other. In a way, they had learned far more than they could have hoped. And time was getting on.

'I just wanted to see where she lived,' Margaret extemporized. 'And we have to go. We're horribly late already.'

'And we were aiming for fashionably,' Reid added, getting up. 'No, don't come down. We can see ourselves out.'

Andrew Rose had almost reached Anthea Crossley when there was a noise outside. It was a little confused at first, the wheels of a hansom coming to a halt, footsteps, voices. All heads turned. There was a rap on the knocker and the butler, sent up by train with the lilies from the country house, flung open the door. He was getting rather tired of opening the door to a ragbag of assorted students, so he was glad to see a rather more sedate couple standing on the step. The age gap was a little larger than he liked to see, but they seemed content enough with each other. He ushered them in, only to see another couple standing behind them. The man was a stunner, the butler would be the first to admit, tall, golden-haired and with shoulders like tallboys. The woman at his side was attractive enough, but clearly not out of the top drawer. This confused him; he had looked down the guest list and no couple seemed to meet these criteria. He braced himself, shoulders or no shoulders, to chuck them out bodily.

But no. The Young Master was bearing down on them, hands outstretched. Reaching them, he positioned himself between them and displayed them like prizes at a cattle show. 'Look, everyone,' he called. 'It's Angela and Constable Crawford!' He had done better introductions in his time, but he had no time for regrets. The guests surged forward, engulfing the happy pair, and Margaret Murray and Edmund Reid only stepped aside in the nick of time, avoiding being crushed by a whisker.

Eventually, the hubbub died down and the edges of the crowd began to peel off towards the supper room. Those in the know walked a little faster than the others, hoping that Ben Crouch had left at least a little for everyone else. Finally, Angela caught Margaret's eye.

'Dr Murray,' she gasped, straightening the comb at the back of her hair which somehow had been dragged askew. 'Did you know about this?'

Margaret chuckled. 'I would be lying if I said no,' she said, 'because, as you see, I am here. I was sworn to secrecy, though. I knew you wouldn't mind.'

Reid and Crawford had gravitated towards one another, like iron filings to a magnet.

Margaret nodded towards them. 'I knew they would be happy enough, talking shop.'

Angela looked at her erstwhile lecturer with a knowing look. 'Are you and Inspector Reid . . .?'

'Good heavens, no,' Margaret said. 'He's a lovely chap, of course, but recently widowed, apart from anything else. As you surely know by now, Angela, my life is too full for romantic fripperies.'

Angela looked at her again, peering closely. 'And yet, you know . . .' she said. 'You do have a twinkle in your eye.'

'I admit I enjoy the man's company,' Margaret said, bristling a little. 'But it is just because we have a lot in common at the moment. The hunt for the killer of Helen, Emma and Norman. And now, of course, getting poor Walter Inkester exonerated and reinstated.'

'I wish you would,' a passing student said. 'I'm in his department and if someone doesn't do something with that wildebeest soon, we'll all be sorry. As it is, you can hardly breathe for the smell on our corridor.'

'My dear boy!' Margaret was horrified. 'It's been there now . . . how long?'

'A week, more or less,' the student said. 'I had a peep in the crate yesterday and the gases have blown it up so it looks like a whale. The slightest touch and . . .' – the boy threw his arms in the air – 'chunks of wildebeest as far as the eye can see. I've witnessed it with a goat that got left over the Easter vac. A wildebeest would be much, much worse.' He took an unconcerned bite out of a chicken leg he was holding and wandered off.

Margaret and Angela watched him go. 'They are a strange lot, the zoologists,' Angela remarked, in something of an understatement.

'Indeed. Just off the subject for a moment, I saw Elspeth Inkester the other day, coming out of a stationery cupboard with a physicist.'

'My goodness.' Andrew Rose poked his head over Angela's shoulder. 'That sounds like that game, you know the one. Did you play it? My Aunt Went to Market.'

Margaret smiled. 'My aunt went to market and she bought an anteater.'

'Yes, that's the one.' Rose planted a champagny kiss on Angela's cheek, one arm draped nonchalantly around her neck. 'I must say, Piers knows how to throw a party.'

Angela screwed her head round to look at him. 'And you live here, do you? You and Ben?'

'We *do*, yes.' Rose threw out an expansive arm. 'Not in quite all of it. The salon' – he jerked his thumb over his shoulder to the gigantic room where the food was laid out – 'isn't very homey, if you see what I mean. Generally, we stay in the yellow drawing room, which is over there.' He pointed again. 'My bedroom is about as large as the entire ground floor of our house, and we do all right, or so I always thought.' He smiled. 'As student digs go, I have known much, much worse.' And with another kiss in the direction of Angela's ear, he was gone into the crowd.

Margaret watched him go. 'He's very charming, Andrew, isn't he?' she said.

Angela turned as well. 'A tad oily for my taste,' she said. 'Notice he didn't comment on my house.'

'Has he been there?' Margaret asked.

'He has, though he doesn't know that I know he has. He is one of the midnight inamorati that Anthea drags home from time to time. She thinks we don't notice, but the addition of various gentleman's folderols in the laundry basket rather gives the game away.'

'Oh dear. It's such a shame. She has a very brilliant mind.'

'Of course she has,' Angela said, in the bland tones of someone who knows what she wants and also knows that she already has it. 'But I don't think that's why they come home with her, somehow. I'm moving out when Adam and I are married and heaven knows what she will turn the place into.'

'I know!' An outraged voice was at Margaret's elbow. 'I don't want to spoil your party, Angela.' It was Janet Bairnsfather in full Presbyterian spate. 'I'm very happy for you and

Constable Crawford. But by the time you are back from your honeymoon, she will have turned it into a house of ill repute.'

'Oh, I don't think it will be quite that bad,' Angela murmured. 'It was just a figure of speech, you know.'

'Yes, she will.' Janet's voice was now a shriek and people were beginning to sidle away. 'But I don't care. I'm going home. Back to my parents. I don't need to be here, you know. I know you all look down on me.' She stamped her foot. 'Just because I don't understand your jokes.'

'Or any archaeology,' Ben Crouch muttered to his companion, a rather big-boned girl holding a loaded plate of canapés.

'I heard that, Ben Crouch!' the girl screamed, her accent becoming more impenetrable as her distress mounted. 'Just because I don't know my Greek from . . . from . . .' and she burst into tears.

'A hole in the ground?' Crouch suggested and wandered away.

Angela tried to pat the girl's arm but was shrugged off.

'Come along, Janet.' Andrew Rose, oily or not, had his uses. 'There's no need to get so upset. I'm sure Anthea will rise to the occasion, be a real little mother to you all.' He glanced over to where the woman in question lounged on a flimsy-looking chaise longue in the shadow of the staircase. It wasn't clear quite what the languid young man leaning over her was saying, but the odds were that it wasn't a question on archaeology. 'Or if not, you could move in here. There is, as you see, plenty of room.' His light-hearted suggestion did not go down well.

'Here?' Janet shrieked. 'With *men*? Don't be absurd. There are murderers about as well.' She suddenly changed tack, as if her previous subject were exhausted. 'Murderers, wherever you look.'

Reid and Crawford, standing in the salon doorway with policemen's portions of delicate crustless sandwiches balanced on Mrs Gibbs's best Spode, looked up like two startled horses.

'No, no.' Andrew Rose patted her and was not shrugged off. He was getting somewhere at least, though not far. The girl was taking huge shuddering breaths and was on the verge of hysteria. What Rose said next would decide which side of the fence she fell. 'I know that people talk a lot about murder, but why would it worry you? One was a girl who was no better than she should be and she lived nowhere near you. All right, you may have seen her once, at a lecture, but I bet you can't even remember her name. Hmm?'

Janet scrubbed at her nose with a scrap of lace-trimmed linen.

'Well, it was Helen, as it happens. The other one – Emmeline, wasn't it? – well, you didn't even see her *once*. She died miles from here. And as for poor old Norman – well, I suppose you haven't been going around making husbands jealous, have you?'

There was no answer. Janet stood there looking at her feet.

'Well?' He put a finger under her chin and lifted her face to his.

'No,' she whispered.

'So, no more silly talk of going home?'

'No.'

'Right. Go and find one of the two dozen bathrooms, or however many we have here, and mop your eyes. Then get a plate of food before Crouch eats it all and the next thing I want to see is you dancing. The music is starting any minute.' Unexpectedly, he kissed the tip of her nose and she scurried away.

Angela was impressed, and Margaret impressed but also not surprised; she had had Mr Rose down for a bit of a rogue since the day he had arrived, fresh from Manchester Grammar. 'Andrew, that was very sweet of you,' Angela said. 'Thank you.'

'Well,' he said, with mock humility. 'Didn't want her to spoil your party.'

His voice was all but drowned out by Ben Crouch banging the side of a seventeenth-century chased silver punch bowl with a ladle. 'Pray silence,' he roared, 'for the groom-to-be.'

And everyone took up the cry.

'Speech! Speech! Speech!'

Piers Gibbs woke that Sunday morning with a hangover the size of the Coliseum. Someone, somewhere not a million miles away, appeared to be banging a gong, very slowly but very, very loudly. There was also a nagging voice at the back of his head, telling him in indistinct words that he had done something really rather stupid.

He chose not to open his eyes for a while. The voice had suggested in all kinds of subtle ways that when he did, the real pain would begin. He started to take stock, to see if there was any part of his body which didn't hurt. He wiggled his toes. They seemed all right, if a little further away than he was used to. He flexed his knees. All present and correct. Fingers, ditto. He moved his head, just a little. Oh, no; too soon, too soon by far. He finally narrowed down the problem areas – excluding the head, which was not going to be working for the rest of the day, he knew – to his back, which was unusually hot and slightly sweaty and his impedimenta, as his house master at school had always chosen to call it. The latter seemed to be in some kind of vice. Opening his eyes to look was not on the cards, so he gingerly felt down there with his free arm. His blood froze. Something very odd was going on; it felt for all the world as if . . .

'Good morning, Piers,' a voice breathed in his ear and the grip on his impedimenta grew tighter. 'So, we're awake, are we?'

He grunted, with the grunt of a small, shy woodland creature facing the predator of its nightmares. Everything was flooding back and not all of it was good.

'Ready to go again?' Anthea breathed.

Piers couldn't shake his head because of the flashing lights. And that would be his excuse, until his dying day.

Ben Crouch also had a headache, a monster sitting with its scaly arms and legs wrapped tightly around his neck and shoulders. But he had never met a hangover that could stop him eating a breakfast of champions. He was pretty sure his grandmother had once told him, 'Feed a cold, feed a fever, feed a hangover' – or something along those lines.

'How're you feeling, Rose?' he asked his only other ambulant housemate.

'Not too bad, all things considered,' the Manchester Grammar man said. 'I may have overdone it a bit with Janet Bairnsfather, though.'

'We were all quite impressed at first,' Crouch conceded.

'It was all going spiffingly until she started on the punch. What happened to the punch, by the way?'

'Oh, I don't know.' Crouch looked modest. 'It may have been the brandy that got accidentally spilled into it. Or the gin. One of those.'

'Janet certainly had a taste for it, before the night was over,' Rose said. 'She was all over me like a rash before she went home.'

'At least she did go home,' Crouch observed. 'Unlike some.'

'Oh?' Rose's eyebrows went up. 'I noticed you had made . . . friends with that rather buxom lass from the Biology department.'

Crouch chuckled. 'Biology is right,' he said with a knowing smirk. 'But I was talking about Anthea.'

Rose laughed. 'Anthea didn't stay with me last night,' he said. 'She wouldn't have been able to dislodge Janet for long enough.'

'Not *you*,' Crouch said. 'Old Gibbsy-boy was the lucky man last night. I'm surprised you couldn't hear them. You'd think in a house of this quality that noise wouldn't travel so far. At one point, I thought they were in the room with me.'

Rose looked mutinous. 'No,' he muttered. 'I didn't hear that, no. My room is along the corridor, if you remember.'

Crouch chuckled and stood up to get some more bacon from the sideboard chafing dish. 'Distance no object, old son,' he said. 'I'd be surprised if they couldn't hear them out in the street. Still, it won't last; Anthea isn't what you'd call a one-man-gal, is she?' He peered at Rose, squinting to try and beat the thump of the monster on his back. 'Oh, I see. I'd forgotten you and she had . . . well, never mind. She's a bit out of your league, wouldn't you say? A bit of an expensive prospect, our Anthea. Never mind,' and he gave a hungover chuckle. 'There's always Janet.'

Breakfast at Angela Friend's was always quite a decorous affair. There was no bacon, sausage or any of the things that made Ben Crouch's life worth living. But there were preserves, warm rolls, toast and coffee. It was going further than usual this Sunday morning because only Angela and Veronica were present, both as fresh as paint.

'So,' Veronica said, buttering some toast, 'did you enjoy your party?'

Angela smiled. 'As a matter of fact, I did. It was so good of you to arrange it all. I wouldn't have said yes, if I had known in advance.'

'I know. That's why we did it in secret. I must say, Piers did us all proud. Or perhaps I should say, his parents did.'

'I couldn't believe how wonderful that house is. Those lilies!'

'And a butler, for heaven's sake.' Veronica had been a little bowled over by the butler.

'I don't think he's a permanent feature,' Angela said. 'He lives in the country house, as a rule. They just have a cook and some housemaids.'

'Just?' Veronica laughed and sprayed crumbs. 'Gosh, sorry. Behaving a bit like Ben Crouch there.'

Angela smiled. 'I know. But Mrs Gibbs worries about her little boy away from home. She doesn't want him to rough it.'

She and Veronica looked at the empty, Anthea-shaped space at the table. Neither spoke, though they were thinking the same thing.

'And Janet. That was a bit of a revelation,' Veronica continued.

'Give a teetotal Presbyterian a pint of spiked punch and stand back,' Angela said. 'I doubt we'll see her before tomorrow lunchtime.'

'Did she and Andrew Rose . . .?'

Angela laughed. 'No, I don't think so. But it wasn't for want of trying.'

'And you and Adam . . . when are the nuptials?'

'If you're asking whether we have been practising, then the answer is no. But to answer your literal question, we are marrying as soon as term ends. I want to stay until then. It seems . . . well, to be honest, I want to see if Margaret and Inspector Reid can solve these murders. It seems rude to leave before they have.'

'Yes,' said Veronica, leaning across the table, avid eyes shining. 'Is there anything there, do you think? They seem . . .'

Angela glanced from right to left and then leaned in as well. 'I have heard a few things, actually . . .'

And they whispered and giggled until the toast and the coffee were cold and forgotten.

Adam Crawford didn't have the leisure to enjoy a hangover, which made little difference as he had been drunk on happiness the night before, not alcohol. As he sat and wrote out his reports that Sunday morning, he almost had to pinch himself to remember that he was about to marry the most wonderful woman in the world.

Blunt stalked past his desk and loomed over him like an avenging angel. 'So, I understand that congratulations are in order, Temporary Detective Constable Crawford.'

'They are, sir, yes. Thank you.'

'I wasn't actually giving you my congratulations, lad,' Blunt grunted. 'I was just checking that you are indeed engaged to marry money.'

'I prefer to call her Angela,' Crawford said, bending back to his task. Trust Blunt to twist a simple congratulation into an insult.

'Hmmph. Well, may all your troubles be little ones, as they say,' Blunt said. 'I would wish you all the happiness that Mrs Blunt and I have enjoyed, but you haven't really done anything to annoy me that much. Yet. Have you written up that report on Inkester yet?'

'Just finishing it, sir.'

'What's it say? Just the gist.'

'That he didn't do it, sir.'

'Hmmph.' Blunt loomed some more. 'Well, let me wish you all the happiness that Mrs Blunt and I have enjoyed. Then tear it up and start again.'

Crawford sighed. This detectoring lark wasn't as easy as it was cracked up to be.

Margaret Murray had allowed herself a lie-in. She didn't often do that, partly because it annoyed the woman who came in to do. Sunday was her day off, though, so there was no one to consider but herself. She popped downstairs, wincing at the cold house. She put some twigs and coal on the fire in the sitting room and ran through into the kitchen. The kettle here was faster, thank the Lord, than the one at University College so by the time the fire was crackling, she had a cup of tea and some bread to toast assembled in front of it. She sat looking into the flames, smiling at the events of the night before. She would miss Angela, but she was glad that she was happy. She would miss Inspector Reid as well, when he went back to his Hampton-on-Sea fastness. What she wouldn't miss was the worry of the murders. She couldn't help but fear that there would be more. Edmund Reid was a murder in inverted commas in her mind; without Thomas, he would have certainly been dead. And then who? She shivered as a goose stepped over her grave. She had never feared death – as long as she had a nice high status burial, she always said – but she didn't want it quite yet. She put another piece of bread on the toasting fork and bent her thoughts back to happier things. She hoped that Angela would stay in touch. She looked forward to taking her babies round the British Museum in their perambulators. It was never too soon to start.

Margaret Murray had been at her lectures and tutorials with her usual punctuality on the Monday following The Party. Somehow, it had achieved capital letter status among those who had been there – and those who hadn't. The Gibbs's home in Furnival Mansions had achieved almost legendary status among the students, some of whom were living three to a room. Even those who were in relative comfort, as in the case of Angela and her cohort, couldn't help thinking that they were missing a trick. Monday morning had seen a shortfall in attendance across almost every faculty, but by the afternoon normality had re-asserted itself, as normality, as befits its name, always will.

Hangovers had been left behind and the grey afternoon had not dampened Margaret's spirits, but the tutorial she had taken just before the end of the day had been a quiet affair. Her usual team were all present and correct, but there were undercurrents which Margaret didn't like. She knew that it was pointless to deny students a social life, a love life, indeed, but when it started to impinge on learning, enough was enough. As she went through the hour, she was jotting down the names of those she would have to speak to. Before the time was up, she had written down every name except Angela's – and even she had been in somewhat of a trance. She would have to bring Flinders Petrie in on this one. There was something about his voice that brooked no argument. She herself was no slouch, but telling a group of a dozen or so graduates and undergraduates to stop mooning over each other, if that was the word she sought, was above her pay grade.

She went along to the kitchen just down from her study and picked up the kettle. Empty, of course. She went along the corridor and up a flight of stairs to the cleaners' cubbyhole and filled it at the tap. She could see that they would need water, but why it couldn't be in other rooms as well she had never been able to understand. Back in the kitchen, she put the kettle on to boil, knowing it would take approximately an aeon before it was ready to make the tea. She got the brown teapot down from the shelf and looked inside to make sure it was empty. No, of course it wasn't empty. It was a mess of congealed leaves which she knew must date from at least the Friday before. She was on the way out of the door before she thought to check whether there was any tea in the caddy. She knew before she lifted the lid what the answer to that one would be, and she was right. Just a couple of dusty leaves at the bottom and a note which read 'IOU T, WFP'. She took the kettle off the primus with a sigh and walked back to her study. She tried not to picture the warmth of the Jeremy Bentham, the curtains drawn against the miserable weather, the candles lit on every table, the faces of friends and lovers lit from below as they enjoyed their cakes and tea . . .

She opened the door of her study and noticed that, to add insult to injury, the fire was almost out. She added some coals and it began to glow sullenly. Even Mrs Plinlimmon seemed asleep, her eyes shrouded in shadow with the firelight so low. Making up her mind, she reached for her coat and left again. A quick cuppa and a slice of Victoria, and she could get rid of this horrible black dog and get back to her study and her long-standing work on the god of the witches.

*   *   *

The Jeremy Bentham looked like a Dickens Christmas illustration that dark and stormy night. Scuds of bitter rain were in the wind and Margaret Murray was glad to open the door and become part of the warmth and candlelight inside. It was not as busy as she had pictured it; the weather had probably put off all but the most determined. But she was right in picturing the faces of lovers and friends; in one corner, Piers Gibbs sat opposite Anthea Crossley, his hand firmly grasped in both of hers. He was looking a little puzzled, as a man will who has stepped on solid ground and found himself on quicksand. Angela and Crawford were at another table and they both gave her a little wave. Towards the back, she recognized the back of Inspector Reid, in earnest conversation with, to her surprise, Thomas, who looked up and caught her eye. He waved her over and got up.

'Pot of tea and a slice of Victoria, Prof?' he asked her and she nodded, shrugging off her coat and draping it over the back of her chair.

'Oh, yes, please, Thomas. If you would.' She sat down and sighed with pleasure. Having a nicely made cuppa brought to you beat having to make your own in a kitchen made hideous by other people's crumbs hands down. 'It's good to see you and Thomas friends, Inspector Reid,' she said, with a smile.

'Well,' he said, 'when a man has saved your life, I suppose bygones are bygones.'

'True. Tell me, have you had any more thoughts . . .?'

'None. I'm so sorry, Margaret.' He had clearly decided not to backtrack on their Christian name decision. 'I think I will head back to Hampton tomorrow. I'm as likely to be able to sort out my thoughts there as anywhere else. Mrs Mulvahey has been in touch asking whether I will be needing my room after next week. I'm comfortable there, so it would be a shame to leave.'

'Yes.' Margaret felt unaccountably disappointed by his answer. She had told the truth when she said there was no romance pending, but she would miss him, all the same.

He saw her face and patted her hand. 'It's not the moon,' he reassured her. 'And I won't forget what we're doing – we *will* get justice for them, Margaret, don't worry. Look, here's your cake and tea. Let's forget about death and destruction for a bit, and have a chat about Saturday night.' He tossed his head a little towards where Gibbs sat under Anthea's thumb. 'Will he escape, do you think? Or has the Gorgon turned him to stone?'

Margaret smiled at him through a mouthful of cake. 'You are a very unusual policeman, Inspector, if I may say so.'

'And you are a very unusual archaeologist, Dr Murray, if *I* may say so.' He raised his cup to her. '*Salut.*'

FOURTEEN

The tea and Victoria cheered Margaret Murray up a little and she trotted back across the road to the frontage of the college feeling quite a lot lighter of heart. Jenkins came out of his booth like a funnel-web spider sensing a wandering ant, but she was ready for him and got to the bottom of the stairs without incident. Everything was quiet. She knew that Flinders Petrie had gone home, because she had heard his voice in the corridor as she finished her tutorial. No one else in the faculty or nearby kept the hours they kept, so if he was gone, she was alone.

Only, not quite alone.

'Good evening, Mrs Plinlimmon,' she said, hanging up her hat and coat. The fire was burning brightly now, and she put a couple more coals on, to keep it in while she worked. When she was engrossed in the god of the witches, as she had been for years, she had been known to sit there in front of a cold grate for hours until the shivering set in. 'It's a wild night out there, so be warned; if you go out mousing, make sure you wear a scarf.' She chuckled to herself. If that owl could talk, her mistress would end up in the loony bin. As usual, she left a gap for an answer. There was no need for rudeness, even when talking to a stuffed owl.

'Oh, good. It's no night to be out. Oh, by the way, do you like my picture? Did Jenkins show it to you when he brought it up? Not our usual taste, you may say, but pretty enough and it will brighten up that dark corner over there, by the window.'

Margaret pulled up a chair to her desk, having chosen two books from her groaning shelves.

'I need to do something about this bookcase, Mrs Plinlimmon. Poor Norman had more of my books than I realized; when I got them all back, it was hard to know where to put them. This one, for example.' She picked one up off the side table by the desk. 'I hadn't even missed it. It's a copy of Juvenal – really, I expect he got more use from it than I ever will, but it's been handy during this latest unpleasantness.' She smiled gently at the owl. 'I know you don't like me using the "M" word, Mrs Plinlimmon, but we have to face facts. There is a murderer on the loose and there is something in history to explain it. Don't *ever* tell any of the history lot I said that, but it's true.'

Mrs Plinlimmon winked in the firelight. She wasn't keen on the History faculty either. She liked to believe that she was in an unbroken descent from Athena's actual personal owl and had heard at least one of the philistines doubt it. If she could have ruffled her feathers, she would have done so. Or taken his eye out, as an alternative.

'We have all the facts at our disposal now, Mrs Plinlimmon,' the archaeologist said. 'I even have a link between the first victim and the second, courtesy of my picture over there. There isn't anything concrete to link Norman, but I think we can go for the slightly less definite and say that Rome is our over-arching theme here. Rome and her outposts, perhaps I should say.'

Margaret closed her books. She wasn't going to be able to concentrate on gods or witches after all. Her article for *The Anglo-Saxon Review* could wait. It had been nice to be asked, but she was finding it hard to make Infangthief easily under-stood by the ladies who lunched, the main readers of the journal as she understood it.

'You know, Mrs Plinlimmon,' she said, reaching down into the bottom drawer of her desk and bringing out the port, the special one she kept for herself. 'You know, I feel I almost have the answer in my hand. The motive is easy to identify. Greed covers it almost entirely, I think. Greed perhaps leav-ened with envy. It's not a good combination. I always try to

make my students see that there is more to life than fame
and fortune. It's nice to have them, I won't deny that. And
those who say that money can't buy happiness have obviously
never tried to bring up a family of five children in one room
in Hackney on a casual labourer's wage. But it should never
be the be all and end all. Look at Norman Minton, for example.
A renowned expert on Rome, published in I don't know how
many journals. Spent the summer months in Italy, speaking
to very prestigious gatherings. I understand next summer he
was fully booked to tour the United States. Not something I
personally would enjoy, but it would have tickled him to
death.'

Mrs Plinlimmon sucked in her breath. *How very tasteless.*

'Sorry.' Margaret looked at the owl to make sure she had
not taken too much offence. 'A slip of the tongue. But instead
of all that, he will still be as dead as a doornail. I dare say
there may even be some who were envious of his romps with
Elspeth Inkester.' She chuckled. 'I *know*,' she said, flapping
her hand at the owl. 'Not everyone's cup of tea, one would
have thought, but she has her . . . adherents, shall we say.
Perhaps she has unique skills. But anyway, long story short,
whoever in the world of academe envied Norman Minton,
there is little to envy now.'

Margaret Murray poured a generous port and leaned back,
sipping it slowly in the firelight.

'I don't think anyone would have envied poor Helen, or
Alice as some knew her. She worked at two jobs – and yes,
Mrs Plinlimmon, being a prostitute, if I may use blunt language,
is a job, like any other.' She paused for thought and took
another sip. 'Well, not that much like mine, perhaps, but you
take my point. She found time to try to expand her mind by
coming to the open lectures. And yet she died, alone and in
pain and distress, in a squalid room in Storey's Yard. Why,
you ask. I think it is something to do with what Emma Barker
found in Hampton-on-Sea, a special something which she
wouldn't name even in her own notes to herself. She hid it
with bad Latin and worse poetry. Josephus is at the heart of
it, but which of the many Josephuses who must have lived at
the time, that is the question? Of the known ones, only Joseph

of Arimathea fits the bill in the timeline. But some scholars say he is only a story anyway . . .'

She closed her eyes and savoured her port. She could feel the fire warming her feet as they stuck out under her desk. She kicked off her shoes and wiggled her toes. She put down the glass and folded her hands on the desk top.

'There is something, something that Emma found which could prove one way or another something which people have died for. That's the feeling I have, Mrs Plinlimmon.' She glanced across to the window and spoke to the pair of feet which stuck out from below the curtains. 'What do you think, Mr Rose?'

The Jeremy Bentham was now almost empty and Thomas had sent the staff round putting chairs on tables. He had shooed Gibbs and Anthea Crossley out some time before that, because she was making him feel edgy. He had never much liked predatory women and she was possibly the most obvious example he had ever seen. He had once read an article in *National Geographic* while waiting to have a haircut and had never forgotten the graphic description of a female praying mantis devouring her mate. The look in the eyes in the engraving of the creature were writ large over at the corner table. Angela and Crawford he left alone. Real young love; he had no problem with that.

He was a bit worried about Inspector Reid, though. Ever since Margaret had finished off her slice of Victoria sponge, he had sat there, looking into the candle's flame and cutting his Battenberg into smaller and smaller bits. Most of it was now simply crumbs, but still the knife chopped and chopped away, first one way, then the other. Thomas had topped up his tea several times and it was being drunk, but neither the waiter nor the policeman noticed quite when. Thomas was in a quandary. Eventually, his resolve cracked.

He approached Angela and Crawford with deference. ''Scuse me, both,' he said. 'Can I have a word?'

'Of course, Thomas.' Angela pushed out a chair and he sat down. 'How can we help? Or is it just Adam you want?' She knew this would be something she would be saying a lot from here on in, and didn't mind at all.

'That's very understanding,' Thomas said. 'You're a

lucky man, Constable Crawford, if you don't mind my saying so.'

'Not at all.' Crawford looked around. 'Are you closed?' he said. He hadn't noticed it happening.

'Clos*ing*,' Thomas said. 'We try and stay flexible at the Bentham. No, what I wanted to ask was, is there anything worrying Inspector Reid?'

'Apart from three murders and an attempt on his life?' Crawford asked. 'Probably not.'

Thomas decided not to meet sarcasm with sarcasm and bit back a retort. 'Only, he's over there, just chopping up his Battenberg.'

'As long as he's paid for it,' Crawford said, 'I suppose he can do what he likes with it.'

'No, no, it's nothing to do with the Battenberg,' Thomas said. 'He can feed it to the pigeons if he likes. It's just . . . well, he's just staring. Staring at the candle. He hasn't said anything since the Prof left.'

'She can have that effect on people,' Angela said. 'You know that, Thomas.'

'Yes.' Thomas smiled. 'But more than her usual effect. He's worried about something. I don't like to ask.'

They all looked at each other and, as expected, Crawford caved in first. 'All right,' he said. 'What do you want me to do?'

'Just go and check on him, Adam,' Angela said. 'Make sure he's well. He had a very serious blow to the head less than a week ago. And he isn't a well man.'

Crawford sat in his chair, undecided. True, Reid had got him his current, possibly temporary, role. But he was a virtual stranger, in the scheme of things. As well as something of a legend. But it was clear that Angela and Thomas were not going to let it lie, so he scraped back his chair and went over to Reid's table.

The shoes didn't move and the curtain gave nothing away, not the merest shiver. 'I admire your sangfroid, Andrew,' Margaret said. 'Perhaps I confused you by using the name "Emma". I noticed on Saturday that you prefer to call her Emmeline.'

After a few seconds, the shoes shuffled and the curtain

quivered aside. Andrew Rose stepped out, as casually as if he had just arrived a tad late for a tutorial. 'You noticed that? I didn't even realize she was known as Emma. She introduced herself as Emmeline.'

'With every reason. It was, after all, her name. How did you meet?'

'It's a long story.'

'I've got all night. Let me put some more coal on the fire and then we can settle down for a good old chinwag. Mrs Plinlimmon feels the cold, so I like to keep the fire well banked up. How about these comfy chairs? A glass of port, perhaps? I'm having another, so do keep me company.'

Rose had not meant this night to go like this. He had watched when she left and had gone into the room to check on her progress. Had she made none, she would live. If she had put even one and one together – well, when you've killed people before, one added to the tally was no big thing. 'A port? Why not?'

Gesturing to the chair, his lecturer topped up her glass and poured him his. 'So, a long story,' she said, plumping up her cushion and getting comfortable.

'It's hard to know where to start,' he said.

'At the beginning, I should,' she said. 'I know that as archae-ologists we never know quite where the beginning is. There always might be that one more layer that lies beneath. But it's knowing when to stop digging that's the key, isn't it? In case you destroy what you already have.'

Rose took a sip of his port. 'It all started last year – last academic year, that is. I wasn't living in the palatial surround-ings of Furnival Mansions then. I was out in Tothill Street, not the most salubrious of digs.'

'I understood your father was a successful businessman. Mill owner or similar, isn't he?'

'Wasn't he, you mean. Cheap imports had been eating away at his business for years and he lost a contract supplying uniforms for our brave chaps. Something about being substandard.' He shrugged. 'I don't know. The War Office are utter bastards over things like that. Anyway, Mother had some money of her own, but . . . well, it was Tothill Street for me until the wind changed, or whatever thing he was relying on.'

Margaret sipped and listened. So far, she was sewing in all the ends without needing to ask questions. They would come later.

'Actually, my digs weren't that bad, if you listen to some of the other students. I had a room to myself. A very pleasant landlady and an even more pleasant landlady's daughter, if you see what I mean.'

'I had always assumed you had an eye for the ladies, Mr Rose,' Margaret observed.

'You'd be surprised,' Rose said. 'I came down from Manchester as green as grass. But it seems there is always some woman who is willing for a roll in the hay, if you aren't too choosy.'

'So, the landlady's daughter wasn't the first?'

Rose laughed. 'The *first*? She wasn't even the *only*. But sometimes you can have enough of a good thing and I went for a walk, to avoid her. I bumped into Alice – Helen, as you knew her. She was just seeing one of her gentlemen out of her front door and without missing a beat, she asked me if I was feeling good-natured.'

'And I assume you were.'

'Not especially, as it goes. But I was feeling disgruntled and there's nothing like a working girl to work off a gruntle with. They don't want to chat and they don't want to kiss and fondle.' Suddenly, he realized who he was talking to. 'Sorry, Dr Murray, but you did ask.'

'I'm a big girl now,' she assured him. 'Let's put aside this idea that teachers get back into the cupboard when the bell goes and assume I am unshockable, shall we?'

'As long as you're sure. Well, she took me up to her room and . . . can we assume the rest? But then, to my amazement, she *did* want to chat. To the extent that she didn't charge me a penny, not that night or any other.'

'You are a silver-tongued devil, Mr Rose. I don't blame her for wanting your company.'

He raised his glass to her. 'Thank you. That means a lot. It turned out she was a model for some artist off the Strand. She wasn't that comfortable doing it, because it turned out she liked women and Alice was never sure whether she would make some kind of pass at her.'

'Would she have minded?' Margaret asked. 'She was being paid, presumably.'

'Dr Murray! Do you mind?'

She had done the unthinkable and outraged him.

'Alice was a lot of things but she wouldn't do anything like that. But, as it happened, this artist, I can't remember her name now, had a permanent girlfriend.'

'Emmeline.'

'The very same. Alice was interested in archaeology; that was what we talked about. It was because of me she started coming to the lectures. She was very bright, actually. In another life . . . well, anyway.' Rose looked into the fire.

'How did the landlady's daughter take all this?'

'Take all what?' He was genuinely surprised.

'Well, it sounds as if you were stepping out with Helen – you don't mind if I call her Helen? – on a regular basis.'

'Good Lord, Dr Murray. I hope I have enough lead in my pencil to cope with two women. Where was I?'

'Helen was very bright.'

'Yes. Well, towards the end of last term, Alice said that this Emmeline had found something she was excited about. She had found it out at a dig in Kent and she had it hidden in the little shack she had there, out on the dunes. She wouldn't even tell the artist . . . what *was* the woman's name?'

'Marjorie. Marjorie Simmons.'

'So you *have* been there. I thought you must have been, when I saw . . . when I saw the picture of Alice.'

'Which I can't help noticing has now got a big hole in it.' Margaret kept her voice level.

'It . . . it upset me.' Rose was briefly on the defensive, then relaxed again. 'It took me by surprise.'

'I would imagine that it did. So, did Helen find out what it was?'

'No, that was the point. She was clever, but she didn't know enough to find out what it was. Didn't know the right questions to ask, if you see what I mean. I taught her all I could, but . . . well, there was only so far I could take her.'

'So you decided to go to the horse's mouth, as it were.'

'Alice—'

'Andrew, can we *please* call her Helen?'

'All right. It's all one to me. Helen reckoned that I would be able to seduce Emmeline with no great difficulty. She said that with my . . . attributes . . . I should be able to get her to fall in love with me.'

Margaret looked at Andrew Rose over the rim of her glass. He was handsome enough, as long as he didn't stand too near to Piers Gibbs or Adam Crawford. If his main attribute was something that was usually hidden, she didn't see how he would be able to use it to seduce Emmeline Barker, who preferred things normally kept up a skirt. But that was an issue which didn't need to be explained in any detail. It just showed the innocence of Helen Richardson and the hubris of Andrew Rose.

'I caught the train with her, one Summer Saturday. It was quite crowded, like these things are, the East Enders all going down to the sea. So I offered her my seat, then offered to carry her bag and, well, one thing led to another. She discovered I was an archaeologist and she took me out to where she was digging. She was very friendly, so I thought that Al . . . Helen was probably right.'

Margaret took a sip of port, to stop herself from slapping his smug face.

'The dig was interesting enough, but nothing special. She took me back to her shack and, to be honest, calling it a shack was doing it a favour. It was only just holding itself up on this dune that was sliding into the sea. She was full of the dig, how she had found something that would turn the world upside down. It was then that I decided she was probably a little bit unhinged. Norman's lectures—'

'Do you mean Professor Minton's lectures?' Margaret's voice was cold.

'Yes, of course.' Rose saw no problem in placating a woman who would be dead inside half an hour. 'Professor Minton's lectures were boring enough, God knows, but he didn't leave us in any doubt that Roman forts, whether just post holes of a wooden overnight bivouac or the stone footings of something more permanent, are ten a penny. It sometimes seemed to us that you could chuck a trowel at any bit of undisturbed dirt and you'd unearth one. That, or a villa. Anyway, I pressed her a bit as to why it was so special. But she wouldn't tell me.' He drank off his port and held out his glass.

Margaret took it wordlessly and filled it up.

'Thank you. Nice of you to share the good stuff.'

'Not at all. Mrs Plinlimmon and I don't get half enough visitors.'

'Where was I? Oh, yes, she wouldn't tell me. So I tried a bit of wooing, to put it mildly. She wasn't having any. She actually got quite violent. Hit me with her spade.' He sipped his port and looked into the fire, miles away.

'And so?' Margaret knew she should just keep quiet, but she had to prompt him or burst.

'Well, I strangled her, I'm afraid. A spade across the head hurts, Dr Murray. I was angry.'

'Angry? And so you killed her?'

He thought it over for a moment, then shrugged. 'Yes. There didn't seem much else to do.'

Margaret had known from the first moment she saw the destroyed picture that she was in danger, but realized the full extent of it only now. 'Did you find what she was so excited about?' she asked, as calmly as she could.

'Oh ho, yes,' he said, patting his pocket. 'It'll make your eyes pop, Margaret. Before I do.' He smiled and put his port down on the fender and winced as he straightened up. 'It's a cracker of a find, I have to give Emmeline that. A cracker.'

'Inspector Reid?' Crawford looked down at the wreckage of the man's Battenberg and saw Thomas's point. He was clearly miles away.

'Hmm?' Reid looked up. 'Oh, Detective Constable Crawford. How nice to see you. No Angela tonight?'

'Er . . . yes, she's over there, chatting with Thomas. We were wondering . . . are you feeling well, sir?'

Reid looked at the policeman, dwarfing the little chair. He smiled. 'I'm well, thank you, just a little distracted.'

'Is it the case? Because I can let you know what we've found.'

Reid perked up. 'You've found something?'

Crawford smiled. 'Absolutely nothing. But we can talk about it.'

Reid laughed and slapped the man on the arm. 'A good try, Constable. No, to tell you the truth, I'm worried about Dr Murray.'

'She *does* seem a bit down. Angela has been saying the same.'

'I don't mean her mood. I mean . . . I just mean I have one of my old copper's feelings about her. I don't know what . . . it's as if I have an itch I can't scratch.' He sighed. 'Getting old, that's the trouble. Getting fanciful.'

'If having a feeling about things is getting old, then I am getting old as well. I feel as if we're on the edge of a cliff, looking down into the dark.'

'Don't look down, then, I shouldn't.' Thomas had joined them.

'It's about the Prof, Thomas,' Crawford said. 'Inspector Reid is worried about her.'

'She did seem a bit down . . .' Thomas ventured.

'Not her mood, dammit!' Reid banged the table and made the Battenberg crumbs jump. 'She's in danger somehow. Where did she go from here?'

Angela had joined them. 'She's probably gone back to her study. She likes to work late, with no one to bother her. You can often find her and Professor Petrie there, about the only ones who are.'

'Working late . . . on her own . . .' Reid suddenly jumped up. 'I'm going over there. If she's all right, it won't matter. If she isn't . . . well, she'll need me.' He looked at the trio around his table. 'Us, then. Even you, Miss Friend. You can get us by Cerberus.'

'Who?' Thomas thought he knew everyone at the Godless Institution.

'Jenkins,' the others chorused.

'Got your coats?' Reid checked. 'It's howling out there. Constable?'

Crawford patted the truncheon in his pocket.

'Tom?'

'Half a mo.' Thomas dived behind the counter and straightened up, slipping something into an inside pocket. 'Ready.'

'Miss Friend.' Reid touched her arm. 'We'll leave you at the door, to get help if we need it. Will you be all right?'

'Probably,' Angela said. 'I'm sure I can deal with Jenkins.'

Crawford had never been prouder of her.

'Then,' Reid said, 'let's go.'

'I've seen things, Mr Rose, that you could only dream about. There are things still waiting to be catalogued that will set the archaeological world by the heels.'

'Try not to build up your part, Margaret. I may call you Margaret, I think, as you and I will be very intimate before the evening is out.' He looked at her and smiled. 'I can't decide how to do it, actually. Apparently, or so I have read, most murderers have a method and stick to it. I offer up as an example Inspector Reid's old friend, Jack the Ripper. Rather boring, really. Same old hack and slash. I have . . . experimented, let's call it. You always taught us, Margaret, that experiment is all-important. If one way of wielding a trowel doesn't bring results, try another way. Well, strangulation was not difficult.' He looked down and for a moment she saw the unsullied boy who had stumbled into her first lecture, a pile of books under his arm and hope in his heart. 'Not difficult, but longer than I expected. It must have taken four, perhaps five minutes. The burying was a pain, as well. It was pointless, too, as it turned out. The whole shack fell into the sea a few days later, so I could have left her there and then none of this would have happened.'

'Tchah,' Margaret said softly. 'Even the rate of erosion lets you down in the end.'

'Don't joke, Margaret,' he said nastily. 'Oh, I know you like to be the funny one, cracking one-liners to make sure the hearties in the back stay awake. But this is serious. This won't lay the world of archaeology by the heels. It will lay the *world* by its heels.'

He leaned back in the chair.

'Let's have a bit more coal on, shall we?' He reached into the scuttle with the tongs and carefully placed the nuggets on the flames. 'It's a shame I've already had a go at bludgeoning – too bloody, by the way, before you ask – because these fire irons are a gift.'

'Have you made a plan, then?' Margaret hoped her voice came through loud and clear, as her heart was in her mouth.

'Oh, yes. I'm going to risk shooting, this time. That idiot Jenkins won't hear it. He spends the whole night asleep if he can manage it. I dodged him easily when I did for Norman, though the cleaner gave me a bit of a turn. Anyway, let's not get out of sequence. Clear thinking, Margaret, that's what you always told us, am I right?'

She nodded. 'Why Helen?'

'You may as well ask "why not Helen?"' he said. 'She was dying to know what I had found and, like a fool, I showed her. Well, of course, she had to say thank you the only way she knew how and – again, Margaret, if I shock you, do say – I have to admit, it was a corker. My goodness, I learned a thing or two that night. So, what with one thing and another, I left my jacket behind. It was high summer by this time.' He picked up his port glass and emptied it. 'Hard to believe, isn't it? Shocking night outside.'

They could have been two friends discussing the weather.

'And your find – Emma's find – was in the pocket, I assume?'

'It was. When I went back the next night, the jacket had been brushed and hung up, but there was nothing there. She denied it ever had been, but I knew she had it. I bided my time for a night or two, then went back with the phial the police found. I told her it was the latest thing to make a good time even better. I had one as well. Harmless, of course. So, when we were . . . again, apologies . . . at the height of things, I tipped it down her throat and the greedy whore swallowed it and licked her lips.'

'And died.' Margaret's voice was low.

'Correct. She had a stupid box where she kept things and sure enough, there it was. I took it, but left the box.'

'I know. I found it. I found the half-used railway ticket and some wood traces.'

'And they got you . . . where?'

'Until now, not very far.' She smiled. 'I have never known you so informative, Mr Rose. If only your essays had ever been this good.'

He chuckled. 'I think, after a suitable interval, I may try to write a whodunit. Doing it is so easy, it seems a shame not to.' He smiled and stretched a little, settling in for the last bedtime story of Margaret Murray's life. 'So many little frills and furbelows you can include, when you stop and think. For instance, the "client list". Remember that?'

Margaret nodded.

'I know it gave you food for thought. And food, that was my inspiration. Living with Ben Crouch, how could it not be? Reginald Glass and James Brisket – for God's sake, Margaret. I didn't even try to make it sound realistic, yet you and that big flatfoot of Angela's swallowed it, hook, line and sinker. I didn't even bother to disguise my handwriting. It worried me for a while, because you have seen so much of it, but no – you saw what you saw and the details passed you by. Oh, Margaret – what do you always tell us? The devil is in the detail?'

'And not only there, it seems.' She spoke more in sorrow than in anger.

Rose sniggered. 'Honi soit qui mal y pense,' he said.

Margaret looked at him with her head on one side. 'Perhaps I haven't always made it clear, Andrew,' she said, 'but I have always had a soft spot for you. From the first, I knew you would go far.'

'Ah, but how far you could never guess,' he said.

'I do wonder, though,' she said, in friendly tones, 'whether you are quite well. Nothing that can't be fixed, but you are just . . . a little cold-blooded, perhaps?'

'Margaret. May I call you Maggie? No, perhaps that's a step too far. Margaret, I have here in my pocket the find of the century. Oh, hark at me! That's not saying much, is it, in 1900? The find of the . . . the find of the for ever, if that's a phrase. But you've interrupted me. I was telling you about Helen.'

It took a while for the four to rouse Jenkins. He had curled up in his booth and was faster asleep than usual, thanks to the half bottle of champagne that Rose had given him, courtesy of the engagement party. 'No need to feel left out, Mr Jenkins,' he had said. 'You're as much part of this college as we are.'

Jenkins was not a connoisseur, and had necked it out of a chipped china mug. Now, in his dreams, he could hear banging, but from very far away.

'You killed her. What else do I need to know?'

'Why, I suppose. She was in many ways, and you'll think this odd, the love of my life. So far, at least. She was pretty, she was eager to learn and, most of all, she loved me. Totally and without question.'

'And yet, she stole from you. Not as loving as all that.' Margaret was done with being sympathetic. As she was likely to be shot in the next few minutes, she might as well speak her mind.

'Well, that's what I thought at the time. But since then, I have come to realize she was simply trying to save me from myself. What I have here' – he patted his pocket and again Margaret noticed him wince – 'won't be to the taste of everyone. I will be hated in many quarters, I know. But . . .' – his smile was beatific – 'oh, the fame. The glory.'

'The money?'

'That too. I don't deny the money will be nice. It's worse, you know, to be brought up with money and then lose it than to never have it at all.'

'Again, I would argue with that. But I can see that it drives you, so it's important to your tale.'

'My *tale*? My *tale*?' Rose leaned forward and she felt a spray of angry spittle on her cheek. 'This isn't a *tale*, Margaret. This is world-changing. World-ending, for you, sadly, but you'll at least die knowing why.'

'True. That's something, isn't it, Mrs Plinlimmon? Pointless death is so . . . well' – she gave a little chuckle though her throat was dry as dust – 'pointless, isn't it? Tell me, can I get you anything for the knife wound? It's still giving you gyp, I can see.'

'Knife wound? What do you know about that?'

'Oh, come on, Mr Rose. Thomas isn't just a waiter, chief cook and bottle washer, you know. He is a cracksman of some repute and he knows some of the most hardened criminals in London, if not the world. What he doesn't know about knife fights can be written on the head of a pin. So if he says he caught someone with a knife, then he did indeed catch someone with a knife. But why Inspector Reid? What had he ever done to you?'

Rose sniffed dismissively. 'Poked. Pried. He found Emmeline's body, for God's sake. If it wasn't for him making a nuisance of himself, she'd still be in that dune. You wouldn't know she went to King's. You wouldn't have had those stupid notes.' He banged the arms of the chair. 'I wouldn't be *here!*'

'Goodness,' Margaret said, sitting up straight. 'It was nothing to do with Inspector Reid finding the body that helped me find the King's connection. No, it was the Herne Bay Decorum Society who helped me there. If you want to take them all on in your vendetta, you will have to go through Ethelfleda Charlton, and with that I can only wish you the very best of British luck.'

Rose frowned. This recital was beginning to get away from him.

'You may be interested to know, by the way, that I have left a note, hidden somewhere only he will be able to find it, for Flinders Petrie. It is to be opened in the event of my death and it tells him that you are the murderer of me and the others. It gives my reasons, and I believe it will easily bring you to the gallows.'

Rose snorted. 'That's insane. You couldn't possibly have known it was me. I left no clues.'

'True. You were most meticulous. Or lucky, I'm not sure which. Because, Mr Rose, Manchester Grammar School and all the glittering prizes then and since cannot stop you being really rather stupid.'

Rose clutched his pocket. 'And yet, I have this,' he hissed. 'And a gun, don't forget.'

'I haven't. Do you want to know my reasoning?'

'If I must.'

'At Angela and Constable Crawford's party, I noticed that you didn't use your left arm any more than you had to. You are not a sportsman, so I knew it wasn't an injury sustained in a game of any sort. Also, you named the first victim as Emmeline. When she was known to all and sundry, except her family and occasionally, in jest her lover, as Emma.'

Rose's eyes goggled. 'That's it?' he said. 'I don't think that will hang anyone, Margaret, do you?'

'But look at the bind you're in, Mr Rose. You have in your pocket something incredible. There will be four dead bodies, all with a link to archaeology. Even the Metropolitan Police aren't so stupid as to miss that connection. Especially when it is pointed out to them by the great Flinders Petrie.'

'I don't care,' he said. 'I can talk my way out of it. Always have. Always will.'

Margaret stood up and held out her hand. 'If so,' she said, 'why not shoot me? But I would quite like to at least see this fabulous thing. If you would let me hold it, that would be a kindness to a dead woman.'

Rose looked at her suspiciously. Then, with infinite slowness, he took a revolver out of his pocket and levelled it at her. With the other hand, he reached inside his coat.

'Jenkins!' Angela screamed. 'Jenkins, for the love of God, let us in!'

'Is he even there?' Tom asked. 'He does rounds or something, doesn't he?'

'Don't make me laugh,' Angela said. 'I fell asleep in the library one night and he didn't find me. Said he hadn't liked to disturb me when he was questioned about it by the principal. But it was obvious he had spent the night in that horrible pit he has made for himself in the hall.' She beat on the door again. 'Jenkins!' The pitch and volume made the men cover their ears and Tom and Reid looked at Crawford with some sympathy.

Finally, they heard shuffling steps across the marble floor and bolts were drawn back one by one. Eventually, the great door swung open and the four barrelled through, knocking Jenkins over like a ninepin. In his champagne confusion, he could never remember how many people had entered, but using the same general rule as Tom always did, by the following afternoon it was at least two dozen, accompanied by a couple of dogs and a horse.

Jeremy Bentham sat in his glass case, watching the chaos with his imperturbable glass eyes. A trick of the light – or was it a trick of the light? – made him seem to follow their progress up the stairs, his neck cricking silently to see them pass. Jenkins decided to put the whole thing down as a nightmare and tottered off back to his noisome bed. He heard the grandfather clock in the principal's office down the hall strike the half hour. But which hour he neither knew nor cared.

Margaret Murray was no stranger to guns. Being brought up in India, she never went outside without her ayah and a havildar beside her, a gun on his hip. She had never known him fire it, but simply having it there, on a level with her bouncing curls, let her know she was safe, was protected from the unknown and fearsome creatures that her ayah assured her lurked in every doorway. Then, at her uncle's parsonage in Rugby, she had gone along with the other girls and women to follow the autumn shooting parties, when men with far too much rum punch inside them blew innocent feathered creatures to smithereens. But this gun was not like anything she had seen. It fitted in Rose's palm as if made to measure and she could almost see down the barrel, where the bullet with her name on it rested mutely in the chamber, ready to be sent on its deadly task.

Rose extended his other hand and opened it with a theatrical flourish. It seemed churlish at such a dramatic moment to be disappointed, but she was, nonetheless.

'That's it?'

'Not what you were expecting, perhaps?' he sneered, and moved his hand nearer so she could see just what it was. In his hand was a box, about five inches long and two in diameter. Its cross section was roughly octagonal, for the simple reason that it had been made of eight slivers of olive wood, roughly stapled together to make a container. There was no lid, though it was possible there had been once.

'I was expecting olive wood, yes,' she said. 'There were tiny fragments in the wrapping paper you left behind.'

He nodded, impressed. 'The thing with you, Margaret,' he said, poking the gun nearer so she could see the blued metal of the barrel gleaming with oil in the firelight, 'you do know who to ask when you have a conundrum. And look where that got poor old Norman.'

'But really, Andrew,' she said softly. 'Have three people . . .?'

'Four people,' he said, smiling.

'Four people died for that?'

'Yes,' he said simply. 'And I think more will follow. Look inside. Go on.' He proffered it to her. 'I don't mind you looking. After all, you won't be telling anyone, will you?' He clicked back the hammer and flexed his finger on the trigger.

Moving slowly, she took the rough box from his hand and turned it up over her own, so that the contents slid out. Inside was a lead sheet, rolled into a cylinder. It had clearly once been wrapped in something and tied with a string, but the fabric and hemp had rotted away. She looked at him, wondering what he would allow her to do next before putting a bullet in her head.

'Go on. Unroll it. Carefully – but I don't have to tell you that, do I?'

With infinite care, she put the side of her thumb under the opening of the roll and eased it open. Writing on the inside began to emerge, as crisp and clear as the day the scribe's stylus had taken the dictation from the Senate in Rome.

'Read it,' he breathed. 'Read it out to me.'

She took a step nearer to the fire, to get the best of the light from the lamp on the mantel. '*Turbator Josephus, ex Judea, hic est. Et turbator Jesus . . .*'

She looked at him, her eyes wide. 'But . . . this . . . this will ruin lives,' she said. 'People will be devastated. It flies in the face of . . . well, everything.' She thought of her uncle, perhaps not the most devout vicar in the church at large, but a staunch believer in every word of the Bible. Of the millions of people who lived their lives as though in the image of the Son of God. If the words on this tablet were true – what of them?

'*Now* do you see why I did what I did?' he said, his eyes gleaming in the firelight. '*Now* do you see?'

Before Margaret could answer, the door of the study crashed back and Crawford filled the space. Behind him, two indistinct figures pushed forward, eager for the fray.

'Oh, for the Lord's sake,' Rose hissed, and Margaret couldn't help thinking that it would take people a long time to stop saying that. 'The bloody cavalry, as I live and breathe.'

'You can't kill us all,' Crawford said, surging forward.

'He can, y'know,' Tom muttered, surging forward nonetheless. 'That's a Bull Dog in his hand. Five shots.'

Rose took aim and squeezed the trigger, just as Margaret knocked his arm up with a swing of the poker. Rose wasn't the only one to see the benefits in a good sturdy companion set. The shot went wild and after that, for quite some minutes, Margaret wasn't sure quite who was doing what to whom. What she did know was that Edmund Reid was by her side, asking in his quiet way if she was all right. What she did not know was that a monumental tussle had gone on in her normally quiet inner sanctum. Crawford had grabbed the gun and Tom had driven his knee into Rose's groin as the quickest way he knew of disabling anybody, short of killing him. The rest was a Metropolitan Police standard procedure movement in which Crawford wrenched Rose's arms behind his back and snapped on the cuffs.

And Margaret didn't hear Crawford say, 'Now then, Mr Rose, come along quietly, there's a good gentleman.'

And Andrew Rose did.

And then, suddenly, Margaret was alone and it was all over. She sat in her chair and reached for her glass of port, miraculously still intact, and knocked back the remainder in one. Only then did she remember what she held in her hand and she put the glass down and straightened it out again.

'The troublemaker Josephus,' she translated aloud, 'from Judea is here. And the troublemaker Jesus, called the Christ. This Jesus was sentenced to death by the order of the governor Pontius Pilate, but Josephus engineered his escape, and a thief, Barabbas, died in his place. There is a price on his head and he has been in hiding in parts of the empire for ten years. He is now believed to be in Britannia. Find him and end it.'

She sat there for a while, stroking the surface of the ancient furl of lead, imagining what it had seen. It had been created in Rome, a Rome that Norman would have been able to walk around like a native. It had gone overland and over sea, to warn the new fort on the coast of Kent who was coming their way. Did they get there? Who knew? But from the date inscribed at the top – Claudius IV, the fourth year of the reign of Claudius – Jesus of Nazareth was in his forties when he had set the empire in a stir. Ten years, she thought. Four thousand days. And did those feet in ancient time walk upon England's mountains green? Who knew? She put the lead sheet between her palms and pressed it between them, making herself remember the feel of it, the smoothness, the very years seeping into her skin. Then, with a flick of the wrist, she threw it into the flames. It bubbled for a moment in the hottest part of the fire and then dripped down and away.

'Four thousand days too much,' she muttered and dropped her head into her hands. And she was still like that when Angela found her.

'I wouldn't have minded so much, William,' Margaret said, the next evening. 'But the madman shot Mrs Plinlimmon. There were feathers everywhere and they can't find her beak at all.'

'Great Scott, Margaret.' Petrie turned to her. 'You could have died and all you worry about is an owl!'

'But I *didn't* die, William, did I? And Mrs Plinlimmon is often the only person I speak to from one day's end to the next who makes any sense at all.'

'Can she . . .' He felt very stupid saying the next thing, but she had had a narrow squeak and deserved to be cut a little slack. 'Can she be saved?'

'As a matter of fact, Walter Inkester came to her rescue. He happens to have whole drawers of oddments and there was a barn owl's beak in there, which he has donated to the cause. She is with his best taxidermist as we speak.'

'Walter has a lot to be grateful to you for. A beak and a handful of straw for stuffing is a small price to pay, isn't it?'

'The police would have seen sense in the end,' she said, sounding less certain than was her usual habit.

'Can you hear yourself, woman? He's lucky to have escaped hanging. As is Andrew Rose, by the way.'

'Well, he is clearly unhinged, William.' Margaret moved to a more comfortable position. She had pretended she was unaffected by her brush with death, but since it had happened she had felt the need for pampering and mollycoddling, if only for a while.

'No one can understand why he did what he did. Can we really have taught him so inadequately that he killed three people . . .'

'. . . and severely beat one, and disembowelled an innocent owl . . .'

'Yes, let's not forget that. Done all that evil, for an olive wood container with nothing in it?'

'It *is* early first century, William. A remarkable survival.'

Petrie shrugged. 'If it had proper provenance. He says it was found in Kent, but how do we know that? Emmeline . . . what was her name . . .?'

Margaret gave a sad smile that Petrie missed in the dim light. 'Barker. Emmeline Barker.'

'Yes. Well, Miss Barker may have claimed she found it at her dig, but we only have her word for that, and that word is silent now. No, Margaret, for my money that box comes from Libya, somewhere like that. They're always finding survivals there. Scraps of fabric. Wood. Rope. He killed for nothing.'

'Isn't that sad, William?' she said, closing her eyes. 'So sad for them all.'

'I found your note, by the way,' he said. 'Not to be opened except in the event of your death. How did you know?'

'Did you read it?' she asked.

'Well, no. You're not dead.'

'Oh, William. You're so literal. That's perhaps your best attribute.'

He grunted. He wasn't an easy man to compliment.

'What's my best attribute, William? Humour me, I'm a woman in shock.'

'It's hard to choose,' he said, ever the diplomat. 'But it's easy to choose your worst.'

'Oh.' She bridled. 'And what's that?'

'You will hog the bedclothes. Now, shut up and blow that candle out!'

THE REAL MARGARET MURRAY

Margaret Murray was born in India in 1863, in what was then the Bengal Presidency. Her father ran a paper mill and her mother was a missionary. Her education was sporadic, largely because women of her social class were not expected to work for a living. She did train as a nurse, however, during India's cholera epidemic and carried out social work in England.

From 1894, despite having no qualifications, she enrolled in the newly opened Egyptology department at University College, London. Here she stayed for many years, lecturing and encouraging the students of her 'gang' and working with William Flinders Petrie, one of the foremost archaeologists of his generation. The work took her to Egypt and led to her publishing a number of works.

On the outbreak of the First World War, Margaret volunteered as a nurse in France. Exhausted by this, she went to Glastonbury in Somerset and became immersed in the Arthurian/Holy Grail legends and her archaeology morphed into folklore and anthropology. She was given an honorary doctorate in 1927 and she travelled extensively before retiring seven years later.

As president of the Folklore Society, she fascinated thousands and shocked several with her publications on witchcraft and demonology, on which she had controversial views. She remained alert, adept and still writing into extreme old age, publishing her autobiography *My First Hundred Years* in 1963, the year of her death in Welwyn, Hertfordshire.

Her legacy lives on today in the writings of H.P. Lovecraft and the whole modern Wicca movement. She was a determined feminist, striking a blow for emancipation in a world dominated by male privilege.

Ingram Content Group UK Ltd.
Milton Keynes UK
UKHW012124030423
419589UK00007B/532

9 781448 307418